Suddenly she stumbled forward and lost her footing in a deep drift that seemed to envelop her. And there above her loomed the big stone arch that marked the entrance of the cemetery.

She sank back wearily, and the great white drift received her and folded cold arms about her. The lights from the stone arches touched her gold hair till it looked like a coronet, and the long sable-edged robe wrapped her round like a winding sheet.

Once she opened her eyes, looked up to the gateway, tried to struggle up again, but found herself too weary and sank back once more, dreaming that her wish for death was coming true. . . . she was alone and safe at last. . . .

Tyndale House books by Grace Livingston Hill.
Check with your area bookstore for these best-sellers.

SPICE BOX

LIVING BOOKS ®
Tyndale House Publishers, Inc.
Wheaton, Illinois

This Tyndale House book
by Grace Livingston Hill
contains the complete text
of the original hardcover edition.
NOT ONE WORD
HAS BEEN OMITTED.

Copyright © 1943 by Grace Livingston Hill. Copyright renewed 1971
by Ruth Livingston Hill Munce
Cover artwork copyright © 1992 by Nathan Greene
All rights reserved

Living Books is a registered trademark of
Tyndale House Publishers, Inc.

Printing History
J. B. Lippincott edition published 1943
Tyndale House edition/1992

Library of Congress Catalog Card Number 92-81009
ISBN 0-8423-5939-7

Printed in the United States of America

99   98   97   96   95   94   93   92
 8   7   6   5   4   3   2   1

I

THE snow was falling heavily in great blankety flakes as the cars wallowed back from the cemetery. Janice sat staring out the window into the impenetrable whiteness, hearing but not listening to the low-toned guarded speech of Herbert, her brother-in-law, and Mr. Travillion, the old family lawyer. She was too weary even to think of what might be in the life that was ahead of her.

Then the car turned into their drive, and stopped before the door, and the girl shuddered and half drew back as Herbert offered to help her out.

"Good night, Miss Whitmore. Good night, Mr. Stuart," said the old lawyer, with an all-too-apparent hand on the latch of the car door. "I'll be seeing you about that matter we spoke of in a few days!" She must not linger. The old man was in a hurry, and Herbert was standing out in the snow. He would be angry.

Out on the walk Herbert grasped her arm as if to steady her steps, but a rush of dislike for him overcame her fear of slipping, and she rushed up the steps regardless of the snow, which had covered several inches deep all traces of the feet that had carried her sister's casket out of the house a little while before. The thought of it came to the girl as she hurried up to the porch, almost falling, and tried to open the door.

But someone had put the night latch on, and by the time the servant arrived her brother-in-law was beside her, his hand on her arm again with a proprietary air.

"What are you in such a rush about?" he asked her gruffly. "Anybody would think you might be a little more decorous, at least until you get into the house."

She shrank away from him into the hall, her handkerchief at her eyes, and hastened toward the stairs. How she dreaded to look about the familiar rooms in their prim funereal order. It seemed so horribly empty in the space where the casket had stood. And there were still flowers everywhere, on the mantel and tables and window ledges. There had been too many to take to the cemetery. Her breath caught in a quick sob as she stumbled forward to the stairs.

Then suddenly Herbert's voice broke on the silence of the so-empty house:

"That's enough sniveling, Janice! We're done with all that foolishness now. I've stood in this gloom for six weeks, but I won't stand it another hour! Louise is out of it all, and there's no call for any sentimental bawling. I want a little cheer in my house and I'm going to have it. You go upstairs and take off those black rags that make you look like a death's-head, and come down to dinner in something bright and cheerful! It's high time things were done to please me! And no long faces, mind you! Get a little color into your face and be prepared to make me have a pleasant evening! I've ordered a good dinner, and we're going to have a little enjoyment in life after all the gloom!"

Janice turned in dismay, her face ashen white against the blackness of her garments:

"O Herbert! I couldn't! Not *tonight!*"

Herbert glared at her, a threatening light in his eyes.

"Don't you say 'couldn't' to me, young lady!" he roared, and took an unsteady step toward her, recalling to her mind that he had had a number of drinks that morning before the funeral. Her experience through the years she had lived in this household had taught her that when Herbert did much drinking, she and her sister might look for trouble.

"A little decent treatment is what I deserve after all I've suffered, and I'm going to have it," he went on in a high-pitched voice. "Your sister lay down on her job and died, but you've got to do *as I say,* understand?"

Janice began to tremble. Well she knew that it was of no use to protest when he was in that mood. She turned to hide the quivering of her lips, the falling of her tears, but she was too tired even to try to stop.

"Put on one of your fancy evening dresses. The coral one, or the turquoise. I guess you look best in that. Put rouge on your face, and lipstick, and try to be attractive for once. I'm sick of your washed-out sniveling looks. I want something cheerful around me. And hurry down soon. I don't want to be kept waiting. *Go,* I say, and *be quick* about it."

He was speaking to her with the tone he had used to her sister Louise so often during those last two awful years before her death, trying to force her to get up and be gay when she was too weak to stand on her feet.

He had never used that tone to Janice before, for she had always kept out of his way when he was in this mood. Louise had seen to that. Though of late his manner with Janice had been admiring and affectionate as if she was a little child, growing constantly too affectionate, till her dislike for him had deepened into first dread, and then fear. This had made her many times contemplate the possibility of going away permanently from the shelter of her sister's luxurious but unhappy home. The sister's certain distress and unhappiness without her had been the only thing which held her.

But the weeks of Louise's final illness had of course separated Janice much from her brother-in-law, as she had been almost constantly beside the sick bed, and had not come down to meals at all while he was in the house.

The past four days of deep sorrow had made her forget for the first time her fear, and as yet she had not looked into the immediate future.

Now, however, she was suddenly face to face with her unnamed fear, and with no frail sweet sister to protect her. What should she do? She must go away at once of course, but not tonight in this terrible storm. And she was in no state of mind either to get ready, or to know how to plan and where to go. Besides, there were servants and neighbors to be considered. What would they say? What would they think? For Louise's sake she must plan so that there would be no scandal, no gossip. Louise had endured everything that no breath of scandal should be spoken about her broken hopes of life. She must for Louise's sake get away quietly and naturally if possible, so that no one would think it queer for her to leave so abruptly the home where she had been for the past five years, an apparently loved and honored member of the household.

Gathering all her forces she faced the angry man, her own sweet conquering expression on her face, the look her dead sister used so many times to wear under such circumstances.

"Herbert, really, I'm almost worn out with all I've

been through. Couldn't you excuse me this evening? I do need to rest."

She was very young and sweet. The dark shadows that sorrow had etched under her eyes only served to bring out her loveliness in spite of her pallor. She spoke pleasantly, coaxingly, as one tries to explain to an unreasonable child.

Usually her gentle tones had a quieting effect upon him, but tonight he was not himself. He had kept up nerve and brain all day by his many visits to that costly decanter in his library. It was not that he loved his wife so much, for it was long since he had even pretended to do so, but his conscience perhaps—if he had any left—must have set up a rebuking clamor when he saw her lying white and still, a lovely waxen shadow of what she used to be when he married her, before he broke her heart. Death had renewed her youth and set a seal of something more upon her exquisite face, that spoke of immorality and condemned his own weakness. He dared not face it so he had tried to drown his conscience in drunkenness. Janice, as she faced him, suddenly realized that she had never seen him in quite this state before, and her spirit quailed within her.

Then his voice thundered out so it could be heard all over the house.

"You'll do what I say, do you understand? I'm not going to have any more nonsense about it either. I'm master in my own house and you're not going to dictate to me the way your nit-wit of a sister tried to do, either. Perhaps you don't know that you're entirely dependent upon me now. Your own money was all invested in a stock company that failed a year ago, and you're absolutely penniless! Your fool sister wouldn't have told you about it, but it's all true. So you see I've been keeping you in luxury all this time and I guess you can see something is due to me. I'm not going to throw you out as long as you obey me, but I want you to understand once and for all that you are *dependent* on me, and when I express a wish for anything it's up to you to grant it."

She stood wide-eyed with anger flashing in her eyes. The blackguard! To dare to take the sacred name of his sweet wife upon his lips in such wise! She was weak with the horror of it! She longed to strike him, to wither him with words. Yet she knew it would be useless to answer him. Louise had never been able to silence him, though she had tried it in many ways. What should she do? Could she possibly hope that if she went upstairs and dressed in gayer garments he would subside and forget some of the things he had said, be more reasonable?

A great fear seized upon her. Dared she stay here overnight? Yet how could she go out in this storm and darkness?

Then she caught a vision of the maid's frightened curious gaze peering from behind the heavy portiere of the dining room door. She must somehow quiet this maniac and keep the servants from hearing what was going on if possible.

Her face froze into sudden haughtiness, and her voice was low and controlled, although the effort it took was almost more than she could endure.

"Very well," she said coldly, and turning hurried up the stairs. Her mind was in a tumult. Somehow she must quiet this fiend, and afterwards she would get out of the house as quickly as possible, no matter how bad the storm.

Hastily she removed her black garments and went to the wardrobe where hung the pretty dresses that her loving sister had provided for her. But she could not bring herself to put on those gay frocks. The sight of them sent the tears stinging into her eyes. Frantically she reached for a little white crepe de Chine, simply made, that had been her graduating dress the year before. She dashed cold water into her face to repair the damages sorrow had made, and hurried into the dress. Her eyes grew dangerously bright with the excitement of her hurry, and the deadly pallor of her face was heightened by a vivid spot of color that flew into her cheeks. But she did not stop to look at herself. She was too anxious about what was before her to care how she looked. She did not know how beautiful she was as she came down the stairs. But the man at the foot of the stairs knew, and came toward her.

Herbert had taken off his overcoat and hung it in the hall closet, paused to take a deep draught from a bottle he had hidden on a shelf behind the door, and then as he heard her descending the stairs, he hastily corked the almost empty bottle, and slid it back on the shelf. Leaving the door carelessly swinging open behind him he hurried out and waited for her at the foot of the stairs, a maudlin delight in his drunken face that filled her with a frenzy of fear. Yet she did her best to come on calmly, not to let him see that she was frightened.

The heavy frown cleared away from Herbert's cruelly handsome face, and something almost gloating took its place, as if he were watching a new possession and delighting in it, a possession whose full value he had not heretofore realized. Trying not to look at him, nor to see the expression of his face Janice came steadily down till she reached the last step. Then suddenly Herbert stepped forward, lifting her hand from the baluster and drawing her close to him. Flinging his arms about her fiercely, he laid his lips on her sweet shrinking ones and strained her to him.

"My darling! My beautiful one," he cried pressing his

face to hers, "you are all mine now! There is no one between us any more!"

With a wild cry Janice tried to tear herself away from his grasp, those circling arms that were so fierce and strong about her, to turn her face away from those disgusting, clinging lips, gasping and crying out, forgetful of listening servants, of all else save the necessity to get away. But she was held as in a vise, and her face was smothered with loathsome kisses.

At last she wrenched one hand loose and beat wildly against his face, his eyes, his mouth, she could not see where, only to struggle her best and get away.

For an instant he struggled with her, angrily, and then one of her blows must have reached his eye for he staggered back, his hold about her relaxing, and the girl slid down at his feet.

"You little devil!" he said fiercely. "I'll teach you! You'll learn to take it and like it, do you hear that?" and with one hand to his eyes he staggered toward her again.

But Janice, her terror giving her new strength, sprang to her feet and fled from his outstretched hands, down the hall toward the front door. Whither she was going she did not stop to think, only to get out and away.

Before her stood that hall closet door, swung wide, as Herbert had carelessly left it, and there on the door hook hung an old evening wrap of her sister's, a long warm circular garment of dull blue. It was richly lined and trimmed with fur, but of a fashion of several years back, and therefore it had fallen into common use. Louise had worn it, she remembered, the last walk they took together around the yard before her final illness, and coming in exhausted had thrown it down on a hall chair where the maid had found it and hung it in the closet. Such a train of thought to flash across her mind in that moment of stress, but it was like her sister's hand held out to help her.

She caught at the cloak now, and dashed out the front door closing it sharply behind her. She knew that Herbert would be following at once. There was no time to pause.

The fierce winter wind met her like a wild beast, breathed its burning-cold breath on her bare arms and throat, searched her shrinking flesh clad in that thin gown. The sleet cut and scratched her face and hands, and the first step of her light slippers from the threshold into the deep carpet of snow that had already drifted up to the very doorway, chilled her through and through.

Yet she dared not hesitate an instant. She plunged wildly down the steps and into the deeper snow of the path, struggling frantically the while to fling the cloak about her. She finally succeeded in stringing it across her shoulders, holding it fast as she fought against the fierce wind and snow, down to the street and on out the road not realizing what direction she was taking.

Something had happened to the street lights, and the way was very dark as she sped on. Her fingers were fumbling to find the fastenings of the cloak. If she could only get it buttoned about her! And there was a capacious hood that would cover her head.

But she was too much afraid that Herbert would come out after her. She was faintly conscious that she heard the front door open behind her, heard her name called fiercely, angrily, and so she sped on into the darkness. The sound made her forget the cold and wet, and she plunged wildly on in the night. She must get away from Herbert. If he caught her he would bring her back and she dared not think of what might happen.

When the baffled maniac rallied from the pain in his eyes Janice's blow had given him, he stumbled toward the front door, pausing a moment to look into the hall coat room, with a vague idea that the girl might be hiding in there, else why should that door be open? His dazed mind utterly forgot that he had left it unlatched when he hung up his hat and coat. But he could not believe that Janice had actually gone out into the storm on a night like this.

And then he flung the front door wide and the light streamed out into the storm, lighting up the snow-filled air till it seemed like a great shaft of gold. Janice, shivering into the shelter of a great hedge, saw it and hurried on farther and farther from the house.

Herbert had expected to find his young sister-in-law near at hand. Perhaps hiding on the front piazza. Or she might have merely gone around to the back door and entered the house again that way. She would likely go up to her room and lock herself in. If she had he would get her, even if he had to break the door down. She should not elude him. He would find her and bring her down again and conquer her!

He had purposely waited a moment to frighten her, if she had really gone out. She would be ready enough to come back out of the cold when she got good and scared, but now as he stepped outside the doorway and gazed up and down the white flurry of the outer world, he could not see any sign of her. The deep whiteness everywhere brought to his muddled mind the scene at the grave and the awful whiteness of the cemetery. He turned angrily back into the warmth and light of the house, shuddering away from that whirlwind of whiteness. She must be in the house somewhere. She must be! He slammed the door shut, leaving her out in the storm. He could never follow her out into that cold and sleet. He hated discomfort. Not even his anger could carry him so far.

Janice heard the slamming of the door, but did not know of course whether he had gone back or was still following her, and her terrified feet kept speeding on, numb with cold in their slight covering, struggling through the deep snow as though by superhuman strength. Corner after corner she turned in her flight, out into the country, not stopping to think where she was going.

Stumbling and blinded, scarcely knowing what she did, she made her way into the road, through drifts that almost brought her to her knees. Only the strenuous effort necessary to keep moving made her unaware of the fearful cold, the sting of the sleet in her face, the numbing ache in her feet. The hood had slipped back from her head and the snow was covering her hair, lashing into her eyes unmercifully.

And then at the crossroads there was the familiar sign pointing the way to the cemetery. Without an instant's hesitation she turned into the road through which she had ridden only a little while before. Ah! Here was sanctuary! There was no place for her in this world, but she could rest beside her sister. Here was peace!

She stumbled on. The snow had drifted deeply here, and in some places was much beyond her depth. But she floundered on, again and again plunging down into what seemed bottomless depths, and then struggling up again, on toward the place where they had laid her sister that afternoon.

The drifts were deeper here, for the wind had been at work, sweeping down the long bare road from the hilltop, hurling the eddying snow higher. At the side there were places where it was even now above her head, with only a narrow path that was wadable around it, and ever as she struggled on, each step seemed more and more impossible.

The tears had frozen on her white cheeks, and her lips were numb with cold. The frozen cry of her heart stifled in her throat, and there was none to hear. "Oh, Louise, my sister, let me come with you!"

Then suddenly she stumbled forward and lost her footing in a deep drift that seemed to envelop her. And there above her loomed the big stone arch that marked the entrance of the cemetery.

She sank back wearily, and the great white drift received her and folded cold arms about her. The lights from the stone arches touched her gold hair till it looked like a coronet, and the long sable-edged robe wrapped her round like a sumptuous winding sheet.

Once she opened her eyes, looked up to the gateway, and tried to struggle up again, but found herself too weary, and sank back once more, dreaming that her wish for death was coming true. For Herbert would never think to seek for her here. She was alone and safe at last.

Was God anywhere about? And did He care?

Then she closed her eyes and the snow softly fell on her face and on her eyelids, and the light glinted down and touched her with unearthly beauty.

2

HOWARD Sterling, the young house doctor from the sanitarium at Enderby, had been detailed to accompany a patient home who was still in a critical condition, but whom for certain reasons, it seemed best to put back among familiar surroundings for a time.

They went in the ambulance. Two nurses had attended on the way, and were to remain with the patient indefinitely. The young doctor was to stay overnight if it seemed necessary. But if all went well he had promised to return that evening so that another interne who was taking his place in his absence might get away to attend his sister's wedding.

The journey was a short one having taken a little over an hour. The patient had borne it well, and did not seem much exhausted. The experiment of bringing him home had proved so far a successful one, and he seemed to be resting comfortably. There was no reason at all why the young doctor should stay any longer. The ambulance had returned immediately but there was still time to make the six o'clock train back to Enderby and take over for Brownleigh so that he could start early for the wedding.

On the other hand there was a girl, Rose Bradford, in whom he was somewhat interested. She lived only five miles from the house of the patient, and there was time, if he hurried, to make a call upon Rose and then return to see how the patient fared, before catching the seven o'clock train from the Crossroads Junction. It was an express and would get him to Enderby a little after eight. He could telephone Brownleigh to arrange for one of the other doctors to take over during the brief interval, only a half hour or so. That would still get Brownleigh to the wedding in time. It was better, perhaps, that he should arrange to do this and so have time to take another look at the patient before he left, anyway. So his decision was made.

There was no difficulty in securing a conveyance to take him over to the Bradford estate. The grateful family of the patient could not do enough for him. In a short time Dr. Sterling was speeding in a luxurious car toward Rose Bradford.

It happened that Rose was even more interested in the young doctor than he was in her, and she was quite anxious for her father to meet him. She knew her father was a man of influence and could if he chose put her young doctor on his way to a name and fame, and place him far beyond the mere drudgery of a common house doctor in a private hospital. So as soon as she received his telephone call she had set about at once planning how she might keep him at her home until her father's return that evening, to dinner, and for the night. Then they would have opportunity to get acquainted.

There was quite a house-party of young people staying at Bradford Gables, and they put their heads together to make arrangements for a brilliant evening affair, that would without doubt beguile the stanchest and sternest adherent to duty that the medical profession could show. So when young Sterling arrived at the Gables he found the stage set for a prolonged stay with a delightful program prepared.

He looked about on the luxurious house, and down on the attractive Rose-girl who awaited his answer with eyes that pleaded eloquently, and felt greatly tempted.

Rose Bradford was small and slender, with wild-rose cheeks and lips like a small red bud. Her hair was dark and curling and fitted close about her face.

He looked down admiringly into her lovely dark melting eyes, and his expressive face took on that indulgent gentleness used in speaking to sweet pretty children.

"How I wish I could," he said wistfully. "It would be most charming. You certainly are an enchantress, and perhaps I should turn and flee at once, for you are making it more and more difficult for me."

The eyes melted their sweetest into his glance, and the pleading began in a soft gentle voice. She was thinking how engagingly the doctor's crisp hair waved away from his forehead. He was handsome as a Greek god. Why did he have to be poor, and a doctor? Why hadn't he been born the son of a millionaire instead of that tiresome Channy Foswick that her mother wanted her to marry?

There was a fresh bright color in the young doctor's cheeks that spoke of abounding health and clean living, but Rose didn't think much about such things. She was admiring the interesting whimsical twinkle in his gray eyes, and she was determined to keep him at the house as long as possible, so she kept up her insistence.

"But I can't possibly stay," he told her. "The man who is taking my place at the sanitarium is due at his sister's wedding tonight. I promised to be back and take over."

Rose shrugged her dainty shoulders, "After all, what

is a *sister's* wedding? He wouldn't be missed," she said. "It isn't as if it were something necessary like illness or death. Can't you make it up to him afterward? Get him a whole day off or something? Besides, wouldn't he think the patient had required you to stay? Isn't it really safer for you to stay a few days and see how the patient gets along at home? Surely you *ought* to stay, at least overnight."

But young Dr. Sterling in spite of his Greek-god features had a strong firm chin under the curve of his pleasant mouth.

"No," he said, "I couldn't do anything like that, not for *any*one. I have made a promise and I will not go back on it. Brownleigh is depending on me. It wouldn't be right."

The melting brown eyes flashed, the lips took on a look of scorn.

"He would never know," she said stormily.

"No," he said firmly.

She argued and coaxed but all to no purpose. The time was going that he had hoped to have filled with pleasant talk, and so at last he left her, quite disappointed that she had been so unreasonable, so determined to have her own way. Of course, she had been brought up to have everything she desired. And he was a fool even to play around for an hour or two with such a girl. She was not for him. He still had his way to make. He could never hope to give her all she would want.

But although he had started away in plenty of time for the plan he had made, the costly car in which he had been sent to Bradford Gables was not equipped for the snow that had fallen so rapidly even in this short time, and a slight break-down delayed them further, so that when they arrived back at the Martin mansion it was quite dark, and he was not a little worried lest he was even now going to have trouble in making his train. Also by this time his mind had suffered a revulsion, and it began to seem little short of cruel to have come away leaving the beautiful girl so unhappy. He began to question his own action. Brownleigh had perfectly understood that it might not be possible for him to return in time. Perhaps it would have been all right to have stayed. Well, he would see how the patient was. Let that settle it. And yet, did he have the face to return to Rose after he had been so decided in refusing to stay?

He went up to his patient and found him sleeping quietly, his pulse steady, his whole condition very good. Well, there was nothing for it but to go back to the sanitarium and sent Brownleigh off to the wedding.

The chauffeur meanwhile had put chains on the car, but the family of the patient were solicitous about him. They begged him to telephone the sanitarium and stay at least overnight. The storm was a real blizzard, they said. He might be snowed in on the train for hours. But when he firmly resisted their appeals, they served him with hot delicacies, and insisted on loaning him a great fur overcoat which they said would keep him warm on the train in case they were snowed in. And at last he was started.

It was not far to the Junction, only a matter of four or five miles, and the man had orders to stay overnight at the Junction if the roads were too bad to return home, so there was no need to worry about him.

Sterling had telephoned Brownleigh just before leaving the house and the relief in the other's voice when he found Sterling was returning left no doubt in his mind concerning his duty. Also Brownleigh's report of one particular patient made him still more anxious to get back to his work.

But as he sat in the dark in the car, continually Rose

Bradford's pretty alluring face kept coming across his vision. The disappointed pout, the tearful eyes. Yet what had he to do with her, child of luxury, who had stooped to coax one of the world's workers to while away a stormy evening?

He set his lips in the darkness and began planning how he might conquer fate, make himself a force in the world, one who would have a right to court a girl like Rose.

The car wallowed through the uneven road, plunged from side to side, and was aggravatingly slow. Sterling studied his watch by the light of his pocket flash and saw it was getting perilously close to the time the train would pass the Junction.

The world stretched white and wide as he looked through the window. White darkness, *terribly* white. And even the lighted windows of the houses they passed made but small blurs afar. The progress of the car grew slower and slower. Then they came to an enormous drift that spread wide and high before them and the driver got down to reconnoitre. A great wall of snow seemed to have reared itself impassably across the way. Sterling opened the car door and leaned out, calling questions, making futile suggestions. And then the driver uttered a sharp cry, a call it really was, and Sterling sprang out and went to his side.

It was then he saw her. There in the full glare of the headlights of the car she lay, pillowed on the snow, her gold hair matted with ice where the velvet hood had fallen back. The velvet drapery of her cloak was fast disappearing under the hurricane of the sleet, and there above her arched the great stone gateway of the cemetery! It was a startling sight on a night like this, the beautiful girl with the white, white face in its setting of blue and gold and snow.

He glanced about him to see if there was anything to explain the phenomenon of a lovely young woman thus attired, asleep in a snowdrift in front of the cemetery in this awful storm, but only the driving sleet and luminous distance of impenetrable whiteness answered his question.

It was as if the heavens had come down in a majesty of snow and lifted the earth up in a deep embrace.

Then his physician's instinct and training instantly began to work. He plunged over to where the girl was lying and tried to lift her, giving directions to the frightened chauffeur who was reluctant to touch what seemed to him like an apparition, but they finally succeeded in carrying her to the car and laying her on the cushions. Then the driver, wishing he were anywhere but on the road a night like this, essayed to find the road. He had taken the precaution to bring a snow shovel along, and working with all his might, managed to clear a way back into the main road. So he climbed to his seat and started his car, his mind still heavy over the burden of beautiful death behind him.

And meanwhile, Sterling knelt beside the silent girl, touching her cold, cold face that seemed so deathlike. He lifted the stiff little hand but no response came. He threw back the frozen velvet cloak from the softly garmented breast, and stooped his skilled ear to listen if there was still life in her body. He could not be sure, but he worked swiftly with what remedies he had at hand. There was no time to lose.

He jerked off the warm fur coat in which his hostess had enveloped him and wrapped it around the girl's still form. He chafed her cold hands, he took off the draggled slippers stiff with ice and held the little icy feet in his warm hands, drying them and finally wrapping them in the fur robe of the car. With his pocket flash he looked keenly into her face again for any signs of life. Then from his case he forced a few drops of stimulant between those white lips, but it was hard to tell whether they got farther than the lips, for he must work almost in the dark.

The face still looked marble-white and peaceful in its unearthly beauty, and there was something so exquisitely pure and almost holy about her that he touched her with awe.

In desperation he laid his own face against the girl's face, and felt the chill of her flesh. He laid his lips upon hers and tried to think he felt a warmth stealing into them.

Then suddenly he was confronted with the problem of what to do with her. They had reached the foot of the long hill below the cemetery. The village could not be far away. He could see dim lights blurring through the storm. He knew it was almost traintime for he had looked at his watch just before they had stopped their car. Would it be possible for him to stop somewhere and leave his burden and still make his train?

He called to the chauffeur:

"Is there a doctor near here you can call before the train comes?"

The chauffeur shook his head.

"Village is half a mile away. I don't know any doctor around here."

"Well, can you take her into the station and get someone to take charge of her at once? I must make the train."

"Station's closed," said the man tersely.

"Well, what can you do with her?" asked the doctor sharply. "She ought to have help at once to save her life, if it isn't too late already."

"Me? I can't do *nothin',"* gasped the man in horror,

stepping away from the sight of the closely wrapped figure.

"Perhaps you know her and can take her to her friends," he suggested, looking anxiously toward the now oncoming train. "They will be searching everywhere for her."

"I don't know nobody down this way," said the man stubbornly with a frightened ring to his voice. "I just been to the house up yonder about two weeks. You'd better take her onto the train with you. I can't do nothin' with her."

Then the train was upon them and there was no more time to think.

Sterling lifted his burden, with the help of the chauffeur who was all too anxious to get it away, and curious startled officials received it and carried it awesomely to a compartment in the Pullman which happened to be vacant.

Sterling lingered on the step of the car a moment, shouting directions to the chauffeur who readily promised anything to have him gone with the strange girl who he was certain was dead. Oh! Certainly he would inform his people at once of the stranger who had been found, and ask Mrs. Martin to give the information to the surrounding countryside. Of course he would go to the police headquarters in the village so that the girl's friends could find her. He assured Sterling that he would do all in his power to locate her folks, and his relieved countenance smiled benignly at the young doctor through the storm, as the train took up its laborious way through the snow.

The man watched the train out of sight, and then hurried to his car, resolved not to say a single word to anybody about the affair. In his opinion that girl was dead, and maybe he would get mixed up with a murder case somehow if he let on he knew anything about it. Moreover he had decided on the way over to Bradford Gables that evening that people who would ask a chauffeur to go out in a storm like this for *any* guy just to see a *girl,* or catch a train, weren't good folks to work for, and now was as good a time as any to leave. He would take that car home and then he would vanish in the morning. What that doctor ought to have done was to leave that girl lying there in the snow and let her own folks find her. She must have been dead long before they got there anyway, and it was none of their concern. What was the use of turning everything upside down and being uncomfortable for someone who was already dead? He believed in looking out for number one always and everywhere. So he went to the village and took a little much needed stimulant, and then managed to get the car back to its owner's garage, so late that he did not come in contact with any of the family. He said not a word about the strange experience he and the visiting doctor had encountered. He spent the rest of the night packing his effects for a hasty departure, and quite early in the morning he announced to his master that he had heard through a cousin he had met in the town the night before, that his mother was very sick, and he felt he should go to her at once. So he received his wages and departed before anyone had time to question him. And long before the doctor had ventured to disturb the family to ask whether they had found out anything about the girl, he had disappeared from the region. So the family knew nothing about the happening in the storm.

Like a frail crushed lily Janice lay in a white bed at the sanitarium and made little response to the treatment given her. It was as if she had gone too far into the world of whiteness and shadows to return.

Meanwhile, back in the house from which she had

fled the drink-crazed man had searched in vain to find her. In puzzled anger he at last pieced together a story. He told the servants and the few neighbors who came to inquire, that his sister-in-law had gone on a visit to the far west with a relative, and it might be some time before she returned. Then he hastily closed his house, offered it for sale, and went his way into a far country.

Some ten days later there appeared in the local papers of the region near the Martins' estate a brief account of the young woman who had been found near the cemetery gateway on the night of the blizzard, but not one of all the host of friends who loved Janice and her dead sister recognized her from the brief description given. A lovely girl attired in thin white and a sumptuous velvet cloak trimmed with fur. The Janice they knew would never have tramped the drifts on the road to the cemetery in a blizzard. It never occurred to anyone that the young woman who had been found and was lying near death's door in a nearby sanitarium could be Janice Whitmore. She would write to them, of course, as soon as she rallied from the death of her beloved sister. This other girl was probably some poor dancer from a cabaret, a sinner, or perhaps sinned against, and in a desperate situation trying to end her life. "What a pity!" they said, and thought no more about it. So the days went on, and only the young doctor who had found her, and was slowly bringing her back to life again, had any interest in her.

Her brother-in-law had no thought of her, not even of wonder as to what had become of the helpless young girl who had been left in his power and had escaped him. His only fear was that Janice had gone to a distant cousin who was a famous lawyer, and knew all about the financial affairs of the two sisters. He did not wish to get under the keen eyes of that lawyer, nor listen to his questioning about the estate, for Janice was scarcely of age as yet, and this cousin had been an executor of the sister's inheritance. He did not care to have that cousin know how he had tampered with the estate, and how greatly it had diminished under his hand.

The wondering servants in his household had shaken their heads and whispered, mindful of the loud voice and the way the master had thundered orders to the girl; mindful of the unwelcome embraces at the foot of the stairs, the wild fright in the girl's eyes. What had he done to her? Had she gone out alone in that storm, and what had happened to her?

Furtively they searched the house, even down to the cellar, every cranny where she might have hidden. But they were dismissed and far away before any news came out about the girl that was found.

Later, when Dr. Sterling communicated more at length with Mrs. Martin, she employed detectives, and did her interested best to find out who the mysterious girl could have been, but nothing ever came of it.

And the girl lay white and listless in her hospital bed, unconscious of what went on about her, utterly forgetful of all the recent happenings, coming out of chill cold and going into burning fever, buried in the oblivion of delirium, opening her white lips only to moan in low helplessness, quiet only when the cool hand of the doctor was laid on her hot forehead. Once or twice she opened her eyes and looked up at him with a frightened glance, fearful, questioning, and then slowly her eyelids drooped and closed over the troubled eyes as if satisfied. She drew a soft little sigh and seemed to rest more quietly. It strangely touched the young doctor, as if somehow she were depending upon him, as if in some occult way she understood that he had saved her from death in the storm.

Yet if she had any memory of what had brought her to this pass, in the midst of her delirium and fever, he could not tell. She was very ill, of course. Pneumonia had taken possession of her and there seemed to be no strength in her to resist the disease. Sometimes he wondered if perhaps death would be a sweet release to her from things worse than death. Of course he did not know anything about her, had no means of even guessing, save from the sweet sad droop of the lovely lips.

Yet more and more he longed to save her, to bring her back to life and see her smile once, to know that he had been able to lift the shadow from the pitiful tired young face.

As a doctor he should not let himself be interested in this way in a patient. Interest like that was apt to cloud his mind and blunt his perceptions. And this girl was nothing to him. Yet whenever he said that to himself he kept seeing her so white and still lying in that snow bank, sinking into a quick death, and his heart reached out and longed to help her. When the disease itself was practically conquered, there was the great weakness to deal with, the utter listlessness and apathy.

Sometimes when her nurse was busy elsewhere he would come and sit beside her for a few minutes and study the sweet quiet face. Now and again he would take the little inert hand in his and hold it gently, and once he fancied that the fingers nestled to his, but perhaps that was mere imagination.

Once as he sat thus he bowed his head and murmured almost inaudibly:

"Oh, God, you know what this is. Grant me knowledge to help."

And when he looked at her again her eyes were open, just for an instant. She seemed to be studying him with a question in her glance, and when he smiled at her there came a faint semblance of a smile to her lips. But then her eyes closed and the smile was gone.

Howard Sterling was not a praying man, and he couldn't understand why he had uttered that sudden unpremeditated petition, but somehow he felt after that smile that God had heard and answered in a way. Afterwards he told himself he was a fool to make so much of this incident of the girl, and he ought to get away from it and let somebody else take up her case. Perhaps it would be a good thing for him to take a few days off and make that promised visit to Rose, get his mind off the sanitarium and everything connected with it. Rose would be off him for life if he didn't do something about keeping his promise.

But somehow he didn't go. He kept putting it off again and again for various little reasons, until one night he told himself that he really didn't *want* to go until he saw a decided improvement in this girl. That would make Rose furious if she knew it, but it was true nevertheless, and of course it was true that he ought not to be so obsessed with the case of an unknown mysterious girl.

But it would soon be spring. The snow was gone, and in places the trees were beginning to take on a semblance of greenness. If the girl could get out into the open and breathe the springtime in the air it would surely give her new life. Perhaps he might even venture to take her out riding some day when she was stronger, and try to coax from her a little of her story. It did seem as if after all this time they ought somehow to be finding her people. If she were strong enough he might take her to the place where he found her and perhaps that would bring back memories. But no, that would not do, for the utter sorrow and abandonment of her whole attitude showed that she must have sustained some great shock or she would not be in this condition.

But the days went by, and little by little Janice came slowly back to life again.

3

MARTHA Spicer lived a little over a hundred and fifty miles from Enderby where the sanitarium was located.

For twenty-seven years she had served, first as saleswoman and then as buyer for women's underwear and stockings in a large department store. That she had been successful was proved by her rapid rise, and the deference that was paid to her by floorwalkers, salespeople and other store officials. But that her temper had suffered through the various trials of her position was apparent in the lines of impatience and discontent written on brow and lips, marring a face that would otherwise have been attractive.

She was not an unpleasant looking woman. Her features were regular and finely cut, her skin was clear and smooth, her hair abundant and becomingly gray, though too severely arranged. She was always immaculately neat, though severely plain. Her lips had that firm set that gave one the impression she thought it was wrong to look pretty. Poor thing! She had been so severely tried by the little snips of salesgirls whose thoughts were on the arrangement of their hair, and the height of the heels *on their shining* pumps, that perhaps one could hardly *blame her. But there was* about Miss Spicer's eyes a kind of fire of repression that danced now and then through the hardness she had cultivated, and made one feel that very many years ago, before she had been obliged to look out for herself and be discreet and responsible, she might have had a lot of mischief in her, and perhaps been almost beautiful.

But if there had been mischief and merriment in Martha Spicer it had long ago retired meekly into the background. If someone had boldly told her that she had been starved for years for a little bit of real fun she would have looked at them aghast and put on her most biting glance, the one she kept for customers who brought back the silk stockings they had purchased declaring that they already had runs in them when they were sent up.

Martha Spicer had been thrown upon her own resources since she was eighteen and the world at first had been most unkind to her. There had been the death of her father and mother, the utter loss of all the property, what little there had been, for her girlhood life had been scrimped from her earliest remembrance. Then the lover to whom she had turned, proved inadequate and she found herself sending him away to another girl, bitterness and defiance in her own heart. It was about that time she began to earn the title of "Spice Box" in the store, and in more modified ways it had stuck to her through the years.

But she had kept herself to herself, been independent and diligent, always within the bounds of refinement, neatness and conventionality. She had lived her dull round of monotony now for twenty-seven years.

She had an aunt and uncle, her only near relatives, a somber couple, who kept up a semblance of being in touch with her, though she never taxed their companionship to any extent. Twice a year she had visited them, Aunt Abigail and Uncle Jonathan, always with some small useful gifts from the store, such as handkerchiefs, neckties and collars. And they on their part had brought out the best preserves for supper and commended her for her diligence and prudence. Then they had gone their separate ways again until the time for the next semi-annual visit was due.

They had suggested years ago that she might live with them and pay her board, but she dreaded the very thought of living with them. They had not wanted her, she was sure, and she did not want them. They lived far from her department store. And they seemed satisfied with her decision and had never asked her again. Perhaps they dreaded any change in the routine of their lives as much as she dreaded to come into theirs.

And then suddenly they both died, Aunt Abigail outliving Uncle Jonathan by only a few months.

It was a great surprise to Martha Spicer after her aunt's funeral to have the lawyer tell her that the house, and quite a substantial bank account, besides some modest thousands in good securities, had been left to her. It had never occurred to her that there would be anything left, or that if there were she would get it. But she was the only living relative, and there was no will, so there was simply no one else to inherit it. Perhaps the old couple, in spite of scripture, had hoped to find some way of taking their worldly possessions with them. But however that was, Martha Spicer, after twenty-seven years of hard work, suddenly found herself independent, a woman of leisure.

She had never thought about inheriting money. Certainly not from her uncle and aunt, and of course there was no one else. Uncle Jonathan had always talked about the house as if it was mortgaged up to its full value, and they were just about ready to walk into the poorhouse. And if she had known that there was any money she would have expected Uncle Jonathan to leave it to his church or a missionary society, or at least to a hospital where it could work for him in the next world as good works. He was a sanctimonious old man, as well as very penurious. So when Martha was told that the old house with its worn furnishings and a substantial bank account belonged to her she was almost stunned. It did not seem right somehow to take it and do what she pleased with it. It was somehow like taking an unfair advantage of Uncle Jonathan and Aunt Abigail.

But after a little it began to seem like having Heaven open suddenly and let down some of its gold paving for her use. She had saved, of course, out of her earnings, and had enough put away to keep her frugally in her old age. But to be able to stop work and live in her own house like any "woman of means" almost took her breath away. She was not quite sure even yet that she ought to accept it. Yet here it was, and the lawyers and the judge said it was hers.

She even questioned at first whether she wouldn't continue on at the store, and just rent the house. Get a better boarding place perhaps and broaden out her life, go to a lecture now and then, maybe give something to missions. That ought to please the dead relatives. But after thinking it over carefully she came to the conclusion one night, why should she? She had always said she hated the store. Of course, she had done her work thoroughly and conscientiously, but she had never loved it the way some of the workers did. She had always longed for leisure to read, to lie down and rest her tired sad heart, nurse her disappointments and get a little comfort for the bitter ache that had been with her so long. She wanted to get a little beauty out of life before it was too late. To take the joy of living that she had always supposed was there for those who had the time to search for it.

And so one day she went grimly to the store head and offered her resignation. It eased her heart a little that he demurred and offered her more salary if she would reconsider, saying some very nice things about the work she had done with them, but she had made her decision and she was not one to change for a mere matter of a little more salary, especially now that she had inherited a tidy sum that would make her quite comfortable. So she agreed to stay long enough to put the one who was to take her place, through the routine, and then one morning in early spring she packed her sparse belongings, paid her board bill, and went on the trolley car to her new home.

But somehow when she arrived it did not give her the thrill she had expected. The house looked gloomy and desolate, and more than once during that first week while she was cleaning and putting the house in livable order, she found herself longing to get back to the cheerful store with its throngs of people coming and going. This house was lonely. She had never thought of it in that way before, but now that she was here alone, even considering all the drawbacks of a third-rate boarding house, it wasn't as pleasant as she had expected.

Of course, there was plenty to be done in a house that had been closed for several weeks, and as it was work that she was not accustomed to doing she found it very tiring, so that by the end of that first week she was tired enough to go to bed early and get up late Sunday morning, trying to luxuriate in the fact that she did not need to hurry to get anywhere. Although the realization didn't seem as alluring as she had expected it would.

She got herself a nice dinner, a bit of beefsteak and a

roasted potato, a few strawberries, telling her well-drilled conscience that it was not an extravagance, for the tiny box would last two days at least, and even if it was extravagant she had a right to it. Hadn't she gone without in plenty of ways all these years? And she was able to pay for an extravagance now and then, anyway.

She ate her dinner slowly, savoring every mouthful, fighting off that empty desolate feeling as she realized that there was no one in the whole world who would be likely to look her up, or care where she was. Glad to be free, of course, from some of the disagreeable fellow boarders she had habited with, yet sorrowful because the new life didn't blossom with new interests. Of course, next week she would likely go to church when she had time to look over the churches in that vicinity and decide where she wanted to go, but just today she would stay at home and have a taste of really resting, and knowing what a leisurely Sabbath was like.

So at last Martha Spicer sat down in Aunt Abigail's patchwork-cushioned rocking chair by the window, in her own house on Sunday afternoon, and took up Uncle Jonathan's religious paper to read a little. The subscription hadn't run out yet, and she somehow felt she ought to use it up. It didn't look very interesting, but she hadn't anything else just at hand that she wanted to read, so she began at the beginning and read conscientiously on through, determined to give her full attention to whatever came. Perhaps she would so be able to understand her uncle a little better.

At her feet sat Aunt Abigail's cat, Ernestine, amply wrapped in ancient fur. Her yellow eyes squinted retrospectively between long Sunday winks, her breast rumbling contentedly, like a time-worn hand organ. So she had sat at the feet of Aunt Abigail since kittenhood, a portly well-conducted cat whose follies, if she ever had any, were all in the past. She had not yet discovered that the careful bowl of milk and the ample dish of meat on which she had been lavishly fed were given from duty now, and not from love. For Ernestine, to her new mistress, now represented that church missionary society, or that needy hospital, to which Uncle Jonathan would surely have left his money if he had had time to realize that he was so soon to be called away from this earth, and would therefore not need the money any longer himself.

The house which Martha Spicer had inherited was in a plain quiet neighborhood, in a narrow unattractive street with rows of other brick houses all alike, all having gray stone steps, and there were plenty of children always noisily abroad.

The house was in the middle of the block with a narrow alley running on its left side. The steps gave immediately upon the brick pavement in front. There were two regulation front windows and many of the householders had adopted the fashion started by one of them perhaps, of having blue paper shades at the windows. They were of various tints, varying from indigo to robin's egg blue. Framed in the grimy red brick of the walls the effect was anything but pleasing to the trained taste of Martha Spicer, for even though her work was mainly among stockings and underwear, she had enjoyed all the beautiful things in the great store and knew when things matched and when colors jarred. So, as she sat at her front window and looked across at her only view her heart was not pleased.

The house consisted of double parlors, so-called, a dining room and kitchen backed by a shed or a laundry, a long narrow dark hall and steep stairs ascending on the alley side. The two front windows and a grudging one in the jog of the back parlor were the only sources of light for those two small parlors, and both rooms were dim and breathless even with the double doors stretched wide. The dining room was brightened only by a single window looking into a neighbor's back yard whose high fence mostly destroyed the view of even that uninspiring spot. Ernestine sometimes took a nap on the top of this fence while the boys of the neighborhood were gone to school.

The second story of the house had three good rooms and a bath, and a tin roof out over the back kitchen.

The furnishings of the house were ancient and worn and dreary. Nottingham lace curtains at the windows, flanked by gray paper shades with many pinholes winking through them. Ugly old tapestry and brussels carpeting, oilcloth on the hall, faded ingrain carpets upstairs.

There were a few pieces of fine old mahogany furniture, relics of Aunt Abigail's bridal days, but the rest were common and ugly. On the walls were cheap chromos, a steel engraving of Washington crossing the Delaware, the twin pictures of "Wide Awake" and "Fast Asleep" framed in black walnut with carved walnut leaves at the corners. Also there were "tidies" on the arms and backs of the chairs and sofa. Martha abominated them, but as yet she hadn't had the courage to remove them. It didn't seem quite polite to the old aunt and uncle to do so. They represented the handiwork of Aunt Abigail since childhood, done in tidy cotton, and were fearfully and wonderfully made.

So Miss Spicer turned from it all with a sigh of almost disappointment at the pall of dreariness that seemed to be over it and went for solace to her paper.

Outside there was a hum of children's voices, the high treble of boys' flute-like changing voices. They were making some kind of a horrid hullabaloo. There was the rattle of a tin pan containing stones, and the loud excited barking of a dog. It was most annoying. She told herself she didn't like children, and especially boys.

And then as she turned a page of the paper she came on an article on saving boys. "A Plea for the Boys" it was entitled, and Martha's lip curled. "A Plea for the People Who Have to Endure Boys" she thought it ought to be called. She would like to write it. There wasn't a bit of sense in letting boys make such a horrid racket in the street. They ought to be complained of. What on earth could they be doing to that poor dog? She was not particularly fond of dogs. At least she had never had anything to do with them, but she didn't want them tortured and she couldn't endure that yelping.

She rose suddenly and put her head out of the window to see what was going on, and found herself the object of attention of a group of boys immediately under her window. As she drew back out of sight she heard one boy say:

"Who's that old party? Ain't she a new one down here?"

And then the deep hoarse growl of the boy next door which had already become familiar:

"That's Miss Spicer. She's the party that owns the house now. The other old 'uns croaked, you know, and she's some relation or other. 'Spice Box' the kids call her. She's some tartar all right. I heard her talking to the milkman the other day."

"Oh boy!" said the first lad delightedly, "let's give her a serenade one o' these nights!"

Martha Spicer sat back in her patchwork rocker and fumed inwardly. What a world this was in which children dared to talk about a respectable elderly woman that way. To think she was obliged to live here and be subject to such unpleasantness. It was unbearable!

Then she turned back to her paper again and began to read:

"If some good women with pleasant homes and nobody but themselves to enjoy them, unless it be a cat or a poodle—" Miss Spicer cast an apologetic glance at Ernestine—"would just try the experiment of cultivating one boy, they would find an ample reward in the joy of doing it. Wouldn't it be a grand thing to save one boy from becoming a good-for-nothing man, or worse? All they need is a pleasant room, a few cakes or some molasses candy now and then, and a chance to bring their friends with them, and your boys are won. It isn't necessary to do much to amuse them, they'll do that themselves. What they want is a decent place to hang around in. You may say their own homes ought to hold them, and so they ought, but in nine cases out of ten they don't, and perhaps it would not need more than one glimpse of some of those homes to show you why. In truth most of their parents are more to blame for their being bad boys than they are; yet the parents either don't know how, or don't care. Why not be a mother to some boy whose mother isn't 'on her job' and save a boy? But there is one thing you must remember. Don't preach! You can't do a thing with a boy if you begin by preaching at him. You've got to win him first, and after that you can do anything in the world with him. Oh, he's like the proverbial robin. You've got to put salt on his tail before you can catch him. But he's worth catching. And isn't it a solemn thought that if you don't do something for that boy that lives next door to you, perhaps he'll land in jail some day, and you will be at least a little responsible, because you might have done something!" Miss Spicer stirred uneasily and frowned. She had left responsibilities in the store and she didn't want to be reminded of any new ones. Besides, those little hoodlums out there in the street were beyond saving. They *ought* to bring up in jail, beginning that way. They ought to be electrocuted or something and rid the world of them!

Her eyes dropped to the printed page again.

"You may think that some of them are not worth saving, but just try it and you'll find out. You will end by loving every mother's son of them, and finding something deeply interesting in them. There is no interest in life so absorbing as a boy if you just set yourself to know him, and help him to the right way. But if you try it you must make up your mind to give up self to a certain extent and be a boy with your boy. You've got to learn his language, adopt his code, and enjoy his sports. But it will pay you as nothing you ever did before. It is better than clubs and bridge. Try it and see."

The clatter outside the window was growing intolerable and the paper on how to save the boy seemed inappropriate. Martha Spicer cast it aside and went up to her room to take a nap.

But before she closed the blinds to shut out the last rays of the afternoon sun, she looked down cautiously on the little throng below, her eye singling out unconsciously, the dark thatch of the boy who lived next door.

"Gee! I'd like to go! Wouldn't that be great? I've never seen the ocean! But no chance for me. It costs too much! Have you ever been to the shore?"

"Oh sure!" swaggered another boy. "I been six or seven times! It's not so great! I'd rather swim in the river. The waves knock you all around."

"Aw, you always did hate to make any exertion," sneered the neighbor-boy. "Bet I wouldn't mind the waves. Gee! I wisht I could go!"

Miss Spicer drew her blinds shut softly then and lay

down on Aunt Abigail's big black walnut bed to try and sleep, but sleep would not come.

It might have been the boy's talk of the "street" picnic that was to be held next week at the shore that set her thinking about a vacation. She suddenly realized that at last it was possible for her to take a good long one now if she wished. There was money enough for her to go somewhere quite comfortably for several weeks and not seem extravagant either, yet somehow the idea did not greatly appeal to her. It didn't seem reasonable. She had a home of her own for the first time in her life and she ought to stay in it and enjoy it.

Enjoy it? That sounded like a duty, and she had been trotting around all her life at the point of that bayonet of duty. And how could she ever enjoy those gloomy rooms anyway, those ugly furnishings, that Aunt-Abigail-Uncle-Jonathan atmosphere of everything? It was all very well for them. They liked that sort of thing. They had been brought up to it and the things were theirs, accumulated through the years. But her soul cried out for other surroundings. Or, at least, why should she not change these as much as she could?

She sat straight up on the bed and faced the audacious thought temeritously. What would Aunt Abigail think if she knew that the ungrateful recipient of all her worldly possessions was contemplating a wholesale destruction of all tidies, antimacassars, and patchwork cushions? That was as far as she got with that first approach to the subject. Tidies and patchwork cushions. Oh, yes, and those horrible pictures, "Wide Awake," and "Fast Asleep" with their unnaturally healthy countenances and impossible auburn curls. She would take those down and burn them in the kitchen range or the furnace the first thing in the morning, frames and all, so that no one would ever suspect if any prying neighbor should chance to come in and take notice.

Having solaced herself with this dire resolution she lay down and slept, while below the street clattered on with its Sabbath noise, and the group under her window plotted mischief.

An hour later she awoke with a start and realized that there was a loud banging at her front door, accompanied by the most unearthly yowling of a cat. At once the thought flashed into her mind, "Ernestine! Those terrible boys!" and she sprang from her bed and hurried to her window.

It was indeed Ernestine in the hands of the enemy. A group of small boys were tying her plumy tail to the front door knob. Their grimy hurried hands knotted the bit of clothesline clumsily but firmly into place, while Ernestine with tooth and claw defended herself as best she could, meanwhile giving forth most unearthly yowlings of distress. She must have put up rather an effective defense to judge by the rough exclamations and curses that came from the young lips as they gave the pampered pet a last yank and fled down the alley.

Miss Spicer exclaimed in horror as the shouts of the boys died away, but Ernestine's furious frightened caterwaulings grew louder and more anguished, and there stood her natural defender looking down angrily upon her, silent and helpless. And then Martha Spicer suddenly realized that she must go down herself and remove that cat from her position of torture, and that this was the very thing that the young imps who had perpetrated this would-be joke had intended.

Then before she could even turn from the window to go downstairs there suddenly burst from the little side gate of the house next door a long lank boy with dark hair, the son of her next door neighbor, Ronald MacFarland by name. She supposed him to be like all bad boys and therefore come to further torment the poor beast in her distress, and it was quite evident that Ernestine also regarded his approach in the same light for her howls grew louder and more intense. Martha Spicer suddenly realized that it would be too late to help Ernestine if she waited to reach the front door, so she leaned from the window and addressed the boy, who by this time had reached the cat. But her words were drowned in the noise of the poor animal, and then Martha Spicer stopped in astonishment as she watched the movements of the boy. He threw himself against the cat deftly to prevent her scratching him, and drew out a big knife from his pocket. Opening it with one hand, as he held the cat under his arm with the other, he cut the clothes-line with a swift clip and set the cat free.

"What are you doing to that cat?" burst forth Miss Spicer angrily, unable to grasp the fact that a boy would do a kind act. "Aren't you *ashamed* of yourself?"

As the words left her lips the cat made a dart for the little iron gate that guarded the path to the back door and disappeared from sight, her clothesline decoration tarrying in view for a brief space behind her like the tail of a comet on its way, and then vanished.

The boy looked up with a grin.

"Ma'am?" he inquired easily. He felt there wasn't much she could do from that height except throw out a pitcher of water, and besides, for a wonder, he had a clear conscience, so he met her gaze undisturbedly.

Suddenly Miss Spicer found herself looking embarrassedly into a pair of merry dancing eyes of the deepest blue with the curliest black lashes she had ever seen, and wondering what she ought to do or say. It suddenly became evident that she was under obligation to this clear-eyed boy for Ernestine's release, and the vituperation that had hung upon her tongue clogged and trammeled her speech.

"I—Why—That is—Excuse me!" she stammered, "I'm much obliged to you for setting my cat free. I thought you were one of those bad boys."

Ronald's face beamed serenely up at her. It did his heart good to be recognized as belonging in another class from the "bad boys."

"Aw—them kids is nutty!" he responded affably. "They'll get sense bimeby."

Ronald was perhaps two years the senior of the eldest of those other boys and he drew himself up with superiority. The lady suddenly realized that he was a pleasant looking boy. There was something too in his tone that gave him the air of being her champion. A quick wonder filled her. She *liked* it! Nobody had ever championed her before. To be sure it was a very subtle thing, and when she had thanked the boy again she wondered just what it had been about him that made her feel so friendly toward him.

4

SHE went downstairs and tried to find Ernestine. She had never been just fond of the cat. It had seemed as if she had taken the place with Aunt Abigail and Uncle Jonathan that a child might have occupied. And that ridiculous name! Ernestine! For a *cat!* She knew it represented all the romance that had no other outlet in poor little narrow Aunt Abigail's life. Ernestine had been the name perhaps that she would have named a child if she had ever had one. But Martha Spicer had little patience for one who could lavish on a cat the affection that should have belonged to a human being. Yet she had cared for the cat conscientiously, and until now had felt only tolerance for her fellow-inheritor. It was her duty to look after that cat thoroughly as long as she lived, but love her she had never intended to do.

Now, however, she felt a sudden sympathy for the injured cat, a sort of fellow feeling. They were strays and lonely ones together with no one to protect and care for them. Her heart smote her for her cold unfriendliness toward the dumb creature. She would never be one to pamper an animal, but her heart was warming toward

Ernestine, and she felt quite distressed when she opened the door to find no cat crouching on the steps.

"Kitty, kitty, kitty!" she called, softening her voice unwontedly.

A sudden stealthy movement at her feet attracted her attention, and two great green eyes peered fearsomely out at her from under the steps.

"Poor kitty! Poor Ernestine!" she said tenderly, using the hateful name for the first time and without being aware of it.

Ernestine's head came a little further out from her hiding place, showing a gaunt haunted look in the furry face.

"Come kitty, poor kitty," went on Miss Spicer, stooping down in earnest now to soothe the frightened beast.

Ernestine suddenly projected herself like a stealthy shadow out from under the step and slid past her benefactor, into the kitchen, taking hasty cognizance of her environments, and making sure of her safety by gliding under the high dining room dresser from whence her green eyes shone balefully out like two green lamps.

Martha closed and locked the kitchen door with a reassuring click and set about preparing their supper. Nice appetizing milk toast and poached eggs—a whole egg for Ernestine. The smell of the browning toast presently tempted the cat, and her mistress was able to draw her forth from her hiding place and remove the fragment of rope still attached to her tail. The cat seemed grateful for this and set up a broken rumbling in her chest intended to indicate gratitude. The lady suddenly realized that it was pleasant to have even a cat grateful and friendly to her.

Perhaps under the circumstances Aunt Abigail might have given Ernestine a seat at the table with a high chair and a bib, but her niece would never go so far as that.

She did, however, find real comfort in setting Ernestine's saucer of toast and egg quite near to her side as she ate her own supper.

Of her own free will she stooped and patted the cat when they were done, and perhaps the wise animal drew as much comfort from the touch as she might have done from more elaborate pity.

After the supper things were washed and put away Martha turned on the light and sat down with her paper once more. Ernestine tucked close to her skirts unreproved, rumbling away her content. Somehow she felt shaken from her beaten path and seemed to have a sweeter more wholesome view of the world. A boy, a simple unregenerate boy had gone out of his way to be kind to a dumb animal, and had incidentally smiled at her, and the whole universe seemed changed.

She read her paper conscientiously through, reading over again the article about how to help boys, and this time it did not seem to anger her so much, for a kindly freckled face seemed to be smiling at her between the lines, and saying in a fascinating drawl, "They're only kids. They'll get some sense bimeby," and the good-natured appeal in his eyes seemed to warm her heart and cool her anger toward boys in general. When she finally turned out the lights for the night she allowed Ernestine to go upstairs with her. Every night so far the cat had attempted it, but had been firmly put back in the kitchen on a cushion in a soap box. Tonight, however, she looked down hesitantly as the great creature purred wistfully about her feet, and then said: "Well, come on. I suppose you're used to it!" And when Ernestine happily jumped on the foot of the bed and curled in a furry mound close to the footboard she did not shove her off, and she absently smiled and patted her as she passed to turn out the light. She was thinking of a freckled blue-eyed face turned up to the window, and a pleasant saucy voice saying, "Ma'am?"

During the hours that she lay awake that night thinking new thoughts, she was dimly conscious of the purring of the cat and strangely comforted by it. Why hadn't she known before how lonely it was in the world without even a cat? Why, even a cat was company.

Bits of sentences from that article about boys floated through her mind ever and anon, and stayed with her in the morning when she awoke. She tried to forget them but they would return at the most unexpected moments and confuse her thoughts. She half resented and half courted the suggestions that article seemed to bring to her.

Monday and Tuesday she got through with quite contentedly going from room to room and burning up or otherwise discarding a few more ancient landmarks in the house. It had to be done a thing at a time, for as yet her conscience was tender with regard to Aunt Abigail's Lares and Penates. But after "Wide Awake" and "Fast Asleep" had been used for kindling the kitchen fire in the old-fashioned coal stove, and several tidies and antimacassars had followed suit she felt better, and a spirit of iconoclasm entered into her. If the house was hers why shouldn't she have it to please her?

Wednesday morning she swept the parlor mantel free from several cheap imitation Dresden shepherdesses, and a purple glass vase decorated with hideous green roses and carried them to the back kitchen where she smashed them in the ashcan. But she left Ernestine asleep in Aunt Abigail's rocker while she did it. She could not quite have done it in the presence of Ernestine.

She felt better after smashing the ancient bric-a-brac, and washed the mantel with vigor and Old Dutch Cleanser, but when it was done it looked bare and empty and she had nothing to put on it. So she went over the house from room to room and finally found an old pair of brass candlesticks rolled in canton flannel in the upper drawer of a bureau. These she brought down and polished till they shone, and then placed them on the mantel where they made one spot of light in the dullness of the room. The dingy old wallpaper of faded maroon with tarnished gilt flowers seemed shabbier than ever though she tried not to notice it. But presently she put on her hat and went down the street to a little art store on Eighth Street and bought a shop-worn copy of the Roman Colosseum, framed simply, and came home triumphant. It was her first attempt in all the years to satisfy the love of the beautiful which had been bottled up in her soul and she felt almost wicked at the happiness it gave her when the picture was finally hung over the mantel. It really did go wonderfully well with the candlesticks, and covered a great deal of the ugly wallpaper.

Ernestine seemed to take kindly to the changes and sat beneath the mantel contentedly with a furtive suggestion in her attitude of how nice it would be to have a fireplace there with an open fire on a cold day.

It was Thursday morning that the dining room shutters stuck and refused to open even with a blow from a hammer. It had rained all night and doubtless the wood was swollen. What a thing it was to be a woman and not know what to do in a case like that! If this had happened in the store she would have sent for the store carpenter, but she had no carpenter.

She went to the kitchen door and threw it wide open to make more light and air, for the room seemed stuffy. As the door swung wide she heard the sound of voices in the next yard and the ring of an axe.

"If you want money for any such nonsense, get to

work and earn it. You'll get none from me!" said a man's voice angrily, and a door slammed loudly.

"I ain't got any way to earn money," said the sullen voice of Ronald. "Oh blame it! I ain't got any way to earn money! I can't ever do anything the other fellows do!" and the axe was slung viciously across the tiny yard.

Something in the boy's tone appealed to the woman. It set a heart string vibrating that had been touched on Sunday with invisible fingers, and the thrill of it had not been forgotten.

Martha paused in her kitchen doorway her brows drawn thoughtfully. She stepped down hesitantly to the brick pavement, and over to the fence, then realized she was not tall enough to see over the fence and went back to the house again. In a moment she reappeared with Ernestine's soap box, a look of determination on her face, planted the box firmly by the fence and mounted it.

The boy had resumed his axe and was bringing it down fiercely on a stubborn stick of wood. His face was dark and dejected. It did not need a prophet to tell that the boy was bitterly disappointed. Martha's heart gave a keen jerk of sympathy.

"Boy!" she said sharply. It was the way they addressed the cash boys in the store. She knew no other.

The boy looked up frowning. He did not wish intrusion in his bitterness.

Martha tried to smile with her strangely palpitating heart in her throat. The effect was curious. The boy forgot his bitterness in studying her. What was "Spice-Box" going to charge him with now?

"Ma'am?" said the boy, his voice still sullen.

She was surprised to find how disappointed she was that he had no smiling response for her, but she tried another smile. She wasn't so used to smiling.

"Why, I thought perhaps you would help me just a minute," she began apologetically. "I can't get my dining room window shutter open. I don't know what's the matter."

"Sure!" said the boy disinterestedly, flinging his axe down with relief and vaulting over the fence before she knew what he was going to do. His suddenness quite took her breath away. She turned cautiously on her box and started to get down, but the boy stepped up and put out his arm. He didn't say "Let me help you," but it amounted to that, and she fairly trembled over the pleasure it gave her. Somehow chivalry had come her way at last!

She led him to the dining room, and Ernestine arose in haste and arched her back when she saw him. But Ronald stooped and smoothed her fur, rubbed her under the chin and spoke in gentle tones.

"Hullo, Old Top! Had a hard time the other day, didn't you? Never mind, Old Sport, you clawed 'em good. Binny Twining's got a ripper all down one cheek. You just missed his eye. And Chuck Frisbie's lost the hide off his nose. Some class to you!"

And wonder of wonders, Ernestine the conservative rubbed her sides against the boy's trousers and arched her head coyly up to his knees, rumbling her affection in no uncertain terms.

Then the boy stalked to the window, gave it one look, grasped hold of the iron ring and gave it a mighty jolt, and behold it opened meekly as if nothing had been the matter. Martha sighed in relief and wonder. The boy had accomplished the impossible so easily.

She handed forth a bright quarter from the little dish of change she kept on the sideboard for incidentals, but the boy straightened up from giving Ernestine a parting touch of affection and she suddenly realized she had made a mistake, for the boy flushed and frowned and drew back.

"Naw, I don't want nothing," he said. "What do you think I am? Take money for just a little thing like that? I guess not! I ain't a gyp. That's all right. Glad to do it for you."

She drew the money back, embarrassed before his generous spirit. He was in need of money for some desire of his heart, for she had just heard him say so, yet he would not take it. He had shattered at a blow one of her fixed ideas about boys. She had thought they were all selfish mercenary little animals, and here he wouldn't accept her money! Indeed she had rather enjoyed the prospect of giving him something to help in the big desire of his heart, and now he wouldn't let her help him! She shrank from his clear eyes and his high-handed way of distributing his favors. She felt ashamed that she had offered him money, and as if she ought to apologize.

"But if you hadn't come in I should have had to send for a carpenter," she faltered, "and you know that would have cost a great deal more."

"You wouldn't need a carpenter for a little thing like that," he said patronizingly. "It wasn't anything."

He started to go back to the fence to return the way he had come, and Martha stood uncertainly in her kitchen door and watched him placing his hard young hands on the fence preparatory to vaulting over.

"I'll tell you," she said with sudden inspiration, "do you like hot gingerbread?"

"I sure do!" said the boy with shining eyes.

"Well, I'm going to bake gingerbread today. What time do you get home from school? You go to school, don't you?"

"Sure I go. I get home about four o'clock when I don't get kept in."

"Well, don't get kept in today and I'll have some hot gingerbread for you at four o'clock!"

There was a smile in her eyes that looked unaccustomed. But the boy understood and his eyes answered.

"Some class!" he answered gaily. "I'll be here!" and he vaulted the fence and was soon heard chopping and whistling cheerily. Martha wondered why she felt all at once so interested in life.

Ernestine came to the door and purred lovingly around her feet, and somehow it was good to have her there. She began to wonder why the cat had not seemed shy of the boy, and was at once convinced that there must be something unusual about that boy. He didn't seem a bit like what she thought other boys were. She was sure she never thought before that a boy could be so likable.

She took pleasure in hunting up her mother's old recipe for gingerbread and getting everything prepared for baking so that it might be ready by four o'clock. She took a pint more milk, and some cream to whip, so that there would be plenty to offer along with the gingerbread.

At four o'clock the boy arrived promptly, walking in the side gate and tapping at the kitchen door with an air of delightful secrecy.

He looked half ashamed as he dragged off his cap and entered. He had been thinking about that gingerbread all day, but he wouldn't have her know it for the world.

"I just thought I'd stop in and see if that shutter's working all right yet," he mumbled, his cheeks growing red. He wasn't embarrassed of course, not a bit, but he had to make some kind of a bluff to carry off the situation.

She led him into the front room where the reconstructed mantel gave an air of newness to the place, and seated him in a comfortable chair near the round center table. The cat arose with a welcoming yawn, and rubbed her back lazily against the boy's foot as much as to say, "Well, this is cozy of you!"

Martha came in bearing a tray on which was a great plate of steaming squares of hot gingerbread, a glass of foamy milk, and a dish of velvety whipped cream. She set it down on the table beside him and bade him eat as much as he wanted to, offering a dish if he wanted to put whipped cream on the cake. She took a piece of gingerbread herself just to keep him company and sat in the rocker to eat it sociably. The boy was not slow in accepting her invitation.

"Gee! This is great!" he said with his mouth full. "Some class to this."

"I guess you had pretty good lessons today," said Martha smiling, and trying to be good company. "You didn't have to stay after school."

The boy grinned.

"No chance," he said gaily. "I never had a lesson in my life. I guess the teacher'd croak if I had a lesson. He sure did have it in for me today, but I shinned out when he wasn't looking."

The lady looked distressed.

"But won't that get you into trouble tomorrow," she asked anxiously, and wondered why she cared.

"I should worry!" shrugged the boy. "Might as well be one thing as another. He always has it in for me."

"Oh, that's too bad!" said the lady in dismay.

"Aw, I don't mind. I'm used to it," he said with his mouth full. "Say," he lifted his eyes toward the picture of the Colosseum. "That's new, isn't it? That wasn't here before."

Her eyes lighted. A boy had noticed a picture!

"Yes, it's new. I bought it yesterday. Do you like it?"

"What is it?" he asked, knitting his brows and holding his judgment in reserve. "Did they have a fire or an earthquake? Or was it some place where they'd been bombing the town? I don't get on to the idea. Queer thing to make a picture of."

"Why, it's the old Roman Colosseum. That is, it's what is left of the Colosseum. The ruins, you know. It's one of the great sights of the world that tourists go abroad to see, or did before this war broke everything up. I've always wanted to go to Rome and see it, and I've always liked the picture."

The boy got up and looked at it more closely.

"Gee, that's where they had those bull fights, isn't it? I remember they had a picture of that in our history book."

Then his attention turned to the candlesticks.

"Those are new, too, aren't they? Some class!"

"You like them? Yes, they're new, or rather very old. I found them wrapped up in a bureau drawer. I like their shape. They are fine old brass."

"They look a lot better than the junk that used to be here," remarked the boy thoughtfully, turning back to the gingerbread and helping himself to another generous hunk.

"You must have been over here a good deal," said Martha, surprised that Uncle Jonathan and Aunt Abigail would allow a boy within their sacred precincts.

"Sure, I used to tend the furnace, and I used to come in this room when she paid me. She used to give me twenty-five cents a week." He stooped and gave Ernestine a fragment of his cake.

Martha's face lighted.

"Oh," she said, "then perhaps I can get you to attend to my furnace next fall. But I think twenty-five cents a week is too little for all that work. How often did you come?"

"Morning and evening." The boy's eyes were shining.

"Well, will you have time to look after mine? And suppose we say fifty cents a week?"

"Oh, gee!" he said, stooping to tickle Ernestine under the chin to hide his pleasure. "But good night! It ain't worth that much!"

"Well, that's settled then. I'm sure it will be worth at least that much to me." Martha had very little idea about the prevailing standards of salaries for taking care of furnaces, but she was sure at first thought that twenty-five cents wasn't enough, even if he did live only next door.

"Now," she said, seeing that the gingerbread had pretty well vanished, and the boy had stopped eating, "suppose we go down cellar and see if the furnace is all right for next fall. I know that's some time away, but it is well to know what to count on, and I always like to have things in good order in plenty of time."

She was surprising herself by making all these excuses for prolonging the boy's call, but somehow the house seemed so much less cheerless with the boy's cheery freckled face in it.

"Did you have the smoke pipe taken down?" asked the young fireman. "I told her it ought to be done, but she said she might want a fire again. And then when she took sick, of course, I didn't come any more. She had a nurse here, you know. The pipe was pretty old last winter."

"Well, now I don't know anything about that, whether it was taken down or not. I never had anything to do with furnaces before. Suppose we go down and look at it."

So they went down. She walked anxiously through

the unknown precincts of her cellar and looked around curiously.

"It's plumb gone," said Ronald wisely, putting a stubby finger through the rust. "See there! You'll have to get a new pipe."

"Well, that ought to be attended to at once, and have it ready to set up when it gets near fall. It's always well to be prepared for changing seasons. I wonder where I'll get someone to fix it? Do you know a good man near here? Could you get me one and see that he does what ought to be done? Of course I'll be glad to pay you for your trouble. Suppose we say your salary begins now, and then I'll feel free to call on you for little things when I need them. We'll settle on a fair rate and you can keep a record of the time it takes. I suppose there will be a lot of things like this before I really get settled here and down to living."

"Aw gee, I'll do that of course. I'll get Bennett, he's a good man. He doesn't charge as much as Simpson either. He's a good friend of mine. But I don't want pay for a little thing like that. That's not work."

"Oh, yes it is, and I must insist that you have a salary or a regular price by the hour, or something or I will not feel free to call you when I need you."

The boy looked at her as if she was a new specimen.

"Okay," he grinned, "have it your own way, only you don't haveta pay me for things that aren't work."

"Yes," said the lady. "I'm paying you for taking the responsibility of little things that I don't understand and might forget, don't you see?"

"Okay, if you're sure it's all right," he said doubtfully. And so it was arranged. But she marveled at his attitude. A sense of financial fairness was not what she had always been led to expect of a boy. Was it possible that there were other boys like him? As she thought about it she vaguely recalled a shadowy sentence from that article on boys which had said something about their fineness of soul. Well, perhaps it might be so. She only hoped it was, even if it meant that she had to revise all her former ideas of boys.

"You've got a good house here," said the boy suddenly, putting his hand on the stone foundation wall. There was a kind of part-proprietorship in the gesture, as though he had entered into a partnership with her and was pleased with the outfit.

"Yes, it's well enough I guess," she answered, and sighed. "It's a little lonely though for me. I've been used to being where there are plenty of people, and the rooms here seem so small and dark."

She was almost ashamed of her confidential outburst as soon as it was uttered, but the boy looked around with comprehension.

"Houses are that way," he admitted. "I don't like 'em myself. I like outdoors best. We fellows go down to the creek about three miles up in the country and camp on a big rock, put up a tent and cook and lie out at night. Gee! It's great! You can't tell which is sky and which is creek sometimes. The fireflies are so big they look like stars, and the stars twinkle around like they were fireflies. Gee, I'd like to live there. The only room I ever saw that was big enough for me was our gym. It isn't all cut up. It's big and high and wide. You can breathe and run in it. Gee! I'd like to live in a house like that up there in the picture!" he pointed to the Colosseum. "Wouldn't that be grand? When it rained you could crawl under a wall till it was over, and other times you'd just have the sky."

She looked down at his eager face and her own heart entered into his feelings. For a wild moment she felt the call of the open, the irresistible longing for something big and free that had never come into her life, and that she had never before even known she wanted.

"Say, do you wantta know what I'd do if I owned a house like this?" the boy went on. "I'd cut out all these partitions and make a big room out of it if it was me. And I'd make one side, or a front, or something, all glass. You could do it easy. You've got an alley next you. Come on out, I'll show you."

She followed out the front door down to the alley and watched his eager face while he pointed to the blank brick wall.

"There's one down on Diamond Street got a baywindow with flowers in it and a bird in a gold cage. You ought to see it. You've got room here for any number of windows. I'd get a carpenter if I was you and knock a hole there." He pointed to the place he visioned for a window. She found her heart leaping with the desire to follow his suggestion, knock out the old dark wall and let in the air and light. What a beautiful thing that would be to do! But what would Aunt Abigail and Uncle Jonathan think if they knew that she even allowed such a thought to be mentioned in her presence? They would look upon it as desecration of their property!

A boy was coming down the street and Ronald put up two grimy fingers to his lips and let forth a shrieking whistle. Martha jumped before she realized what it was. But the boy's attention was no longer on baywindows and elderly female neighbors. Something was evidently attracting his attention down the street.

"I gotta beat it," he said hastily. "If you want anything let me know. I'll see you sub-se! So long!" and he was gone like a flash.

Martha Spicer recovered her senses eventually and realized that she was standing alone in her alley gazing after a vanishing boy. The neighbors might have cause to think her crazy if she stayed here. She gave one lingering, comprehensive, considering glance at the ugly wall which reared above her, and turned to go in.

Ernestine met her at the door as she went in and she stooped to pat her lovingly. A sense of well being and a new zest for life had entered into her.

Yet as the night latch clicked the shades of Uncle Jonathan and Aunt Abigail met her with accusing eyes. Would she tear to pieces a good respectable house in which they had lived a lifetime? She, a poor relation? What was good enough for them ought to be good enough for her! And there were the dull old curtains and the solid respectable furniture. They all seemed to chime in with the protest. All except Ernestine, who seemed glad, rubbed up against her lovingly, and when she sat down made a sudden spring into her lap, and curled down purring happily. She looked at the cat wonderingly for an instant and then laid her white hand on the thick fur and let the warmth of the friendly creature comfort her.

After that she sat for a long time rocking back and forth and thinking: "What if I *should* tear down the partitions and make one big room? What if I *should* have a baywindow? What if I *should* make a bright spot in the world for myself, and maybe some other people? What if I should?

Suddenly she looked at the clock and the habit of a lifetime was upon her. It was time to go to bed.

But as she gave Ernestine a good night pat, and reached to turn out her light she said to herself, "Tomorrow I will go down to the store and get the best Roman History I can find and read up about the Colosseum."

5

JANICE Whitmore was creeping very steadily back to
life and every time that Dr. Sterling went in to see her
he felt more and more encouraged about her. It was
almost like a miracle, he still felt, for she had been down
at the very depths, and it had seemed so impossible to
save her. It perhaps gave him more real professional
pleasure than any case he had yet cared for. But there was
a personal element about it too, as if he had been given
special supervision over this girl, the only one who had
been present to do anything for her at the crucial moment, and he felt his responsibility was great.

He had spent much time thinking about her, wondering what her history might be, and how soon he dared
begin to question her a little. He had been letting the
matter drift until she should seem to rouse from the deep
apathy that had been over her since she first began to be
conscious.

But there came a morning when he entered her room
to greet her as usual, and she turned to him with a faint
smile on her lips, making her face for the instant almost
startlingly beautiful. There was a reminder of the lovely

beauty he had seen in that face lying against the snow that first night. He drew a quick breath and recovered his normal calm, but somehow he felt the time had come to go forward in the case. To that end he sat down a few moments to talk.

"You are feeling better, aren't you?" he asked. "I knew the day would come when I should see the look in your eyes as if you really wanted to live again."

He was watching her very carefully, and he saw her start and catch her breath.

"Oh, no," she said with a slow quivering breath. "No, I don't really want to live, only I know it is right to go on as long as God wills it so."

"Yes," he said, "it is. God knows what He has ahead for you, and there is a reason why He put you here, I suppose. I don't know so much about these things, but I'm sure there was a reason when God made you. But now, what is it that has made you feel you do not want to live? Wouldn't it be better if you were to tell me? Can't you trust me? I shall not make it public."

"Oh," she said, and great tears suddenly welled up into her lovely eyes and fell slowly down. "Yes, of course," she said sadly. "You see, my only sister died, and her little baby girl died too and I'm quite alone in the world."

Her lip quivered pitifully as she spoke, though she was evidently struggling for self-control.

"Oh, you poor child! That is very hard," the doctor said sympathetically. "I know those things seem very terrible, especially at first. Were these deaths recent?"

"Yes, the baby died three months ago, and my sister was just buried—" she was going to say "today" till she realized that it wouldn't be today any more for she had perhaps been here on this bed for a long time. "She was just buried the day—I came here—I guess. I can't quite remember. It was in a storm I know."

"Yes," said the doctor quietly, "it was in a storm. Do you know where I found you?"

She gave him a startled look.

"Did *you* find me? Where?"

"You were lying in the snow at the entrance to the cemetery near Willow Croft. Do you remember enough about it to know what you were going to do?"

She was quiet, thoughtful a moment.

"Yes, I remember a little. I think I was going to my sister. There seemed no other place to go then, and the storm was terrible. I couldn't go any farther. I was so very tired."

"Poor little girl," said Howard Sterling, gently laying his hand on her white one for an instant. "I know. And perhaps this telling about it is too hard for you yet. Would you rather wait till you feel stronger?"

"No, it's better to get it over," she said with a sigh, closing her eyelids quickly and shaking off a couple of tears that were rolling down her cheeks. "It's all right. If I've got to live I've got to snap out of this. I thought perhaps I could die and go away where Louise went, but since I can't I've got to get strong enough to get a job and earn my living. I want to repay you people for all you've been doing for me. I realize it's been a lot."

"There, now, you're not to think about that," he said soothingly, "we've all been glad to do everything we could to help, and we're so happy that you are really on the mend now."

"You've all been wonderful!" she said with another of those quivering sighs.

"But haven't you any friends? Wouldn't you like to have us send for some of them?"

A great fear came into her eyes.

"Yes, I have a lot of pleasant friends, but not such very close ones. You see, my sister was sick for quite a while before and after the baby died, and I stayed at home with her most of the time for a couple of years. We didn't go out much. They are nice people, but I don't want any of them now, please."

"Well, of course you do not have to have them if you do not want them," said the doctor. "I just thought there might be a few who are missing you and greatly pained that you have disappeared."

"No," she said. "They weren't as intimate as that."

"I'm sorry," said the doctor. "I was hoping there was at least one or two who would come and cheer you up if they knew where to find you."

She shook her head sadly, and Sterling felt that the interview for the present was at an end, till suddenly he bethought him of another question.

"Do you know, my friend, you haven't told me your name?"

"Oh," said the girl and a look of fright came into her eyes. "Do I have to?"

"Well, of course we've got to call you something," he said smiling genially. "We have to have something to put in the hospital records. You don't want to just go by a number as if you were a convict, do you? The nurses and officials would think it was very queer if you had no name. Would you want to use an assumed name?"

"Oh, no, I wouldn't like to do that," she sighed. "But—I seem to have arrived here in such a dramatic style. I wouldn't like to be talked about, nor have it get into the papers. My sister would have hated to have that happen to me. You see we are only quiet people."

The doctor bowed gravely.

"I can quite understand how you feel," he said gently, "and I thought you would be pleased to know that I told only the officials of the hospital when I brought you here. I told them that you were found at the entrance of the cemetery as if you were going to the grave of a dear one. You have a right to your own privacy of course, but haven't you a middle name that you could use in some way? I think that would be pleasanter for you while you are here. Do you have any friends who live about here, that is in this immediate vicinity, who would be likely to come to visit someone and perhaps see you or hear of you?"

Janice looked up with a sudden faint smile.

"I don't know where *here* is, you know," she said quaintly.

"Of course, I forgot. Well, we'll have to remedy that as soon as possible. How soon do you think you will feel well enough to take a ride with me? When you are I'll drive you around and give you a glimpse of the place. It is called Enderby, and it is about ninety miles from the place where I found you. Enderby is a very pretty spot, especially at this time of year. I really think a drive might do you a lot of good, put some color into those white cheeks, and a little brightness in your eyes. Then we can talk more about all these things and perhaps settle on some name by which you can be known. Be thinking up a few questions you would like to ask me if you want to. How soon do you think you would enjoy getting out in the spring air?"

Janice smiled gently.

"You are very kind," she said, "but you don't need to go to all that trouble. I am all right, and I'll be up and around soon now. But there is one question I would like to ask you. Would you be likely to know of any place around here where I can get a job so that I can pay the hospital what I owe them, and pay you? That is the only question that interests me now."

"Well, perhaps I might," said the doctor thoughtfully, "but I wouldn't want you to try any hard work at present. I want to keep a close watch on you for a while to make sure there are no complications lingering around to make trouble for you later in your life. But I'll be thinking about it. I wonder—How would you like to be doing something around the hospital for a while? There are light office jobs, work at the desk, meeting the parents of the child patients, something like that. Would that interest you? And later you might even start to take nurse's training if you are interested in that."

A light came to Janice's eyes and a quick flush of color to her cheeks.

"Oh, that would be wonderful! Could I really? Yes, I should like to do anything like that, in fact anything you feel I can. At least until my bills are paid."

"Well, don't fret about bills. That will all come in good time. Get well first. And in the meantime, take a little nap right away and then begin to think about the name you want to be called."

Janice looked up with a quick smile.

"I don't have to think any more about that," she said. "You may tell them I am Mary Whitmore."

He looked at her keenly for an instant, wondering if that was real or an assumed name, but he took it in his best style, with an easy smile.

"Fine!" he said. "That sounds good. I think it fits you nicely. Now, close your eyes and go to sleep. Set your thoughts on getting ready for that drive in the country as soon as possible."

Then with a cordial smile he left her, and she lay there thinking how very kind he had been, and how easy he had made the matter of her name. After all she had not had to tell him whether that was her real name or not, and she didn't feel worried now about it, for Mary was her middle name, although she never used it. The people she knew would not remember it. They had never known her as Mary, and she doubted if Herbert had ever known about it either. At least he wouldn't be looking for her under that name.

Drifting into a restful sleep she thought again how kind and helpful that doctor had been. She owed her life to him, and she supposed she ought to be grateful, although it would have been such a happy release if she could have gone on to Heaven with her sister. But then that was not a thing she had any right to think about. God had put her here, as the doctor had said, with some purpose, and she must stay until He took her away. That was practically what the doctor had said. He must be a Christian. It was what her Christian mother and father had taught her before they left her. It was what her sister believed, and what she had been trained to believe. Of course it was right. And of course she must be glad that her life was saved. Maybe some time she would reach the place where she could be thankful about it. But certainly the doctor was kind, for apparently he could very easily have left her lying in that snowbank to die and not taken all that trouble to bring her here. Well, of course, God had been good to her, and probably there was going to be a way made for the next things that had come to her.

So thinking, she dropped asleep, and dreamed there were angels somewhere near, and her sister with the baby who had gone to Heaven such a little while before.

When she awoke later, she felt a pleasant hope at the memory of the job the doctor was going to help her get as soon as she was strong enough.

These thoughts made a brighter outlook on life and she began to feel decidedly better. It wasn't long before she felt quite equal to the ride the doctor had suggested.

It was a beautiful morning when the nurse came up to say that the doctor wanted her to take a ride, and donning a borrowed uniform, she was soon ready. To think she was to go into the great out of doors again! It seemed so very long that she had been here in this little hospital bed. And spring was now come. There would be nothing to remind her of that awful storm in which she had arrived.

The doctor drove into quiet lanes, and away from houses. Indeed there seemed to be very few houses even in the distance. It was just sweet countryside. Farmers plowing and harrowing ground, planting seed. The low even furrows in the wide fields seemed restful. And then they drove through wooded land with perfume of wild growing things in the air, the pine trees' resinous tang, slippery elm, and the mingling of fresh earth, newly washed with rain.

The doctor watched her furtively, saw the sad look fade out of her eyes, and a sparkle of interest in the beauty about her grow in its place.

"Oh, there are blue violets all over that bank!" she exclaimed. "How many there are! Oh, I would like to get out and pick them."

"Well, you may try it," said Sterling, drawing up at the side of the road. "Just for a minute. Not too long, and if picking the first one tires you, stop immediately!"

He helped her out and stooped down beside her, picking with her, watching her white fingers moving among the broad green leaves. And when he put her back in the car he laid his own handful of purple blossoms in her lap, and smiled to see how eagerly she arranged them and drew them up to her face to touch them, and smell their freshness.

They did not talk much that first ride, just spoke now and again of the blue of the sky, the loveliness of the hills in the distance. Quite casually he pointed out the notable spots in the landscape, but he did not make much of them. He wanted to ease her back into the world again with as little ado about it as possible. To make her feel that she was back into living, and had been a long time, and that the sorrow and sickness were far behind her. When he brought her back to the hospital her face seemed really bright, almost happy.

They hadn't talked personalities at all, until just as they turned into the drive of the sanitarium grounds, and then he said quite casually:

"Well, if you are still of a mind to go to work I think I can promise you that there will be a place for you, perhaps by next week if you feel strong enough for it."

"Oh!" she said, catching her breath with a pleased exclamation. "I am so glad. I'm sure the knowledge of that will help me to get strong quickly."

He smiled down at her.

"You've a better color already," he said. "We must try this again. How about day after tomorrow? I have to take Dr. Severance over to see a patient near Crystal Springs, and there is no reason why you shouldn't go along if you are so minded."

"Oh, thank you!" she said with a quick appreciative look. "I'll be glad to. I wouldn't want you to take any extra trouble for me but if you have to go anyway I'm sure I shall enjoy it."

And so it was that Sterling managed to get Janice out in the open frequently, sometimes when he was taking others, sometimes alone. And when they went alone he would always manage somehow to get a bit of information about her family, and her life with her sister, or her early upbringing. Yet he never appeared to be seeking for such information. It seemed just to happen into their talk, and he stored all such knowledge in his mind in case there should come a time when he might need further information about her for her own good.

So little by little and without consciousness of what was happening they grew into a good fellowship, which both enjoyed.

By this time Janice was beginning to have little duties assigned to her every day, and she enjoyed feeling that she was doing something really useful. The doctor watched her carefully, making sure that she was not overdoing, and rejoiced to see a light growing in her eyes as if she was really interested in living again. There was a spring in her step now as she went on some duty, and more and more they were beginning to assign real duties to her, till finally she began her training in earnest, and was very proud of her success.

Of course, now that she was on duty a good deal, she had less time to take rides, and less opportunities to talk with Dr. Sterling. And of course she couldn't expect to have as much attention from him now that she was well as when she was a patient. She told herself that perhaps it was a good thing, for he certainly was an attractive young man, and of course she mustn't get to admiring him too much. He was a busy man, and going to rise in the world, and she was a penniless girl with her living to earn. He had been a kind benefactor, and she must not consider him in any other light ever, of course.

Still, she was very happy. Here in this safe sweet place, with real work to do, and a chance to rise perhaps, nothing to fear. She was very grateful to God for what He had done for her. And more and more she remembered to take time for prayer morning and evening. She must not get away from God. The world just wasn't a safe place without God.

They talked about that one day on a drive.

They had been watching the sky with soft floating

clouds that formed into lovely groups, and pointing out that some of them looked like distant cities, and mountains, and then they were both still for a few minutes. Suddenly Janice said:

"God has been so very good to me. I feel such days as this as if I cannot thank Him enough for giving me such wonderful friends, and helping me to a place where I can go on living."

Sterling looked down at her with a tender light in his eyes, and thought how sweet she looked under her little white starched nurse's cap. Then he asked, half amusedly:

"You really believe that God takes notice of His creatures and follows their lives, arranging things for them, don't you?"

Janice looked up startled.

"Why, yes, of course, don't you?"

"A great many do not," he said with a speculative look and a kind of sigh as if the matter had sometimes troubled him.

"Oh!" she said almost sorrowfully. "I suppose they don't. I know some that I am sure do not think anything about God. But I'm sure that if I didn't believe God was there arranging things for me I wouldn't have the nerve to go on."

He looked at her thoughtfully.

"I'm glad you feel that way," he said soberly. "My mother used to believe that. She tried to teach it to me. But life came along and taught me the opposite. I saw so many good people suffering."

"It isn't being good that puts you under God's special care," said Janice. "It's whether you accept what Christ did for you in taking your sins on Himself. Haven't you ever done that?"

He looked at her curiously a moment and then said:

"Well, I joined the church when I was a kid. Is that what you mean? Perhaps that was the old-fashioned way of saying it then."

"No," said the girl decidedly. "Joining the church is only the outward act to show what you have done in your heart. It hasn't really anything to do with the actual being saved. I don't know a whole lot about it, but I can remember that was one of the things they emphasized. It was not being good that saved you. You did that as much as you could because of what Christ had done for you, and you wanted to please him. It wasn't joining the church nor being baptized, because they were outward witnesses for others to see. It was believing what Christ had done, in making atonement for our sin. Not just head belief that He once lived on earth and died, but the actual heart belief that accepts what He did as yours, when He took our sin on Himself and bore the shame of it as well as paid the penalty of death for it, that we might go free. If He did all that for us He wouldn't let us wander around after that and get lost, would He? Not if He ever loved us enough to die for us. I've been thinking a lot about that lately, and it has been a great comfort."

Then she suddenly grew shy at the look of wonder and tenderness in his eyes.

"I should think it would be," he said gravely. "I never heard it explained just that way. I'll have to think about that. In the meantime, I'm glad you have that to help you out. I'd like to talk about it again sometime. But now," glancing at his wrist watch, "I guess it's time we are due to come in and get to work. Thank you for this little talk. Perhaps it has helped me too."

As they drove in one of the nurses came hurrying out with a message for the doctor, and he had to hasten in. But somehow that talk stayed with Janice and came back to her again and again when she was by herself, and she found herself wishing that Sterling knew more about these things and could tell her instead of her having to tell him, for she felt as if she knew so little about it all, and she knew it was important to tell it right. She felt that she had been paying too much attention of late to this world, and how one could have everything desirable, and all the loved ones safe and happy, and she had been getting away from her first faith. She must pray that God would put her right with His truth.

Then she went to her work in the ward and put these thoughts away to be checked over another time.

But Sterling, as he quickly rushed in to see the emergency case that had just been brought in, kept thinking about what the girl had said. Sweet Mary Whitmore—if her name was really Mary—he didn't much believe it was. But how sweet and earnest she had been as she talked, and how well she expressed her thoughts! She certainly must have had unusual training in her young life.

6

JANICE had been a probationer in the Enderby Sanitarium for just four months and three days when she became aware that some of the other nurses were talking about her. She had been on duty overtime and had been sent by the head nurse to take a sleep. How long she had slept she did not know, but she was awakened by a whispered conversation just outside her room door, carried on under her transom so that every word was distinctly audible. It was two of the nurses talking, and otherwise the large dormitory was very silent.

"Did you know that Sarah Brandt has come back from that Martin case up in the country where Dr. Sterling took the patient home?"

"No, when did she come?"

"About an hour ago. I've been up helping her unpack, and was she mad! Oh boy!"

"What was the matter? I thought she was so set up that she got the chance to go."

"Well, I guess she was, but she is fed up with it now. She says she simply couldn't stand the old lady Martin, she was so particular, and she asked to be relieved. Of course she didn't give that reason, though. It seems she wrote a letter to Dr. Sterling saying that she thought Mr. Martin ought to have a man nurse, he was very violent. So Sterling sent up Armstrong this morning, and now Sarah's back."

"My word! She has her crust, hasn't she? How did she dare do that?"

"Oh, she'd dare anything. If you ask me, the real truth is she was bored to death up there in the country, and then you know she's got a crush on Dr. Sterling and can't bear to have him out of her sight."

"H'm! I wonder what she'll think of the way he carries on with our little probationer? It's Mary here, and Mary there, and all the time taking her out riding. I suppose Sarah'll get in on some of those rides now. But it's a cinch she won't want that Mary around underfoot all the time. I'm sure I don't see what he sees in her. Oh, she's pretty enough, but not a particle of style. Just a baby face, and the most childish ideas, not in the least sophisticated!"

"Well, and what do you think, Ray, Sarah says it's reported at Martins that Dr. Sterling is engaged to a girl up there somewhere. Really *engaged!* And she's simply rolling in wealth and stunningly beautiful, so it won't do little Mary any good to go out riding with him, if he's engaged to a rich girl. I sure was surprised. I never thought Dr. Sterling was like that. He seems so kind of grave and dignified. The girl's name is Rose Bradford."

"Oh, all men are that way," sneered the other girl. "Out of sight, out of mind. You can't trust one of them! I think women are fools to run after any of them."

"Well, all I have to say is that I haven't seen Dr. Sterling rushing back to Martins since this little Mary person came. I don't think he's so dead gone on his fiancée as you seem to think, or else he believes in having more than one string to his bow."

"Of course," said the girl who was called Brynie, "that's it. They all do. I wouldn't trust any man an inch from my nose. But I don't see what he sees in that Mary person myself. Little milk and water thing!"

"Hush! Maybe she's back. Her room is along here somewhere. What if she should hear us! My soul! Let's get out of here!"

There was a sound of swishing starched linen skirts and scuttling rubber-shod feet.

Janice opened her eyes, looked around and tried to think.

That was Brynie and Ray. Two nurses who had been here a year longer than she had. They had been talking about herself and Dr. Sterling. How horrible! What would Louise have said if she had known? Louise who was always so anxious for her to guard her good name.

Sudden desolation seemed to engulf her. Why, the creamy walls of her room instead of being lovely and restful had grown somber and gray, and the white curtain but a foglike barrier to the sunlight. Where had flown the joy she had felt when she lay down, joy in her work, in the fact that she was getting on, would soon have her debts paid and be on the way to be self-supporting. And the greatest joy that she had a friend who was wise and kind and always ready to help her. And now like a stifling blanket of sorrow a terrible appalling fact began to settle down upon her.

Doctor Sterling! They had been talking about him. They had been sneering at him. And they had said he belonged to a girl, some rich girl, and was disloyal to her when he asked a nurse to take a ride now and then.

The vision of his handsome face, kindling with

friendly interest, came to her, surely that face could not be untrue. There must be some explanation.

And yet, what had he done? A look now and then, in fact only that very morning, a look that held intimacy, tenderness—had she ever dared to think of it as a loving look? Oh, not really bringing such a thought out in the open even to herself. In fact she had just been drifting and enjoying the pleasant friendship, without trying to analyze it and name the emotion. Her cheeks grew crimson with the thought, shame for the joy she had dared to feel over the intimacy of that look.

She remembered she was a stranger, alone and friend-less, and he knew it. To a certain extent she was dependent upon him. Her position was a strange one. She had not explained her presence on that hillside alone in the storm in flimsy evening garb. He might think almost anything of her. Of course he might like her, admire her, wish to bring her back to health, but at the same time have very little respect for her.

Her life had been an unusually sheltered one. She had known evil mainly through her brother-in-law's ways. Perhaps the covert sneer in those other girls' voices had enlightened her more than anything that had come her way, and she lay quite still, trembling from head to foot. It was plain that she had been most indiscreet. Perhaps it had been all her fault that these nurses had begun to talk and see evil in what had been a perfectly innocent friendship, but she suddenly saw that it must come to an end. Especially since she now knew that the doctor who had made such a strong impression upon her, and seemed to be so very friendly, belonged to another girl. Well, that ended her right even to think of him, or allow herself to watch and admire him. Had she been letting herself fall in love with him unaware? Had she been taking too great pleasure in being near him, and calling him friend? Well, her eyes were open now. She must somehow bring this intimacy to an end. She must not allow him to be talked about, even so much as a breath. He probably looked on herself as a little girl whom he had saved from death, and therefore felt he had a right to help her to have a good time. But it was always in the hands of a girl to control those things, to keep them from getting out of hand, and she must see to it from now on that he had no more opportunities to show any particular interest in her. She would miss his friendship of course, but that had to be. Yet the break must seem so natural and normal that he would not notice that she was holding off. It was going to be difficult, but she had been a fool to let herself get so interested in him, so she must take the consequences.

For the next three days she managed to be very busy whenever the doctor came her way. She gave him brief bright smiles, as a sister might have done, and he could not guess that she was starting a deliberate plan of keeping away from him.

It was easy to do at first for she had, of her own accord, asked to be allowed to do some extra work that was a bit confining, and when he appeared in the offing she was always just running off to get something, or go to another part of the building.

At first the doctor took it all in good part, but then he began to notice that it continued, and though her smiles were just as bright and cordial, they were ever briefer in their passing. She certainly was taking her training with a vengeance, and it began to worry him, for sometimes he noticed her cheeks were too white and she had a tired look under her eyes. He could not know that it was the alarming discovery that she had fallen in love with a man already engaged to another girl that had wrought this devastation in her young face. The long wakeful nights that she had mourned over this and tried to work out ways to undo the mischief were to blame for the dark shadows under her eyes.

But she had hurried on through her days, and when things got bad in the night watches she was learning to take the whole matter to the Lord in prayer, and tell Him to please take it over for her because she couldn't do anything about it herself. She wanted Him to have His way with her, and wouldn't He please take anything wrong out of her heart and help her to go on?

But one day Dr. Sterling came upon her unaware from an unexpected direction when she was passing through the hall with a tray. He laid his hand quietly on her arm. She started and flushed at the thrill his touch brought, and then with her cool little smile she prepared to go on her pleasant, almost distant way again. But he still detained her.

"Wait!" he said peremptorily. "I want to speak to you," and he turned and walked the way she had been going.

She flushed and looked up wistfully.

"Yes?" she said, casting a quick glance about to see if other nurses were observing her.

"I haven't seen you in a long time. I want to know how you are feeling these days. How about taking a ride with me this afternoon when you have time off? I am afraid you are working too hard."

"Oh, no, I'm fine!" she said determinedly. "And thank you for the invitation, but just now we're pretty busy in our hall, and I've promised to take over for someone else this afternoon. I guess it's impossible."

He looked at her startled.

"Look here," he said with a puzzled frown, "just what has been the matter with you lately? I've scarcely seen you at all, and I'm your physician, you know. What has happened? Have I offended you?"

"Oh, no," she said in distress. "You couldn't offend me. I've just been busy—" She hesitated and he looked straight into her clear honest eyes.

"You might as well tell me," he said, with his old friendly compelling smile.

"Well," she said, looking frankly up, "yes, something has happened. I've been overhearing some of the nurses talk, and I feel that they think it is unseemly for me to be going out with you so much. You're a doctor and I'm only a probationer, and I don't think I should do it. You're always so fine and understanding, I knew you would approve. And of course, it isn't as if I really needed medical attention any more. You've been so very kind to me that I don't feel I should presume on your attention any longer."

"Now look here, child! That's all nonsense! You've certainly been discreet in every way, and I've taken many patients out to ride. Just yesterday I had a little girl from the ward out, and she enjoyed it a lot. So don't be silly. I really want you to ride with me."

Janice wrinkled her brows thoughtfully, gravely.

"Well, I'm sorry, but I just couldn't go today. I do appreciate the invitation though."

He looked at her in a troubled way.

"Do you like your work? Isn't it hard for you?"

"I love it," she said with a glow of enthusiasm in her eyes. "No, it isn't too hard. I enjoy every bit of it, and I realize that I owe it all to you that I'm able to do it. I'll never forget that."

"There! You needn't begin on that again," he said with a smile, "but I want you to promise me something. Take care of yourself, won't you?"

"Oh, I will indeed," she said fervently. "Don't I look well?"

He looked at the soft curve of her rounded cheeks, the glow that his words had brought into her face, and smiled.

"Yes," he said, "you look all right, but I don't want you to take this training business too seriously. Remember you've been pretty sick."

"I will," she promised sweetly. "I'll be very careful, truly."

And then there came a call for Dr. Sterling and he had to go.

But in the days that followed Sterling noticed that he saw less and less of the girl who had been on his mind and heart for so many weeks, and though she continued to look fairly well she was full of gravely sweet dignity, and always hurrying off to some duty. More and more, as he thought about it, he felt that it must have been something pretty serious that she had heard to make her so afraid even to stop a moment in the hall to talk with him.

As the days went by Janice seemed withdrawn and distant, and it troubled him whenever he had time to think about it, so that he began to try to plan some way in which he might bring about a change in her attitude.

Twice during those months the doctor had been away and once Janice heard that he had gone to that Mr. Martin up in the region where Bradford Gables was located, and she could not help but wonder if he had also gone to see that girl Rose.

Then one day Rose herself arrived in a beautiful car, arrayed in the very latest sport clothes, and accompanied by a group of stylish friends.

Janice was sitting on the great wide side piazza with a convalescent, supposed to be taking her for a walk, but the patient was openly interested in the beautiful car and the pretty ladies, and would linger, so there was nothing for Janice to do but linger also.

"That's her, that's the one they say the doctor is engaged to," whispered one of the nurses in passing. "Her name is Rose. Isn't she some doll baby?"

Janice took one swift look at the beauty who was descending from the costly limousine and knew that this was really what was the matter with all her sorrowful nights and feverish days of hard work. It was this girl. And oh, she wasn't the right girl for that wonderful doctor-friend of hers. She was just a spoiled beauty, and would never help him on his way. They would never drive through perfumed spring bylanes, and watch the marvelous sunsets and clouds. That girl would be bored by little white clouds like feathers drifting over a sea of ethereal blue.

Then she realized how unworthy her thoughts were, and hastened to urge her patient to walk to the other end of the piazza. But as they slowly stepped along she could hear the other girls calling "Rose, oh, Rose, what time did you say you were going back?" So she was perfectly sure the nurse had been right in her identification. But her heart was heavy in spite of her best philosophy, until she remembered the Lord was looking after all this for her, and she need not worry.

Rose Bradford stayed almost all day and hindered the doctor a lot with his work. Her tones were eager and gushing and she talked rather loud, and in a possessive way. Janice kept out of the way as much as possible but she couldn't help hearing and seeing a lot that went on. And even if she had not heard and seen herself, there were plenty of interested nurses to run and tell her. In fact some of them felt it was rather interesting to tell her about this other girl and see how she would take it. But

Janice held her faith between them and her heart, and tried to be serene.

Sterling looked worn and weary when they finally left, and wondered at himself. Somehow Rose Bradford's eyes did not seem as beautiful as he had once thought, since he had come to know the quiet eyes of the girl whose life he had saved.

It had been the little probationer's painful privilege to witness from her patient's window the gay farewell when the visitors left. Something had gone wrong with the window blind and Janice had to lean far out to fix it, just as the Bradford car swept down the drive and out into the highway. She had a full view of all the gay garments, and heard the sharply sweet voice of Rose as she called out a lot of languishing farewells, finally lifting a dainty hand to her lips and flinging a playful kiss to the winds as they drove away.

Sterling, drawn by some occult influence perhaps, lifted tired eyes to the window just in time to see the white face of the little probationer disappear from sight, and then the color came richly, annoyedly, back into his own face. He wished she had not witnessed that parting scene. And yet there was nothing about it that he could have helped.

The next time that Sterling went to Martin's house he brought the sick man back with him, and sent for Janice to help him get him settled in his room.

She worked swiftly, with downcast eyes and was glad when the head nurse came in and the doctor's attention was turned away from her.

"By the way," he said, as she was about to go to her duties in another direction, "I've been so busy here I forgot to tell you. We're having a new patient on this floor. He comes this evening and ought to be here about now. I told Sam to meet the train. The corner room is ready for patients, isn't it? Well, we'll put him there for tonight at least. No, he's not helpless, but he's in a bad way and ought to be put to bed at once. It's alcoholism. Manning is to be the nurse. Will you tell him to be here, ready, and will you see that a supper tray is prepared? Bring it right up. It will probably be needed at once. Something hot, coffee, soup, I think you understand."

Janice bowed and hurried away. Just after the new patient arrived she returned with the tray. The chauffeur who had brought the man was bringing in his luggage, the doctor was there with the man-nurse giving directions, and the patient stood angrily swaying in the middle of the room, straight in the path that led to the small table where Janice was expecting to put the tray. She paused, looked up at the patient, and then stood frozen with horror, the tray trembling in her frightened hands, her face as white as the cap she wore, for there before her stood her dreaded brother-in-law, Herbert Stuart, glowering down at her with stormy eyes. Then, without warning, the tray fell from her nerveless fingers, and the little white nurse in her pretty blue uniform crumpled down in a heap at the feet of the patient.

It was all so silently, unobtrusively done, that only the tray with its muffled clatter as it thumped upon the thick rug called attention that way. And the silent little probationer lay still as death, without even a quiver of her eyelids.

The doctor with stern white face sprang forward instantly and gathered her up. He gave a quick look at the wild, dazed, drunken man who stood glaring angrily and muttering loud profanities about the way nurses behaved, frowning down upon the girl's white face with startled eyes as if he were looking at a specter.

With a hurried direction to the nurse the doctor strode away with Janice, carrying her to her own room, followed by another nurse.

As Sterling worked over the girl he was trying to think what could have been the cause of her sudden collapse. It evidently had something to do with the patient, for he had seen her face when she first looked at him, and the sudden terror in her eyes was unmistakable. The man had supposedly come from New England, at least that was where he was registered as living at present, and not from anywhere near the region in which he had found the girl. Yet there must be some connection. As soon as she was able to talk calmly he must find out the whole situation. He could not have a mystery like this going on. Somehow he would have to make her tell him the whole trouble.

Sterling knew very little of the new patient, but he had taken an instant dislike to his face. Even allowing for the dissipated life he must have lived, he had the look of one who was utterly selfish and almost cruel, who would stop at nothing to gain his own will. But if he was the secret of the girl's fear, what possible relationship could there have been between them. Not her lover. No, that was unthinkable! He was not old enough to be her father. Her brother, perhaps, but how could a brother hold such a power over his sister that would put a terror like that into her eyes? They did not resemble one another in the least. But, of course, brothers and sisters did not always look alike. Lover, or husband? He shuddered at the thought. Poor little girl if she were in any way tied to this drunken beast of a man!

Suddenly she opened her eyes and looked vaguely around the room, then up into the doctor's eyes with a question in her own, and then with returning memory there came that awful fear again, followed instantly by concealment. She was not going to explain that fear either.

"What happened? Did I fall?" she asked fearsomely. "Did I drop something?"

The doctor gave her a reassuring smile and bent to speak quietly so the nurse would not hear.

"Did something frighten you, child?" he asked gently.

"Oh? No, I guess not. I must have been a little tired. It's been a warm day," she said evasively. "I stayed overtime with the little lame girl in the east corridor. I'm so ashamed!"

It was a simple enough explanation and at another time he would have accepted it without a question. But now his eyes were keen with anxiety for her. He was sure she had not given the right reason for her disturbed state.

"You don't need to worry," he said gently, "it's all right. I am sure you have been working too hard. But now don't think anything more about it. Just lie still and rest. Some time tomorrow, or when you feel really strong again, come to my office and we will talk it over. I want you to know that I am your friend and you need not be afraid of *anything* or *anybody*. Now, go to sleep. It will be all right when you wake up."

He stepped over to the nurse and gave directions that the room was to be kept absolutely quiet and the probationer allowed to sleep as long as she would. Then he turned toward Janice again and flashed her a reassuring smile. Janice, watching him with those wide eyes that still held fright in their depths, answered with a look of gratitude, and then the old reserve dropped down like a veil over her face.

He went away to his office, but all the evening his mind hovered over the thought of the girl, and tried to plan what he could do for her relief.

Meanwhile Janice lay broad awake staring up at the ceiling in the dim light that came through the transom, her heart beating wildly, as she tried to think what she should do.

The fact was startling. Her enemy was under the same roof with her! So much she remembered plainly. Whether he had recognized her or not in his befuddled state, she wasn't sure. All had gone blank with her after her first look at him. The same Herbert only more selfish perhaps, more bestial, heavy eyes, thick sensuous lips, devilishly handsome even in his stupid drunken state. If he saw her he would use his villainous tongue to tell awful lies about her the way he had sometimes done with Louise. She *could* not stay here! It would be impossible to keep out of his sight. She must get away at once. He was, of course, the new patient. She recalled the doctor's word, "Alcoholism!" Then he must be trying to stop drinking again, or to get over a terrible spree. Perhaps this was the very place where he had been twice before.

And Dr. Sterling would find out. He had probably found out already that her fainting was connected with the stranger. She must *not* stay here another *hour*. Her enemy, and the jealous nurses together would make it impossible. It would only make trouble for the doctor if he tried to protect her. She must go! But how? "Oh God! I can't plan, I'm so frightened! Please help me. Please show me what to do!" she prayed.

And then like an answer to that petition came the sound of the ambulance driven to the side entrance. She knew it had been ordered to take a nurse who was convalescing from a slight illness, to the train for a little visit home to her mother, to rest for a few days before returning to her duties. Dare she try and get Sam to help her away?

She sprang from her bed, weak and trembling as she was, and locking her door slipped a few necessities into a little overnight bag that a grateful patient had given her, fastened her uniform that she had been wearing all day, adjusted her white cap, and snatching up a dark blue cape that was a part of her nurses' outfit, softly stole out of her room.

Her rubber-soled shoes made no sound as she went down the quiet hall and out the side door where she knew Sam must be sitting in his ambulance.

Walking down the stone steps briskly she spoke in a low decided voice to the supine Sam.

"Sam, you're to take me just as quickly as you can to the Junction station to catch the express. *Quick!* There isn't a *minute* to lose."

Sam sat up astonished.

"But I was to wait here for Nurse Wiley. She's going home and she's going to take the local from Enderby. Those was the orders from the head nurse."

"Yes, I know," said Janice with dignity, climbing hastily into the back of the ambulance, "but you're to take me first to the Junction. I must catch that train. You'll get back in time for Miss Wiley."

She closed the door of the ambulance, sat back, and was relieved to hear Sam starting his engine. Was she really going to get away as easily as this? "Oh God, was this the way you wanted me to go? Are you keeping me now? Shall I ever be safe again?"

And back on the side piazza they came out with Nurse Wiley, looking around for Sam and the ambulance.

"Now where in the name of sense do you suppose that Sam has gone?" asked Nurse Ray. "I told him to be right here in plenty of time so you wouldn't have to hurry getting in."

"Oh, there's plenty of time. I'll run out to the garage and call him," said Brynie.

But the ambulance with Janice inside was disappearing down the highway in the darkness.

And in his pleasant room enemy number one was calling loudly for a drink, and cursing his new nurse, and the place, and all the doctors and nurses.

7

MARTHA Spicer felt that it was good to get down in the heart of the city again and enter the old store. She felt as if she had been away from it for a year, though it had really been only a few days. Many of the old clerks looked at her and smiled, and some of those who didn't know her so well hardly realized that she had really gone yet. There was something strange about it though, going around in her old aisles, watching another woman in her place facing a stout old gaudy purchaser who was insisting on returning some silk underwear after it had been worn.

She had been away only a little over a week and yet she felt a superior freedom when she looked about on their tired faces, watched the flying hands putting up goods and stacking boxes for the night. Another day was almost done and they were nearly free again to live their own lives for a few hours. She knew exactly how they felt. She had always felt so. And now she was out of it all. Had she actually dared to be restive and unhappy in the house and with the fortune that had made her freedom possible? She was a fool and in ingrate.

There was a smile on her face as she walked among her former fellow workers. They turned weary eyes of surprise after her as she passed from their midst.

"Well, my word! Did you get on to the smile?" called one young salesgirl to another as she smoothed rumpled silk stockings into their boxes.

"Sure I did! What do you think of that? Isn't that the limit? Spice-Box *smiling!* I never expected to see that. I didn't suppose she *could* smile. She musta found a silk lining to her nest. Well, I don't blame her. If I could get out of this dump I'd smile too, wouldn't you, Nannie?"

"Sure I would," answered Nannie, patting her bunch of curls over her forehead to make sure they were engaging as she saw a young man coming down the aisle, headed her way.

And yet both of these girls had fairly agonized to get these jobs, less than a year ago!

"What you going to do? Join a reading circle?" asked an insolent sales boy at the book department when Martha asked for her Roman History. He hadn't forgotten how Martha Spicer had once called him down for having a bit of fun when he ought to have been working. He remembered her biting sarcasm.

The color rose in Martha's cheeks and she almost opened her mouth to make a sharp answer, but as he grinned at her, some motion or a look on his lips, reminded her of Ronald just after he had turned on his heel to "beat it" and given that fearful whistle. Then she remembered he was only three or four years older than Ronald and closed her lips. After all she was no longer connected with the store and had no right to speak. She lifted her eyes to the young man's face. He was white and thin with dark shadows under his eyes. He didn't have Ronald's ruddy color. She recalled that this boy was supporting a widowed mother and had to struggle to make both ends meet. Suddenly a miracle happened in her heart and she smiled up at him as if he were a comrade.

"I don't know but I shall, Albert," she said. "I haven't quite decided what I will do. I'd like to have you come and see me sometime if you are anywhere around near me."

Albert's face was a study of wonder.

"Gee! I *will,*" he answered heartily. "That'll be great! I'll come to supper sometime. May I?"

It was like Albert to invite himself, but it was not like Martha to answer with a smile and say *"Do!"* cordially and give him another smile as she took her package and went on her way.

It was queer, she thought, but that boy Ronald seemed to be in the back of her thoughts all day and to change the look of everybody. Was it the boy-charm that the article in the paper had talked about? Whatever it was, it made the going back to the little brick house not half so desolate as it had been before.

And there would be her new picture and the candlesticks and Ronald and Ernestine. She actually felt a warmth in her heart for the cat! It was astonishing!

She paused at a counter near the door where they were selling pictures at reduced rates, and there was a picture of a bull fight! And right beside it a splendid etching of a great stealthy lion stealing along a jungle place. Something told her those pictures belonged with the Colosseum and the brass candlesticks. They were framed in dull brass beading. All the way home she blamed herself for having spent good money for useless junk. She did not know that they were well-executed masterpieces of great artists, but in spite of her self-reproaches she felt an exultation that she had them.

There were chops for supper that night, two of them,

and a roasted potato. Ernestine had a chop to herself and sat with her tail girdled around her feet chewing away contentedly.

After the dishes were washed Martha went eagerly to the Roman history. The glistening new binding intrigued her, and her solitude did not seem half so forlorn now that she had something to do.

It was eleven o'clock when she finally closed her book and decided she ought to go to bed. Not that it mattered so much when she didn't have to hurry off to the store in the morning, but still she felt as if she had been dissipating.

She went to bed with the pleasant reflection that tomorrow's delivery wagon would bring those pictures, and she would have something to show Ronald as well as something to tell him about the Colosseum. But would he come without a lure of gingerbread? Of course, it wouldn't do to offer gingerbread again so soon. She must think up some errand for him to do for her.

But she did not have to lure Ronald with gingerbread. He appeared at the kitchen door promptly next morning with a cheery whistle and an impudent boy-knock, the kind that seems to imply that he owns the place and expects you to open at once.

He bore over his shoulder a great branch of dogwood blossoms which he had arisen early that morning to get, and handed them out to her quite casually.

"I thought you might like to see these," he said with a flourish, "I was out of town a ways last night and they looked real pretty so I clumb up the tree and got 'em for you."

"Oh, thank you so much, Ronald. They are lovely!" said Martha, her face shining with pleasure. She was as pleased as a young girl with flowers from her young man. It had been a long time since anybody had brought her flowers. "Come in. I was just wishing I could see you. And suppose you help me put this branch up over our picture first. I've got a little bottle that will about fit around that branch, and I can fill it with water and keep the flowers fresh a long time if I watch and keep the bottle refilled."

"Gosh, that's an idea, isn't it," said the boy. "Wait! I'll get the stepladder. It's in the cellar."

Martha laughed.

"I guess you know where my property is better than I do."

The boy grinned.

"Well, I know the cellar all right," he said.

So they arranged the bottle behind the picture frame, and stuck the branch in the water, at such an angle that it swept out over the ugly wall paper and made a lovely bright spot of beautiful blossoms, giving a festive air to the whole room.

Ronald stood back and surveyed the finished work.

"Some class!" he said. "That picture's all right! You say that's a real place?"

"Yes," she answered eagerly, "it's Rome, Italy. I bought a book about those old ruins yesterday and now I can tell you all about it if you have time to spare pretty soon. I've bought two more pictures too that I think you will like. They are to be sent up today."

"I'll come," he said tersely. "It's about school time. I guess I better beat it." He turned to hurry away. "So long!" and he was gone.

After he left, Martha stood for some time looking at the beautiful white blossoms, her heart swelling with a new joy. The boy had taken the trouble to climb a tree to bring her those flowers!

She spent the morning going over the house and doing away with a number of archives that hurt her esthetic soul, and felt better when the rooms presented a less cluttered appearance.

"If it wasn't so small and dark and ugly," she sighed as she looked around, with Ernestine purring about her feet. "I feel as if I couldn't breathe. Ernestine, don't you?"

"Meow!" said Ernestine fervently.

"Well, we'll have to do something," said Martha aloud. "We might paper the walls with some light paper perhaps."

"Meow!" said Ernestine again, and then—"Meow— but if you *should* put in a fireplace!"

"Why, yes, of course," said Martha. "It would be all to do over again if we papered first. We better wait till we decide. If only we could get rid of some of those partitions and have more space!"

"Exactly—*Meow!*" declared the cat.

Ronald breezed in about five o'clock to see if the furnace man had done his work right. The new pictures had come, and he hung them, and admired them very much apparently, but all he said was, "Some class!"

"I might bring a fellah down tonight if you're going to be home," he said.

Martha hesitated. Ronald was one thing but a "fellah" was another. Her old prejudice about boys arose and protested to her, but the look in the boy's face, though enigmatic, was eager and she said, "Why, yes, I'm going to be at home."

"He's an arch-iteck fellah, just started, and he wants a job bad. He's all right. You'll like him," and the boy was off again, leaving her standing with a troubled countenance looking around on her rooms in a kind of ecstatic consternation.

An architect! And she hadn't even made up her mind whether she wanted anything done to the house or not!

It seemed too soon after taking possession, anyway, for her to begin to make changes. It seemed hardly decent.

Yet, if he really *did* come, there could be no particular harm in asking him a few questions of course, finding out what such things would cost. Then if the price was high that would help her to put the idea out of her head. Thus she reasoned with herself. Yet all day she was in a flutter, staring at the walls and thinking how it would look if they were down; trying to fancy a staircase with landings, and a bay window with a window seat and geraniums on the window shelf, white muslin curtains! And how would Ernestine regard the advent of a canary in a brass cage? A canary singing while the yellow sunshine played in the now dark hall and parlor, that would be thrown open to the light?

And what about another big wide window below the staircase, more toward the front of the house? A window with a single large pane of plate glass and a wide cushioned seat below it? With low book shelves each side, and a bit of statuary on the top shelf. Her soul suddenly longed for a little head of Joan of Arc she had seen when passing through the art department at the store, a face of uplifting sweetness and purity. Such a face as that in a room would be an inspiration. Perhaps some day if the other changes didn't cost too much she would buy that lovely bit of art just for a center and inspiration for her home. That would be another story to tell Ronald. She would like to see his eyes when he looked at the holy beauty the artist had put into the eyes of that marble face.

By seven o'clock she had got herself into a state that she started at every noise. It almost seemed, too, as if Aunt Abigail and Uncle Jonathan had come in and were sitting on the two opposite big rocking chairs with folded hands and severe brows, as they used to sit and ask her polite questions about herself on the few occasions when she had visited them. It seemed as though they were there watching to see what she was going to do to their property now that they were gone where they could no longer control it. She almost decided to call Ronald over the fence and tell him she was going out that evening and could not see his architect friend. Then she wavered and tried to decide what questions she would ask him if he came.

No one would have recognized the former composed head of the Underwear Department, in the flushed face of Martha Spicer as she opened the front door to Ronald and his friend.

The architect was young and inoffensive. He bowed deferentially and followed Ronald into the stuffy little parlor, which in spite of the glowing lamp in the middle of the mahogany table, had the air of continually approaching you to smother you with its surrounding nearness.

He cast a quick glance around as if to get ready for any questions that might be asked him. She could see he wanted to please her.

"You are intending to make some alterations in your home?" he asked embarrassedly.

Martha caught her breath at the bald statement.

"Well, I am *thinking* of it," she said with a reassuring smile at Ronald. She didn't want to let him down. "I wanted to find out whether what I want would be at all feasible, and what it would likely cost. It will probably be far beyond my pocketbook however, and it seems hardly fair for you to take your time to talk about it until I am a little more certain."

"Oh, that's all right," said the young man, "I'm glad to take all the time you want, and I'm sure I can do it as cheap for you as anyone else, and do good work. You've got a good solid house here to start with. The boy said you wanted to take out some partitions and put in some windows."

"Yes," said Martha, catching her breath as the daring idea was launched into words.

"I should think it might be done without great expense," said the young man. "May I look around and see just what partitions there are?"

So they started on the rounds and Ronald sat back in a big chair and watched and listened. Ernestine came and jumped in his lap and he sat there tickling her under the chin, as she purred contentedly. The voices of the architect and the householder came pleasantly from the dining room, and Ronald studied the picture over the mantel and dreamed his boy-dreams about bull fights and lion hunting, glad in the thought that he was serving his two friends by thus bringing them together. He had no doubt but that Miss Spicer would enjoy her house better if it was made over, and he was sure it would help Will Roberts to take his sick baby to the shore and pay his doctor's bill. It gave him pleasure to help such things on.

They came back presently into the living room and the architect got out pencil and paper and drew a rough sketch of what could be done.

Martha watched fascinated as the windows she had dreamed, and the staircase appeared on paper as if by magic, with here and there a windowseat or china closet tucked in. And then the crowning touch of all, the big stone fireplace, made of rough cobble stones, but dignifying the place wonderfully. Did Ernestine understand about that, and did she vision a flickering fire for her to sit beside and dream? She uttered a soft "Meow" as she nestled down in Ronald's lap as though everything was going all right for that fireplace and there was no need to worry any longer. She had "Why Worry?" written all over her fur countenance.

When at last the young man looked up from his figuring and announced the result, Martha caught her breath. Could it be possible that she was actually contemplating spending all that money? And yet it was less than the probable figure she had set—*far* less.

"That's approximate of course," he added eagerly. "It could be more or less according to the material you want in it. This is only a rough estimate."

"Well, I must think about it, of course," said Martha, looking down to hide her delight that the figures were no higher.

The builder's pink countenance fell and paled. He tried to think of something else to say, opened his lips tremblingly but closed them again. He wanted this job mightily. He looked appealingly at Ronald, and then down at his pencil, and then began unconsciously to draw another fireplace on the corner of the paper.

"I might work it out, make an estimate. Perhaps I would find some place where I could cut it down," he said. "You see, I'm just getting started. I'd do the work-part cheap. It would mean a good deal to me to have the job right now—"

His voice trembled a little as he cleared his throat.

"His kid's been awful sick—" put in Ronald irrelevantly, dropping his own pencil with a clatter and disturbing Ernestine's repose as he stooped to pick it up.

With sudden insight Martha saw that to Ronald much depended on his protégé's getting this job. Such knowledge a week ago would have been enough to finish the whole matter. She would have suspected that the work would not be well done and she would be cheated. But so great a miracle had the boy's smile already wrought in her that she immediately became possessed of a desire to please these two and give the job at once without further words. All her long years of business training were scattered to the winds by a simple desire to please a rough friendly boy. How startling, if she had taken the time to think about it. Instead she was merely impressed by the way the boy's dark hair tossed itself up over his sunburned brow, and she felt impelled to answer at once.

"Why, I don't know. Yes, I guess you might do that. It's rather sudden, but I guess it will be all right. You may go ahead and make an estimate if you don't mind."

The young man's face relaxed and he arose awkwardly, terribly conscious of himself and of how much hung on this deal.

Ronald stood up gravely and put down the reluctant cat, but there was a look not altogether of satisfaction about his expressive young mouth, and somehow it penetrated to Martha's consciousness and her soul responded to its suggestion.

"I'm sorry your child is ill," she said pleasantly. "Do you live near here? Is there anything I could do to help in a neighborly way?"

Ronald's lips relaxed a trifle.

"No, ma'am, thank you," said the father, growing pink again. "Johnny's better now, but I'm pretty anxious to get him and his mother off to the seashore for a few days. The doctor says that's the thing for him now. And his mother's pretty well run down nursing him so long. He's been sick all summer."

"Well, that *is* hard," said Martha reflectively. And then after a pause and another glance at Ronald whose eyes were averted, she added:

"Well, now if it will help you any with your planning, I think you can just count on this job right away. Begin tomorrow if you like. I really want it done, and I guess I shan't be happy till I get it. We can talk over the details and get them settled later, but you can count on the job. I guess we can fix the terms all right. I don't want you to cheat yourself."

Then out beamed Ronald's smile, on the averted side of his face first, so no one would see it. But it was too big to stay there and it spread all across from ear to ear, so he had to reach down and scratch Ernestine's ear to hide it. Nevertheless before he left he lifted adoring eyes to Martha Spicer's face and the glory of them was reward enough for her.

When she at last shut and bolted her front door and turned to meet the accusing eyes of Aunt Abigail and Uncle Jonathan from the shadows of the hall, her heart was so filled with joy over the relief she had given that she didn't care at all. Just sailed on upstairs, with Ernestine threading her assertive way underfoot, and never thought how reckless and unbusinesslike it was to spend so much money without consideration.

She was very happy as she began to prepare for rest, happier than she had been for years. She was happy at the thought of the lovely place she was going to make out of her gloomy little house, but happier than all at the joy she had seen in Ronald's eyes, and the relief and ecstasy she had seen in the eyes of the anxious young father.

And then, just as she was beginning to take out her hairpins and arrange her hair for the night, there came a timid ring at the doorbell.

8

JANICE huddled in the corner of the rapidly moving
ambulance was trying to think her way through. She
knew she had taken a big chance, and so far she seemed
to have gotten away from the sanitarium without suspicion, and now the next thing was to get rid of Sam
without delay. She had told him he was to take her to
catch the express, but *was* there an express at this hour?
She couldn't remember. He hadn't demurred, so perhaps he didn't know, or perhaps there was one. If there
was one she must without question take it to *somewhere*.
Even if she didn't have money enough to pay her fare
they could put her off somewhere, couldn't they? And
if there wasn't a train and Sam did as she told him and
went back to take Miss Wiley to her train, she could at
least sneak off in the darkness and lose herself, and by the
time anybody responsible knew about it she could be
well hidden somewhere.

But it was a wild drive, for Sam seemed to have an
idea that there wasn't much time to make her train, and
he was making the old ambulance fairly gallop.

But as they neared the Junction she was relieved to

hear a whistle in the distance, and then the headlight of an engine came into view. She could dimly see the station just ahead and a few dark figures ranged on the platform, evidently about to board the train. She drew a breath of relief, and began to think ahead. How much money did she have with her? Enough to carry her to Boston or Buffalo or somewhere far enough away so that Herbert could not trace her? She knew she had two five dollar bills and some change inside her dress, all these were parting gifts which grateful patients had given her, but would that carry her far enough? Yet she must not spend all she had or she would have nothing to live on till she found a job.

The train rushed up to the little Junction station, and on by, and Janice had a moment of fright lest it was not going to stop at all. But she clambered down from the ambulance and dashed across the platform chasing after the last car as it glided by her, going slower now. It *was* going to stop!

"Hurry back!" she called to Sam as she went flying down the platform. And then the train came to a halt, and she hastened to climb up the steps of the last car puffing and panting, all out of breath. She struggled with the door, but it would not open, and to her distress the conductor shouted "All Aboard." Then the train lurched and began slowly to move. It was too late to get off and run to another car. In horror she gripped the doorknob and struggled with it again, but it would not open. She couldn't understand it because there was a light in the car. Surely there must be somebody in there. She began to pound on the glass of the door, and rattle the knob, to kick against the door, but the train roared on and nothing happened. She was definitely locked out, and the train was going so fast now that the dark world outside seemed to be simply flying by. Well, she had gotten away from the sanitarium all right. Sam had gone back and would tell how she just made the train. Nobody could very well trace her, for no conductor would remember such a passenger as she wasn't inside. But how long could she stand this ride? She could not endure standing up clinging to the doorknob very long, for she was trembling already when she got here, both from the shock of seeing Herbert, and from her wild run down the platform to the train.

Carefully she tried to sit down on the top step, but it was a precarious seat, with only a slender handrail just above her head to hold to, and the danger of being thrown off whenever the train went around a swift curve, which seemed to be nearly all the time. They were plunging through the mountains now, and she could feel the depths beneath her even with her eyes shut. She might at any minute be hurled into space. She shook the door and cried out again but no one could possibly hear in all that din and roar, even if there was anyone there to hear. The wind took her voice and tossed it in fragments from crag to crag, flinging it far into the valley below in weakly mocking sounds.

On and on they thundered, rocking and tossing. The train was like some wild beast upon whose back she clung, who fain would rid himself of her. It appeared to plunge and rear and do its fearful best to fling her off.

It seemed hours that she crouched there clinging to the metal doorknob, her feet braced on the doorframe, half crouching, half sitting on the cold platform. Until at last the great untamed thing on which she rode suddenly slowed down and came to a dead lurching stop beside a wooden platform, whose shadowy outlines led to a dark little station.

Scarcely believing her dazed senses, she crept stiffly down the steps of the car, and tried to hurry along the station platform to climb into the next car before the train started on again. But as if the train had been aware of it and would have none of her, it gave a snort of warning, grinding its wheels menacingly, and started ramping on its way again, leaving the girl trembling, sore, chilled to the bone, and ready to sink down in the dark and die.

It was a horrible feeling to be left alone in this wild deserted spot, she knew not where, nor how far from any human habitation, surrounded by no knowing what awful perils. Yet she could not have remained longer on that train platform. She would have lost her mind, certainly her strength, and been flung off into some ravine to die. Perhaps after all she had been wrong to run away. But no, there was Herbert! Oh, perhaps the doctor would have found some way to protect her if she only had had the nerve to tell him all, but it would have been such shame and disgrace to have the story get out among those gossiping nurses. Not that the doctor would have told, but those nurses seemed to have uncanny ways of sensing out stories and carrying them. No, she could not have stayed. She must just be thankful that she got away so easily. But she was still fearful. Somehow she half expected to see Herbert come riding down that track in the darkness after her.

In her terror she shrank close to the silent door of the deserted station. Inside she could hear the quiet tick, tick, tick of the clock, the intermittent click-click-click of the telegraphic instrument, like two friendly watch dogs asleep and snoring. But the wind that swept down the mountain side and whirled through the railroad cut was cold and her blue cape was thin. Moreover her body was worn with watching and excitement and the terrible ride she had just experienced. She had had no supper but the few spoonfuls of broth before the doctor left her. She was trembling from head to foot and ready to cry, crouched down in a corner by the station door her head resting against the little overnight bag she carried.

She must have fallen asleep, for when she awoke she was stiff and sore, with the full glow of a great headlight swooping down upon her. In her bewilderment it seemed a living being, an enemy come to destroy her, but as she gazed in terror her senses came back alertly and she saw it was just another train. Her heart leaped high with hope, and then fell with fear. Suppose it was a freight train and it was going to stop! Suppose she should be discovered by the train hands.

A moment more and the train slowed down and she saw it was a passenger train with sleeping-cars, and some people were getting off. Strange that anyone should choose to get off here! But suddenly now she became aware of a car driving up to the other side of the station, and she arose with new fears clutching at her heart. How was she going to explain her presence here alone at this hour?

This was evidently a through train that had stopped to let off some officials or people of consequence perhaps. It would go away at once of course, and she must get on if possible. Already the conductor was about to swing aboard when Janice hurried from her shadow and slipped like a wraith past him and up the steps of the car nearest her where some people had just got out. She cared not where it was going, only to get away from this dark desolate spot. And so far she had not had to spend any money, but she prayed that she might have money enough to get somewhere away from Herbert.

It was a long time before the conductor found her, seated in a day coach.

"Where did you get on?" he asked gruffly.

"Just back there," she said innocently, lifting frightened eyes.

"But you had no right to get on there. This is a through train to Boston and doesn't stop at that station."

"But it did stop," said Janice with a puzzled frown.

"Yes, it stopped by special request from the president of the road. We have no right to take on passengers from that station."

"Oh, I'm sorry," said Janice. "I didn't know. And it was so cold and dark there, I was afraid."

"But how in the world did you happen to come there at that hour alone? Didn't you know there was a train an hour ago going this way?"

"I missed it," said Janice with troubled gaze.

"Well, where were you going?"

"Why, I was going to Boston. Doesn't this train go to Boston?"

"Yes, but you have no right on this train. I'll have to put you off I suppose, and I really haven't the time to back up. I've already lost as much time as I ought."

"Oh, you needn't put me off if you don't mind. It's very dark and lonely back there, and the station is closed. You see I just came here to get the first train I could catch. I am in a great hurry. I didn't know whether there was any train tonight or not. I just took chances and came. I'm a stranger around here."

The conductor eyed her keenly.

"Are you a nurse?" he asked.

"Yes," said Janice hoping he wouldn't ask where.

"Well, all right, in that case we'll let you get by this time. Have you a ticket?"

"Oh, no, the station was closed. What is the fare to Boston?"

He mumbled the price and Janice with thankfulness handed out the money, leaving her little pocketbook much depleted. But then she still had a little money pinned in her dress.

She put her head back on the seat and slept fitfully the rest of the journey. But a little before they reached the city the conductor came searching her out, putting a kindly hand on her shoulder:

"Did you tell me you were a nurse?" he asked with a note of anxiety in his voice.

Janice sprang up startled.

"Yes," she said, "I'm a nurse."

"Well, there's a woman in the drawing room back there in the parlor car who has been taken very sick. Her daughter saw you go through the car awhile ago, and she wants to know if you can come and help her take care of her mother until we get to Boston and go with them to their home and see her mother settled in bed. They had a nurse engaged to travel with them, but she didn't turn up at the appointed time. They'll pay you what you ask."

To Janice the conductor looked like an angel from Heaven sent to relieve her necessity. In the position of a nurse she would be at least in a measure protected, and she would be relieved from that fearful feeling of being utterly alone in the world.

"Oh, yes," she said eagerly, "I'll be glad to help anybody. I was going after a job."

She arose at once and followed her grim guide to the second car ahead, and was welcomed by a querulous little old lady and her anxious daughter.

She was frightened at first lest her small skill and her so-brief training would not be equal to the case, but she found she was needed more to give confidence than anything else. The daughter was not used to looking after her mother, and was bored and tired by the constant fretful demands upon her, so Janice found it comparatively easy to drop into the ways she had learned at the sanitarium. And when at last the invalid was resting quietly, Janice was approached by the daughter as to the possibility of coming to her mother permanently.

"I can see that mother likes you," she said. And so Janice sat by the window and watched the train roll into Boston, with great relief in her heart. God was caring for her. He had not forgotten her. This seemed to be a way out from her troubles. At least for the present.

She had told the daughter, "Why, yes, I was coming to Boston to look for a job, and I have nothing definite in mind yet. I'll come for a few days anyway and you can see if you really want me. You know I am a stranger to you."

"Well, we are strangers to you, too," said the woman, "but I'm sure we're going to like you. You see what mother likes is the test, and she definitely likes you."

So Janice, out of her distress, arrived at Boston, was taken in a taxi to a great cool luxurious house where there was every comfort. She went to work just as if she were still a probationer on training, only she had no head over her but the whims of an erratic old lady, and her worldly daughter. That night when she lay down to rest at last, she was so weary that she had no time nor strength even to think it all over. God had cared for her, that was all. For the rest she must not even think of Enderby or Doctor Sterling and the work she had left behind her, for Herbert was there, and she *had* to get away from Herbert.

But the next day and the next, and all the days that succeeded brought vivid pictures of her life at Enderby. She tried to keep her thoughts from the young doctor who had been so kind to her, and to make some plans for her future, but try as she would his tender glances, the memory of his kindness, the gentleness of his tones, would keep coming back until tears would sting into her eyes and overwhelm her. But her first waking thoughts would be of Sterling, till one day she realized that this must not be. Probably God took her away from Enderby because she was getting too fond of him, and he engaged to a beautiful wealthy girl! She must remember that and put him forever out of her thoughts. He was not for her, not even as a friend any more. She would probably never see him again now, and she must cease to think of him.

So she filled her days with duties, and made herself indispensable to the Whittiers.

Not that they allowed themselves to grow fond of her in the sense that they had much companionship together. She was in the position of an upper servant to them, and they were people who held themselves aloof from all who served them. So that Janice was practically living her life alone, with no one to question or care about her. It was enough for the Whittiers that she was a good nurse, and ready to meet all possible demands. Why should she have any life of her own, anyway? That was their attitude. And so Janice was lonely and more and more her thoughts drifted back to her dear sister and the precious baby who were gone to Heaven.

Back in the sanitarium her flight was not generally discovered until morning. The nurse who was looking after her stole into her room about eleven o'clock in the evening, and finding the bed empty concluded that Janice had felt better and gone back to her duties. She so reported it to the doctor. But the doctor immediately on the alert, sent orders that she should go back to bed at once. The messenger asked the head nurse if she knew where Mary was, and she said with a cold sneer, "Oh, no! She isn't on duty. She's gone to her room," and so the messenger let it go at that and took no further pains to find out whether it was so or not.

But in the morning it was discovered that Janice was not anywhere about the place, and no one knew just when she had last been seen. The nurse who had been told to look after her was frightened when she saw the steely blue in the doctor's eyes. It made her think of his flashing instruments when he had an operation to perform. She finally confessed that she had not gone back the second time to see if Mary had returned. She went away from the doctor's eyes with a revised idea of duty.

The doctor, now thoroughly alarmed, began a quiet investigation, cross-examining every nurse and employee on the place, and finally reaching Sam.

He listened quietly as Sam told his story, remembering the way gossip could fly through the institution, and when Sam's story was told he said in a matter-of-fact tone:

"That's all right, Sam. I wasn't sure whether she got off safely or not. I was busy in the office and no one seemed to know whether she had succeeded in finding you."

He asked a few questions about whether she caught the train, and exactly what time it left the station, which train it was, whether an express or local, and then thanked Sam.

"I'm glad you looked after her, Sam," he said pleasantly.

But after Sam had gone back to the garage he went to the telephone and asked a few questions of the station agent at the Junction. The agent told him the station was always closed after the seven o'clock train went down and he went right home. He couldn't say whether anybody from the sanitarium went on that train or not. He saw Sam drive up just before the train came but he didn't take notice whether any nurses got on the train or not. The doctor thanked him and hung up. This of course confirmed Sam's story as far as it went.

The doctor told the head nurse that Mary had been called away suddenly, and it would be necessary for her to put someone else in her place. It was very possible that she might not return for some time. He spoke as if he had just received a message to that effect. The head nurse eyed him suspiciously, but asked no questions. She knew that he expected her to make this information known to the other nurses, and she did so. It was a great relief to her to have "Mary" out of her way. Mary was entirely too conscientious to suit her purposes, also the doctor never seemed to see *her* when Mary was about. But she suspected that there was something more behind all this than appeared on the surface.

So the doctor silenced the brief excitement about Janice's disappearance, but the tumult in his own heart grew as the day passed by and no word came from her. He had hoped against hope that she would send him a telegram, or a note, or perhaps telephone, though something warned him that she would not.

And more and more he was convinced that this all connected in some way with that new patient who was an alcohol addict.

So that afternoon he made a visit to Herbert Stuart's room, satisfied that he was the cause of Janice's flight.

The man was nervous and irritable, complaining that his old hallucinations of vision were upon him. He constantly saw a face that he knew to be dead. Once he querulously inquired what had become of that nurse who had fainted on his arrival, and when told she had left he drew a sigh of relief. Said he was glad, that her face looked like someone he used to know.

Sterling stayed by him an hour, trying to soothe him, talking with him of his home, gradually getting bits of information that made him more and more sure that this man was somehow connected with his probationer.

When the day passed and no word from Janice arrived he placed Brownleigh in charge of the house and took a short trip on his own account. The nurses said among themselves that he had gone to see Rose Bradford, and it was high time for him to show a little belated devotion, now that his pretty little nurse who had turned his head completely was out of sight.

However, Dr. Sterling did not go to Bradford Gables, but to Willow Croft, where his new patient owned to having lived at one time. He took a room at the hotel, plied the landlord with a few judicious questions which helped out the information he had got from the unsuspecting patient.

It was not hard to get the landlord started. He spoke volubly of the family of Stuarts, although he said the man, Herbert Stuart, was "no good!" and led his lovely wife a life of it till she died. He bewailed the fact that her beautiful sister Janice Whitmore went way to visit friends on the Pacific Coast as soon as the funeral was over. Poor thing! She was just wrapped up in her sister who had been more than a mother to her. Yes, Mrs. Stuart was buried up in the cemetery. The hotel cab was at his service if he wanted to go anywhere. They had a pretty cemetery, it was really worth seeing. The town was proud of it.

Sterling thanked him, declined the cab, but a little later wended his way on foot to the hill road where in front of the great stone entrance gateway he had found the girl in the snow. It was a very different scene now from that stormy night when he had brought the little white girl back to the sanitarium. The trees were in full foliage, and the hillside was covered with well kept grass.

There were flowers planted everywhere, and nothing about the place to suggest death.

He wandered in among the graves, and was not long in discovering an ostentatious monument, the kind the new patient would be likely to put up, ornate and showy, with the words:

Louise Whitmore
Wife of Herbert Stuart,
In the thirtieth year of her age.

And close at hand a simple but beautiful white stone bearing the words:

Caryl,
Daughter of Louise and Herbert Stuart,
aged three years.

After that it was easy to piece the whole story together, and as he turned away and walked back down the road to the hotel, the doctor was relieved beyond measure to know that the man at the sanitarium fighting drunkenness was neither the husband nor the father of the girl he had now come to know he loved. But why had she turned so deathly pale at sight of him, and why had she fled from his home in that awful storm, the night her sister was buried? He must be an awful beast.

When he returned to the sanitarium and found there was still no word from Janice he engaged one of the best detectives he could find to search out information concerning the Stuart family, and especially as to the present whereabouts of Miss Whitmore, the sister.

In due time there came back plenty of information about Herbert Stuart, his activities, gay, crooked and otherwise, including his several marriages, or near marriages. But there was not a word as to the whereabouts of his sister-in-law Janice Whitmore, except the rumor originating with Herbert Stuart, that she had gone West to visit with relatives.

So days passed with no word from Janice. And sometimes the doctor would waken from a dream of her, the look in her lovely eyes, the softness of her white hand when he had taken her pulse, the frightened look in her white face! And it seemed to him he could not bear it. He must go somewhere and find her. He must be able to tell her how he loved her.

But finally there came a time when he felt he must do something to get away from the thought of the girl, and so he accepted an invitation to a houseparty at Bradford Gables, for Rose Bradford had besieged him with invitations all summer.

It did not take long to show him that Rose Bradford's power over him was gone, and the second day of the houseparty he knew that the only thing he wanted in the world was to go out and hunt for the girl he loved. She might not love him of course, for she had seldom given him any encouragement, but at least he must know that she was safe, or he could never again go on with his work.

So he went back to the sanitarium and arranged for a prolonged absence, planning to search for Janice until he should find her.

And meantime in Boston, change had come again to Janice.

The old lady for whom she had been caring suddenly took pneumonia and died, and Janice's work there was over. The daughter announced her intention of selling the house and going to a hotel for a time, after which she planned to take trips wherever trips were possible in these war times. But definitely she would be going to the shore, to the mountains, and to Florida or California in the winter. So she would no longer need the services of Janice.

Janice packed her few belongings, and tried to think where to go, what to do. It wasn't as if she were penniless, for she had been paid a small salary. Though the suggestion of the conductor that she would be paid whatever she asked had not come to pass. The Whittiers had not proved as generous as he thought. But she had some money, and need not feel that she was going to starve if she didn't get a job immediately. She had had to buy some clothes for she had brought so very little with her from Enderby. But God had cared for her so far, He would guide her, and would bring her something to do. She was not afraid.

And she was glad to get away from these people. The querulous invalid she had cared for had demanded her presence day and night, almost continually, and she had been exceedingly hard to please. She was very tired. She wanted to rest a few days before she decided what to do.

So Janice looked up a few trains to places she thought might be comparatively safe from meeting Herbert, and was ready to start. Then she heard herself called by Miss Whittier.

"Nurse, the doorbell is ringing. Would you mind answering it? I can't think what that stupid Katie is doing that she doesn't answer it. She surely must have got back from that errand I sent her on. You see I'm expecting a caller and I'm not quite ready to go down. If it's a gentleman take him in the small reception room, please, and say I'll be down in a minute. He always expects me to be late anyway."

She laughed pleasantly and Janice hurried down to the door. It was the first time since she had been with these people that she had been asked to do any service outside her profession, and she couldn't of course refuse. Besides she was leaving at once. She had already said good-by.

She opened the door with her mind still dwelling on the unusual friendliness of Miss Whittier, and there before her, dapper and trig, his whole attire the perfection of what a man of the world should wear, his handsome face haughty and expectant, stood her brother-in-law!

As she stood there in the doorway and looked up for one swift second it seemed to her that all the forces of her body were suddenly paralyzed. She had visions of herself fainting at his feet again, and this time with no friendly doctor to rescue her from his presence. She must not, *must not* faint! She must be calm. Perhaps he would not recognize her in this simple dark blue dress. Anyway why should she fear him? He had no power over her. Or—*had* he?

With a tremendous effort she rallied and stepping to one side in the shadow as he entered, reached her hand for his card, and tried to speak in a servantlike voice.

"Miss Whittier will be down very soon. Step into the reception room please."

She did not look up but she felt him start and look at her curiously as she spoke. She motioned toward the reception room and hurried away up the stairs. She knew he was still standing in the hall watching her as she went up, and her trembling limbs could hardly carry her up. She laid her hand on the railing and tried to steady herself. But just as she reached the top step she heard his voice calling her from the foot of the stairs, guardedly, but distinctly: "Janice! Janice!"

She had reached the top of the stairs now and was almost reeling with fright. What if she should fall backward, now that she was almost out of his sight! She took one more step and was on the top landing. Could she keep back this blackness that was swimming before her eyes until she reached a place of safety?

Miss Whittier was much too absorbed in her make-up to notice the whiteness of Janice's face, the wildness of her eyes, as she laid the card on her dressing table and slipped away again silently to her own room.

She set her hat quickly on her head, seized her overnight bag and purse that lay ready, hurried down the backstairs and out at the rear door, escaping through the driveway behind the garage. She was thankful that Katie was having a conversation with the ashman over the back fence and did not see her. She hurried down to the next street and boarded the first bus that came along.

This was now the third time that she had escaped from Herbert, and suddenly it seemed to her that she must from now on be in perpetual flight to escape him. How did it happen that he was everywhere when she tried to hide from him? She had thought Boston far enough away from his home to be safe from him.

She began to reflect. It must be that he was the young man who had been calling on Miss Whittier from time to time all winter! Oh, poor soul! Could it be that she was going to be caught in his toils the way her sister Louise had been? Perhaps she ought to have warned her. But it wouldn't have done any good. Her word against Herbert's never had counted. And she would have been the only one to suffer. Miss Whittier would never had believed her.

The bus had gone some distance before she realized that she had no idea where she was going, but why not just stay on it until it reached somewhere that might give her an idea. Perhaps she would just go on till she found a place that attracted her. She would ask her Heavenly Father to show her the way.

"Are you a Fall River passenger?" asked the conductor's voice at her elbow.

She started and answered, "Why yes!" Well why not? That would do as well as any other destination.

She paid her fare and sat back comfortably trying to get calm. She was away again, and was surely safe for the present. Fall River. It would be a quiet boat ride and she could get rested and think. When she got to New York she could go almost anywhere she chose.

So, while Herbert Stuart was trying to calm himself in the little reception room, and get rid of this vision of Janice that continually haunted him wherever he went in spite of the cure he had just completed, and while he prepared his mind to pay court to Miss Whittier and win her over, fortune and all, Janice was riding quietly down the river in the boat, and thanking God that He had saved her once more.

MARTHA Spicer had an impulse to open the upper window and look down to see who might be at her front door at that late hour, and if she had perhaps this chapter in her life would never have happened, for it is easier to be hard-hearted from a height than face to face with misery. But there was nothing of the coward in Martha, and if there ever had been, her business training would have taken it out. All her life long she had forced herself to face unpleasant duties and look them squarely in the eye. The fleeting thought that a caller at so late an hour in the evening boded no good to her was not permitted to remain in her well-ordered, highly-disciplined mind.

She therefore replaced the four hairpins she had taken from her abundant gray locks, and shutting her lips firmly on any excitement she might have felt at the ringing of her bell, she went downstairs, turning the light on ahead of her as she went. The second feeble clang of the bell stopped at the illumination, and the lady walked to her front door, gaining confidence as she went. She even grew cheerful at the thought that it might be Ronald come back for something he had forgotten.

She flung the door wide as if to assure herself that she was afraid of nothing. And there on the doorstep in the full glare of the hall light stood a white-faced girl, looking at her with eyes that seemed to be full of appeal and terror.

"Would you let me come in a minute and tell you something?" the girl said, and her voice was low and sweet.

There must have been something in Martha's face—it was perhaps her store-face she was wearing—that told the girl she was going to say no, for while she hesitated the girl went on pleadingly:

"I *must* come in," she said desperately. "I *must* tell somebody, and I don't know anybody else. A boy told me this morning to come to you."

Ah! What magic was this? A different look began to dawn in the lady's face. Her hand had been on the door drawing it shut, but now she swung it open again.

"A boy told you to come to me?" she asked in awe, as if the sentence had been a talisman, an open sesame to her heart and home. "What sort of a boy?"

"He was a big nice-looking boy with dark hair, lots of it all tossed up over his forehead, and big blue eyes with long curly lashes. He said, 'You go to her. She's a good scout, and she'll tell you what to do,' and I've waited around here all day, hoping you would come out the door, to see if I dared speak to you. But I couldn't get up courage till just now to ring your bell. I hated so to trouble a stranger. But just now a drunken man spoke to me, and I was so frightened. *Oh*—" the girl looked furtively behind her as if she feared he might still be lurking near.

"Come in," said Martha, swinging the door wider open and casting a hasty defiant glance into the darkness of the street. "Come in quick!"

The girl stepped into the hallway shyly and gave a keen look around to make sure the place was all right. Martha slammed the door shut hastily and pushed the big bronze bolt and chain before she turned to survey her unexpected visitor.

"Now," she said with her don't-you-try-to-cheat-me-for-you-can't-do-it air on. "Tell me all about it. How does it happen that you are walking the streets alone at this time of night? You're only a very young girl. What are your father and mother thinking about to let you wander around like this?"

The color flickered up in a faint wave over the pale cheeks and then retreated, leaving her face whiter than before.

"Mother and father died over ten years ago," she said sadly, "and my only sister died last winter." She spoke in a dull hopeless voice. "I came here four weeks ago hoping to get some work to do. I had had a little training in nursing, but not enough to do me any good, especially without recommendations. And I had studied stenography a little, and typing. I used to do typing for my father when I was quite young. But I found I couldn't get a job unless I had graduated from some school of stenography that would recommend me. I only had a little over money enough to get here. I thought if I could get to a big city I would have no trouble finding something, but I've walked the streets, and even been to other towns, and couldn't find a thing! I only had five dollars left when I paid for my ticket to this city, and that's been gone three days now, though I've been very careful, eating only milk and crackers, or something very cheap. But I can't find a thing! I suppose I look pretty shabby, but I can't help that until I can earn some money. I spent my last five cents yesterday morning for a glass of milk, and two crackers they gave me with it. This morning I started from the downtown station, where I stayed all night, to walk out here to answer an advertisement I saw in a paper that a man left on the waiting room seat, but when I got here someone else had taken it. It was a kind of a waitress job, in a restaurant, but he said anyway I didn't look stylish enough, and besides I had to furnish my aprons or make a deposit of five dollars to pay for them. I couldn't have done that of course, and so I came out. I am afraid there were tears in my eyes, for I guess the smell of the food in the restaurant made me feel rather ill, and I stumbled and sort of fell, and then that boy came and took hold of me and took me into a drugstore and made the man give me aromatic ammonia. Then the boy ordered me a cup of tea and some toast, and said if I didn't feel all right for me to come down here to this house, that you would help me feel better and tell me what to do."

The girl caught her breath and reached out her hand to the stair railing as if she thought she was going to fall again, and Martha's heart smote her. Ernestine, too, chose that very minute to appear at the top of the stairs inquiringly, surveyed them a moment and then descended hastily, with soft plush-padded footfalls, as if it were a matter that demanded her personal supervision.

"You poor child!" said Martha Spicer suddenly, drawing the girl into the little parlor and turning on the light. "Sit down!" and she guided the trembling girl to Uncle Jonathan's big chair and put her into it.

The girl sank back whitely against the patchwork cushion as if she had reached the limit of her strength, and her eyes fell shut as if they never wanted to open again. Martha saw the blue-veined temples and the hollow dark circles under the sweeping lashes. She saw the lovely disordered hair under the little crushed black hat, and the delicate refined features of the sweet face.

"Wait! Sit still!" she said, "I'll get you a cup of soup!" She hurried into the kitchen, Ernestine trotting after her with a show of bustling haste, after nosing about the feet of the stranger and deciding she was all right.

Martha lit the gas stove, put on the kettle, poured some soup into a bright little saucepan, and began cutting some bread for toast, when she heard a clear, piercing whistle in the region of the back fence.

She opened the back door quickly and called:

"Ronald! Is that you?"

"Sure is," said Ronald appearing over the fence, "anything I can do for you?"

"Why I just wanted to ask about a girl who came to see me just now," she said in a low tone going over to the fence. "Did you happen to send her to me?"

"Oh, gee! Did she come? I meant to ask about her and forgot. You see I found her on the sidewalk leaning against the fence this morning. She was all in. I took her to the drugstore and got her some kind of dope, and then something to eat, and when I had to beat it I told her if she didn't feel all right pretty soon to go and tell you about it, and you would tell her what to do."

"Yes?" said Martha. "Well, she's come! Then you don't know anything about her?"

"Not the first thing!" said Ronald cheerfully, "only she seemed a good sort and was all in. I thought you'd fix her up, or find out if she was crooked."

Martha surveyed her newly acquired man-of-all-work fixedly, and perceived he had not the slightest perception of the situation. Suddenly she realized that his standards were all so different from hers. He wouldn't realize what he had done. But it occurred to her that perhaps his natural instincts were more human than her own. He had found a girl who was "a good sort," and a woman whom he thought was "a good scout," and he had brought them together, that was all. Perhaps she ought to be thankful for the privilege of ministering to this waif of the street.

"Anything you want I should do?" he asked innocently, and Martha suddenly gave him a radiant smile:

"No, that's all right. I just wanted to make sure you sent her. You might stop over in the morning if you have time. Good night!"

The boy whistled cheerily as he turned back to the house, and murmured happily, "She's all right. I thought she'd be game." Then he slammed the back door and went joyously up to his bed.

Martha heated a bowl of delicious soup, toasted several slices of bread delicately, made a cup of fragrant tea with plenty of cream, and took them into the other room on a small tray. But as she entered the door Aunt Abigail and Uncle Jonathan seemed to have accusing eyes fixed upon her. She could almost hear their voices saying:

"Do you mean to say that at the instigation of a mere wild boy you intend to take in and encourage a girl from the streets? A girl about whose reputation you know nothing, except that she is hungry? Remember your family has always been r-r-r-respectable!" She could even hear the way Uncle Jonathan used to roll his r's.

"Don't mind him," purred Ernestine, winding furrily around her feet, "he always meant well, but never quite understood." Then she tucked herself down cozily at the stranger's feet with an eye to a possible midnight repast. She didn't mind having her rest broken on a special occasion like this. A bit of toast was one of her perquisites.

But Ernestine had reckoned this time without knowledge. The girl was fairly starved. Not a crumb was left!

"There's no use trying to tell you how grateful I am,"

said the girl. "I don't suppose you ever got that near to starving and wouldn't know how it feels, but now I'm all made over new. I feel as if I could go out and try again to find something. And I'm sure I will. Always I've been taken care of, and you have been so wonderful to me! I can see what that boy meant. He seemed so sure you would help. I can't thank you enough for just being kind to me, and after I get a job I'll be able to repay your kindness somehow. I shall not forget what you've done for me, letting me come in, speaking pleasantly to me when I was so downhearted. And your food was wonderful. Just real home food. That soup was so heartening. And now, I must be getting on out of your way, for I know I must have kept you up beyond your regular bedtime."

The girl arose, holding to the back of the chair to steady herself. Martha arose so suddenly that Ernestine had to scuttle precipitately out of her way to escape personal damage.

"But—my dear! Where are you going? Have you a room somewhere?" said Martha.

The girl drew a deep breath and tried to laugh, but it was a sorry little mockery of laughter.

"Oh," she said, "I'll find a place. There are always railroad stations, and they let you sit there all night. I shall be all right and rested in the morning," and she gave a brave little imitation of a smile.

Suddenly Martha came close to the girl and flung her unaccustomed arms around her.

"You poor dear little girl!" she said compassionately. "Did you suppose I would let you go out again in the streets tonight? You are going to stay right here with me. I've got a spare bed upstairs in the room next to mine, and it won't take a minute to put clean sheets on and make it nice and comfortable. The bathroom is right next, and there is plenty of hot water. You take a good bath and that will rest you a lot, and then in the morning you may sleep as late as you want to, all day perhaps, if you will. Come, let's go up. You are all worn out and ought to be in bed this minute!"

Martha Spicer stalked upstairs, head up triumphantly, leading her strange guest of unknown reputation, and perhaps it was at that time that the shades of Aunt Abigail and Uncle Jonathan slunk away ashamed, for they seemed not to trouble her again.

And Ernestine followed apathetically upstairs with her head bowed dejectedly. Things hadn't turned out the way she had hoped, and she still felt in need of a little sustenance. It didn't seem fair when she had encouraged the whole thing.

An hour later, Martha, arrayed for the night, stepped into the next room and stood for an instant bending over the bed, listening to the gentle breathing of her guest. The bath had indeed rested the girl and taken some of the hard lines out of her sweet face. Arrayed in one of Martha's immaculate night robes—(it was strange but Martha had *had* to give her one of her best ones, the one with embroidery and pink ribbons run in, which she always kept put away "in case of anything happening")—Janice lay with her gold hair like a soft cloud over the pillow, the long lashes dark on the white cheeks. One girlish arm was thrown out over the counterpane.

The sheets smelled of lavender flowers, and the girl looked a different creature. She was really startlingly beautiful. The heart of her hostess went out to her. Even there in the semi-darkness of that room, with only the light from the hall night lamp, Martha felt that she was entertaining an angel unaware. The breathing was so quiet that Martha stooped above the face and listened to make sure it had not stopped entirely, and drawn by a sudden impulse came closer and softly kissed her in the darkness.

The girl did not stir, but the warmth of her face and the softness of her cheek reached into the lonely heart of the woman and almost frightened her with a new kind of joy.

She fled to her own room and knelt for her usual formal prayer, but somehow the cold words which she had used since childhood failed her, and her heart gushed forth in new expressions, ending with, "Our Father, bless that dear boy, and this little lonely girl, and show me how to be different."

As she lay in the darkness afterward for an hour, staring wide-eyed at the things which had come to pass she seemed again to feel that there was a Presence in her room, and that a radiance glowed above her. Once more she heard the quaint old word, "Inasmuch!"

The feeling of awe remained with her next morning and she arose and tiptoed around her room getting ready for the day's campaign. A strange sense of having become an employee in a new firm under orders the most holy and sacred, possessed her.

She had in her house a stranger, drifted in from the wide world, in need and alone, and she felt she had been as distinctly commanded to attend to her needs as though a voice from Heaven had spoken audibly to her soul. And though she had never been a woman of deep religious fervor nor given to more than formal worship, she had no question of demurring. Indeed a kind of elation had come upon her and a light shone in her eyes, a smile hovered about her lips.

The half open door revealed the quiet form on the bed in the guest room, but the hostess would not go in and disturb her now. Let her sleep as long as she would. She had been utterly exhausted. When she had prepared a dainty breakfast it would be time enough to waken her.

As she went downstairs she was conscious of a longing for those bay windows in the wide wall that they had been talking about the night before. If there were only a flood of sunshine pouring in, how pleasant it would be for that poor little white child in the guest room to waken to. All sense of hesitation and rebuke with regard to the changes had departed from her. She felt no doubt but that it was quite the right thing for her to do. She was only anxious to have the work begin. She remembered what a radiance had overspread the face of the young man when she told him he might count on the job. Where were all her caution and good sense? How was it she no longer felt that she had done a dreadful thing to engage a man to do so important a job, about whom she knew nothing, and whose only recommendation was that a strange boy had brought him to her and she liked his face. Well, and wasn't that enough after all? What was that old legend she had heard once in a lecture, about a man who was born a king and people didn't recognize him, the story gave this rule to follow: "Whom children love, whom animals follow,"—and she thought of Ronald and Ernestine. It floated through her mind now as she put the tea kettle on. Somehow she felt sure her intuition had not deceived her, and that her chosen architect was all right. Besides, he needed the work. What if he was young and inexperienced? He looked as if he had good sense, and she would always be there to watch. She might not understand carpentering, but she would risk but what she could see if anything really went definitely wrong. And too, she couldn't help feeling glad that she was going to give that little child a chance to go to the seashore and get well, and his tired young mother too. They ought to get off at once.

Couldn't she manage somehow to suggest that to the father?

She was still thinking about it when she heard the back door of the next house fly open, and just for company she set her own door ajar, smiling to herself to think how strange it was that she should actually have reached the place where she liked to hear a boy whistle.

But there was no whistling this morning. Instead there were angry bitter words.

"You oughtta know better than to anger your dad that way when you could see he was in a bad humor. You're always getting up some fool thing you wanta do, spending money when we got all we can do to keep the clothes on your back. What's a picnic when you ain't got shoes good enough to wear to school? You'd oughtta be thankful you don't haveta quit school and go to work the way Johnny Mason has. The idea of your wanting to go traipsing off to the seashore and spending a whole dollar and a half in carfare. I don't see what you're thinking of!"

"I don't care! I think it's mean!" That was Ronald's voice now. "I never can go anywhere. Every other boy in this block is going and I don't see why I can't go too. I didn't ask dad to *give* me a dollar and a half. I just asked him to *lend* it to me. I got a job for the winter tending furnaces, and I could pay it back. Besides it don't cost a dollar and a half, it only costs a dollar for carfare. I want the half dollar to spend. When I go off with the fellows I gotta have *some*thing to spend. There's movies, and all sorts of amusements, and I wantta hire a suit and go in bathing. If dad was like other men he'd take you and me and Teena and go too. Most every man on this street is going."

"Well, it'll be a long time before your dad ever does a fool thing like that with his money. And I advise you to keep your mouth shut about your picnics if you don't want him to give you a good whipping. He's pretty mad already. He wants you to quit school and get a job—" and there was a plaintive wistful sound to the woman's voice, in spite of her harsh words.

But a man's voice calling angrily from within drew the woman away, and there was only left the low mutterings of the boy as he set about his morning's work.

So that was what the boy had been wanting to do! Go on a community picnic to the shore! A harmless enough thing of course and little enough money to spend on an outing for a good boy who seemed to be well-intentioned and kindly. What an ugly father and an unnatural mother to refuse him! But then perhaps the mother was harassed with cares and didn't know how to get along.

And to think the boy wanted money so badly as that and yet had refused her proffered quarter! What a fine sense of honor. Well, he was surely a boy to be proud of! She felt a thrill of pride and pleasure in his friendship. And then she fell to planning. How could she help that boy to get to that picnic? Wasn't there any way? Perhaps she ought not to try, but somehow it hurt her dreadfully to have him disappointed. If she had only known sooner perhaps she could have found a way to help him. But this was Saturday, and Monday would be the day of the picnic. A half-formed plan came flickering to her mind, how she might concoct some work for him to do for her. But there was hardly time now for him to earn enough in anything she could ask him to do.

She was still pondering it as she took the tray upstairs. A delicate piece of toast on which reposed a beautifully poached egg, a cup of coffee, a glass of milk, and a bunch of purple grapes with the bloom on them. It looked nice enough to tempt any appetite, and Martha was glad as she set it down softly on the little mahogany table by the bed.

The girl on the bed had not stirred, did not stir now. Indeed she lay so white and still Martha could not tell if she was breathing. The little lace ruffles and gay pink ribbons over her breast did not seem to rise or fall, nor flutter with a palpitating heart. Could it be that the child had slipped away out of an unfriendly world into the light and warmth of the Father's house of many mansions?

Martha had had all kinds of experiences with living human beings, but very little with the dead. Since her own parents had died she had lived so much in the world of business that the possibility of death seemed remote and unreal. With awe she knelt and laid an unaccustomed hand trembling on the girl's breast, put her ear down and listened, then threw up the window shade to get more light, but her own pulses bounded so frantically that she was unable to tell whether the girl was breathing or not. She even held a small mirror before her lips, but was so excited she couldn't be sure whether it was dimmed with vapor or not. There seemed a chill to the flesh when she touched it that sent a pang of fear through her heart, and she remembered suddenly that if the girl died here in her home they had no means of knowing who she was or where she came from.

As a last resort she laid her lips on the lips and forehead of the sleeping girl and they seemed to strike a chill through her very soul.

Thoroughly frightened now she fled downstairs, out the kitchen door to the fence, and called: "Ronald! Ronald! Come quick!"

The boy threw down his axe hastily, and his dark head appeared over the fence.

"What's wrong?" he asked capably.

"Can you get a doctor quick? I'm afraid that girl is dying!" said Martha.

"Sure, I'll get him in three jerks of a lamb's tail," said the boy. "He's the doctor of that architeck's little kid. Doc Blackwell. He's swell," and Ronald was off like a flash.

10

MARTHA turned helplessly back to her kitchen. The kettle was singing cheerily. She stopped to put on the large preserving kettle full of water. It might be needed. Then she hurried back upstairs. What else could she do? Aromatic ammonia? Yes, she had some. She wet a handkerchief and waved it in front of the girl's face. She put a few drops in water and tried to get a little down between those closed lips, but most of it ran down her white chin and was lost on the pillow. She tried camphor on a handkerchief but there was no change in the white face and a terrible desperate fear was taking possession of her. Suppose Ronald couldn't find the doctor. Would he get another one?

And then she heard the doorbell ring and she hurried down to meet Ronald and the quiet-eyed, young doctor.

The boy and Martha stood very still while the doctor made his examination, but at last it was over.

"I think there is still life here," said the doctor turning to Martha, "but we shall have to work fast. May I have a glass and water and a spoon? Hot water, have you? Boy, you go back to my office and get the little black case on my desk. I need something from it. Miss Spicer, have you a hot water bottle?"

Gravely, quietly, swiftly they obeyed orders. Ronald was back from the office in almost no time, and busied himself in bringing hot water and running errands. And yet with their best efforts it was a full half hour before they were rewarded by hearing a soft sigh from the sleeper, and it was a full hour before she opened her eyes and looked at them with a puzzled expression as if she had come back from another world, then dropped the lids slowly shut again and went on sleeping. But her breath was coming now, regularly and normally. The doctor whispered a few directions about feeding her. It was some time later that he turned away from her again and said with a sigh of satisfaction:

"I think she will be all right now, but that was a close call. I thought for a few minutes there that it was no use, she was too far gone, but she had youth in her favor. She must have been running on the edge of things for a long time, and can't have been eating very much."

"Yes," said Martha, "I'm afraid so. She didn't tell me much last night, but I think she is a lady, suddenly thrown on her own resources. She lost her job and went walking all over after another without taking time or much money from her small store to eat."

Martha was surprised to find that her own voice was trembling, and she felt all unnerved. The sudden relief from suspense had left her feeling weak all at once.

"Well, she's evidently been overtaxing her strength tremendously," said the doctor. "Ronald tells me he saw her nearly fall in the street. It's been loss of sleep and lack of nutrition."

"Yes," said Martha, "she told me last night that there

were always railroad stations one could sit in all night and sleep."

"Yes, I guess that has been the tale," said the doctor sorrowfully. "She's almost finished herself. But she's young. I think she'll pull through now. It was good of you to look after her. But let me know if she seems to be sinking again. She needs good food and lots of sleep. Don't hesitate to call me at any time, day or night. I'm just around the corner, you know. Ronald will bring me word. Of course you understand I make no charge for a case like this."

"Oh!" said Martha, strange tears springing into her eyes, and feeling as if he had done her a personal favor. "Oh, that is good of you. But I'm looking after her you know. I was the one who sent for you."

"Yes? But this is my part of the job, you see. Just call me whenever you need me, and in any case I'll look in again after lunch. I want to make sure that that pulse keeps steady."

"I'll be back after a bit," said Ronald, following the doctor down the stairs. There was a comfortable assurance in his voice and Martha turned back to the room to find the forgotten Ernestine lunching calmly off the stranger's breakfast. Ernestine thought there had been fuss enough made over that tiresome girl who lay in bed at this late hour of the morning, and if nobody wanted that toast and egg and glass of milk, she did. It was time she took things in her own paws.

The rest of the day Ernestine sat apart with an offended air. Things hadn't gone her way at all and she was faint and deeply jealous. She had been summarily swept off the stranger's bed and sent downstairs, and even Ronald hadn't had time to pat her. She tucked up her fur collar, blinked dismally, and forgot to wind up her music box. Life had taken on a strange aloofness, and everything seemed to center in that dark guest room upstairs.

When Ronald came back Martha asked him to go to the grocery for her, and then they had a little talk about the architect and his family.

"He's tickled to death to think he's got the job," said the boy. "He's been wanting to send his wife and the kid to the shore. Doc said they oughtta go right off. Doc wanted to lend him the money but he couldn't see that. But Doc's a good sport. So now Bill Roberts thinks if you are pleased with his plans he can begin work right off and maybe they can go in three or four weeks."

"But they ought not to wait so long," said Martha. "This is just the lovely weather and the child ought to be out in it. Why don't they go at once? I could let him have a little money in advance."

"Gee! Couldya? Maybe he'd take it that way."

"Have they any idea where they want to go and how much it will cost?" Martha's business training came to the front at once.

"Well, he was asking me about a place where they are going to have a street picnic next Monday," said Ronald meditatively. "He said he heard there were good places to board cheap down there. He thought maybe I was going down Monday with the rest, and maybe I'd look him up a place. But—I *ain't*," the boy added, a sullen cloud coming over the brightness of his face.

"Oh, why aren't you going?" asked Martha innocently.

"Couldn't work it this time," said Ronald evasively.

"You would like to go?"

"You bet I would, but dad don't see it that way. Costs too much."

"That's too bad. I'm sorry," said Martha.

"Aw, I don't mind," said Ronald looking down indifferently. "Well, I gotta beat it! I'll be back again after a while. So long!" and he was gone before she could say another word.

When he came back the next time she was ready for him.

"Ronald, I've been thinking. I can't bear the idea of that baby waiting till I get the house fixed over before he goes to the seashore. Besides if this girl is going to be sick for a while that will delay the work, too. I've decided to suggest that he go next week, take his family, and stay a week or ten days himself with them. They'll need him if they are to get the kind of rest they ought to have. I can advance him some money on the job, you know, and he can be working the plans out while he is away. He'll do better work after his mind is set at rest about his child, and I shall be better satisfied in every way. After they are comfortably settled down there he can run back every other day and attend to anything up here that needs him, or if the girl gets well enough he can start his men to work on the house, and keep his wife and child down at the shore a little longer. Do you think that would please him?"

"Oh, boy! I should think it oughtta! That'd be great!"

His eyes were shining for the woman who could work out and propose such a noble scheme for the good of humanity. She was the first one of her kind he had met. And indeed she was a surprise to herself as the joy of her unselfish thought welled up in her heart and flooded her soul. She hadn't known that the giving of a little kindness would be like this, bringing its own reward in joy even before the act was accomplished. Why hadn't she done things like this before? She had often had it in her power, but had always been obsessed by the idea that the world owed *her* all she could get out of it, and everyone less fortunate than herself was trying to cheat her out of her rights. What had changed her?

"Then, how about this?" she said. "I'd like to send you on ahead to find a good boarding place at a reasonable rate for them. He probably couldn't be persuaded to go unless everything was all mapped out for him. I should think this time of year one could get a good boarding place for a very low price. Would you be able to go down to the shore for a day and look around and see what could be done? How about that place you were mentioning this morning? You said he asked about it. I suppose that would please him as well as any place, and you have heard it is nice you say. Perhaps you would find it easier to look up places. Do you think your father would object to your going? I would pay your fare of course and pay you for your day's work. And of course it wouldn't take all day to find a place and you would get a little fun by the way."

The boy's face was all sparkles of delight. His eyes grew larger and larger. And she was offering him money for a day like that!

"Gee!" he breathed as if he could hardly believe his ears. "D'you mean it? *Sure* I'd go. Pa wouldn't even know I'd gone. He don't care what becomes of me, only so I don't cost him nothing. But you wouldn't need to *pay* me besides. It would be great just to go. If I was to go Monday I could get the round trip for a dollar, along with the excursionists, you know."

"Go Monday, by all means," said wily Martha, trying not to show her delight that she had succeeded in getting him off on that picnic after all. "But of *course* I shall pay you for the day. You will need some spending money too, and what I want you to do will take a good deal of your time, so you won't have as much fun as you would if you just went with the others. Besides, you will need something for your meals. I will pay you for the day besides your fare and meals. Will that be all right?"

"*Swell!*" said Ronald, overwhelmed. "*Too much!* Oh *Boy!*" and he turned away to hide his emotion.

As she watched the sturdy young shoulders and the fine strong boy-profile against the fading evening light from the window her heart was filled with a strange new emotion. A sense of what it would have been to have been his mother, and have a right to give him things and receive his affection came to her in hungry boundings of her heart. She was half afraid of her own emotion and turned away to rattle some dishes she was putting on the table, to hide her own feelings. So, they had silence between them for a full minute, like two boys. They were as far apart as two human beings could well be, and yet were in many ways much alike, this gray haired lonely woman, and this boy of fifteen breezy years.

Then Martha turned back with her ordinary tone of voice and said almost coldly:

"Well, then, that's fixed and you can go Monday morning. I'll depend on you to find a suitable place as reasonably as possible. It had better be near to the beach, and you better get your dinner there and see if the eating is good. I'll maybe want to send this girl down for a few days later, so you might ask what it would be for her in a room by herself in case she needs to go."

Ronald accepted this astonishing statement calmly, but his eyes shone. It almost seemed to him as if God must have come to earth to work through a mere woman, and do some of the things that ought to be done. He drew a deep sigh of wonder and awe.

"Sure! I'll find a dandy place! You leave it to me!" he said with a swagger.

It seemed as if he was in a hurry to go then, for he did not even notice the cat who hovered apathetically about his feet. He left the kitchen door ajar in his haste, and it slowly swung back. Martha was making beef tea at the moment and did not notice, until she heard a scrambling over the fence and the neighboring kitchen door flung open, followed by a clear young voice:

"Ma, have I got a clean shirt? I'm going off early Monday morning on a business trip—Be gone all day, and I gotta have a clean shirt! If I ain't got one I gotta wash one *now!*"

The next kitchen door shut suddenly on a surprised voice of remonstrance, and Martha pouring her beef tea into a delicate china cup, smiled to herself over the working out of her scheme. Ronald was to have his picnic and he had never suspected that that was why she got up this "business trip." Somehow that made her happier than ever she had been when she had made a good business deal at the store.

She cast a look of passing anxiety toward the neighbor's house as she shut her own kitchen door. Was there any possibility that Ronald would have trouble at home in getting his parents' consent to her plan? Then the look on the boy's face as he said his father didn't care what he did if he didn't have to pay for it, came back to her and she felt reassured.

She had a sudden fierce longing to have that boy for her own, to educate and uplift him and watch him develop. Then in the dusky kitchen she smiled at herself to realize how her own point of view had changed during the past week. Here, for instance, she was, carrying a cup of hot beef broth to an utter stranger who lay in her guest room bed too weak and sick even to tell her own name. A week ago she would have considered this an imposition on a respectable woman, and would likely have sent for the police to get an ambulance and take the girl to a hospital. And all this difference had been brought about by that boy! It certainly was queer!

After supper Martha sat down in the parlor near to the hall door where she could easily hear every sound from above, and looked about her. Life seemed to have taken on an entire revolution during the last twenty-four hours. Great changes were impending, the very walls about her thrilling with the idea of change. In her mind's eye she could already see bay windows and stairs with landings.

And upstairs in her guest room was that nameless stranger sleeping, having partaken of her beef tea with disinterested submission and closed eyes. Her heart thrilled that the girl was getting better and was likely to live. She wanted her to get well. She wanted to see her beautiful eyes open and sparkle, and color come in her pretty oval cheeks. She had been praying all day for her recovery, and sitting here alone she bowed her head and prayed again. And once begun she found a great many other things to pray about. She wanted the boy to have a good time on his picnic, to be successful in finding a nice cheap boarding house, and return in safety. She wanted the architect to be able to fix her house at a price she could afford, and to be willing to accept some of his pay before hand so that he could take his wife and child to the shore.

She prayed so long that Ernestine got worried and sprang up in her lap to see what was the matter. And being taken in gentle arms snuggled down contentedly and set her music box to rumbling. After all, thought Ernestine, there were compensations, even if one could not understand all the actions of people.

And then Martha got to wondering if she, just plain Martha Spicer, who had never really been much of a Christian, had a *right* to ask for all those material things?

Whereupon she bowed her head again and added to her prayers that she might be made into the kind of woman that the Lord desired her to be, to fulfill his purpose for her life.

The next few days were a curious experience for Martha.

Up in her guest room the stranger lay like a breath of vapor between life and death. Most of the time she slept softly, her gentle breath coming so faintly that often it was a question whether the doctor ought not to be called again. Apathetically the girl partook of the nourishment that was given, lifting languid eyes now and then to Martha's face, eyes that seemed to see only things afar, and not to sense the present in the least.

Now and then the doctor looked in, touched the pulse with a practiced hand, left some fresh medicine and went his way again.

Ronald was in and out ten times on Sunday, and started off proudly on Monday morning with his money in his pocket, and a spic-and-span clean shirt adorning his handsome young shoulders. His cheery "So-long! See you sub-se," rang in Martha's ears happily all day long. She sat up late that night and kept her light burning till he came home whistling, hoping he would drop in and give her news of the day. And he did. He gave a timid tap at the front door, and she, like any *girl,* was there on the instant, her eyes shining, to greet him.

The two conspirators talked for several minutes. Ronald's eyes were bright and his face was ruddy with the day's experience.

"Found a dandy place all right!" he announced as he entered, "right on the beach front, second story front rooms with a big wide piazza almost like sailing on a ship. It ain't much to look at, needs painting and is out of fashion, but the man that keeps a swell place on the

next block has been using it for an annex, till this year
and he says if they don't mind its being shabby he'll take
'em real cheap. He said if the other girl was to come
down too she could have a room across the hall. Here's
the prices, in ink where he crossed off the printed ones
but you must keep 'em under your hat. He doesn't want
those prices known. I jollied him along till I got him
where I wanted him, and he's all right. And the eats are
great! The man has a farm and they had real peas and
beans and tomatoes, and corn on the cob, and plum pie
and ice cream for dessert. They have chicken and ice
cream every Sunday and Wednesday he says, and it'll be
a dollar a week for the kid's milk, and her to go down
and cook it in the kitchen. Boy, but you oughtta see the
ocean out that front porch! It's *great!* You can see three
lighthouses in clear weather. I had a peach of a swim.
There's bath houses belonging to the house, and they
said we could use 'em, so we went in swimming twice.
We had a cracker-jack dinner, and the supper was some
class, just as fine as the dinner. Hot muffins, deviled
crabs, peaches and cream, fried potatoes, and chocolate
cake! Say, you oughtta go down yourself. Say, why
dontcha?"

"Well, maybe I will," said Martha, warming to the
idea. "We'll see when my sick girl gets well. Perhaps I'll
get you to take us both and take care of us a few days.
How would you like that?"

"Swell!" responded Ronald eagerly. "Say, how is the
girl?"

"A little better I think, but she hasn't talked yet except
to say 'No, thank you,' when I ask if there is anything
she wants."

"Good *night!* She was all in, wasn't she? What's her
name?"

"I don't know her name," said Martha. "I wanted to

find out because there might be somebody who is worrying about her somewhere, and I ought to let them know, but the doctor says not to bother her till she talks of her own free will."

"Gee! It must be fierce to be like that!" said the boy frowning. "Well, now, what's the idea? Do I get Bill Roberts here in the morning?"

"Oh yes, does he live far away?"

"No, only a couppla blocks away. I'll have him here at eight o'clock if you'll be on the job that early. He said he'd have the estimate all done by tomorrow."

"I'll be on the job," said Martha.

"Well, I gotta beat it now. Gonta hit the feathers hard tonight. Had a great day, thanks to you! Okay! I'll be seeing you!"

II

RONALD appeared on the dot of eight the next morning, with the apprehensive young architect handing out his estimate apologetically.

They sat down in the living room and Martha read it over carefully. When she had finished she looked up pleasantly:

"Well, that's even a little better than you gave as your first estimate. Are you sure you will make anything on the job at this price?"

It wasn't at all a businesslike question, of course. It wasn't the way she had been taught to buy and sell underwear, but everything in her world was upside-down today.

The young man reddened.

"I'll make a little," he said shyly. "At least I will if things don't go up in price."

"Well, of course I want to deal fairly," said Martha, "and if things go up I want you to tell me. We'll be looking this over again of course, and I guess we can settle it between us all right. I certainly don't want you to lose anything. And now, I think we are ready to go ahead as soon as possible. But unexpectedly I've got a very sick girl upstairs. It may be a few days, perhaps a week, before she will be able to have the noise going on, but we can get everything all planned out, and meantime I want to talk to you about another matter."

The young man's face fell. Was there to be more delay? Farewell fond hopes of sending his baby to the shore if that was so! He could not do it without money. He sighed involuntarily.

"I've been thinking about that baby of yours," went on Martha. "The doctor has been telling me he ought to get to the shore this hot weather."

"Yes," said the young man, the shadow of despair in his eyes, "yes, I know it, but I can't manage it just now."

"Yes, but you *can* manage it, excuse me," said Martha in the tone she used to use to the floorwalkers in the store when they kept her waiting. "You see your wife can't very well go down to the shore all alone, not with a baby, you know, and it wouldn't do *you* a bit of harm to have a little change yourself. You look as if you had done some worrying over that baby too. Your wife would have a great deal more rest if you went along, wouldn't she?"

"Yes, but that's out of the question of course," he said hopelessly. "It will be all we can do to send her and the baby, if we can manage even that."

"Nonsense!" said Martha eagerly, "that isn't the way to talk. You *ought* to go, you know you ought. In fact you *must* go! And I've got it all planned out. I can just as well as not let you have fifty or seventy-five dollars, or even more, in advance on this job. It isn't just convenient of course for me to have the work started for a few days, but when my friend gets well I'd like to have it begun at once. Meantime you could perfect your plans, get your orders in for materials, have the stuff sent here, and you could engage your men. You could do that by letter or telephone, or perhaps see them before you leave. And then day after tomorrow morning you and your wife and baby could start for the shore! It ought not to take her any longer than that to get ready. She won't need any fancy clothes because it is late in the season and there are not so many people left there now. If there is any shopping she needs, either for herself or the baby, I can help her out if she hasn't time to see to it herself, and then she can just pick up the baby's things and put on her hat and go. You see Ronald went down to the shore yesterday, and he found a plain house right on the beach where they won't charge much. When you come home with a well baby and a happy wife you'll see it pays."

The architect's eyes were sea-blue with whitish lashes, and his face was salmon pink from exposure to the weather, but the sea-blue eyes were swimming with salt tears now and the tears were running down his pink cheeks. He got out a large red and white handkerchief and blew his nose vigorously, wiped his eyes many times, choked and coughed.

"I-I-I—c-c-can't—thank—you—!" he spluttered.

"Well, don't try," said Martha getting up and going over to the window to push the shade up a little higher, just to hide her embarrassment. "It's just common sense you see and there's nothing to thank me for. The money will be yours, and you happen to need it just now, so why not take it? Now, you better go right home and tell your wife and give her a chance to get ready. You better plan to take the morning train day after tomorrow if possible. Tell your wife if she needs any help to run over. I can sew something for her and I can order things for her at the store where I used to be, but I can't of course leave here to go away while I have that sick girl to look after. Now, run along and get things going. You've a lot to do."

He blurted out his inadequate thanks and hurried away, and in a short time a slender girl with tired eyes, and a baby wrapped in a shawl appeared at the front door.

"Oh, you've been so good," said the young mother. "I had to come and tell you how happy you have made me. It doesn't seem as if it could be true that we're going to the shore, and that Will is going with us. You don't know how hard it is to go away alone with the baby. I haven't dared leave him alone a minute since he was so sick."

Martha drew her into the house.

"Never mind thanking me, child," she said briskly, "there isn't much time and I know you've got lots to do. How can I help you? Have you got everything you need?"

"Oh, I haven't got anything," laughed the tired young mother hysterically, "but that doesn't matter. I don't mind. Do you suppose I care how I look now that this great thing has come to us? I've prayed—Oh, how I've prayed—but I never believed anything like this could come."

"Why, this is nothing great," said Martha briskly. "This is just common sense. Come, let's get to work. Have you got something to travel in? You'll need a good warm coat too at the seashore this time of year you know. Have you got one? I have one I could lend you, only maybe you'll think it is a little old-fashioned. I bought it five years ago, and it used to fit me, but I'm getting stouter and I've had to get a new one. I'm sorry it's not the latest model."

"Old-fashioned! Why should I care about fashion? If

the baby gets well I don't care what I wear. Thank you so much!"

"Well, you'll care what you wear, too. You ought to. It's only right you should with such a nice husband as you've got. But I guess you can get by with my heavy coat for now, it isn't so bad, and that will be one thing you won't have to bother about now. I'll shake it out and hang it in the yard to get the mothballs out of it, and you can get it later. Have you got a suit?"

The girl flushed.

"Why, yes—that is I had one, but I burned the front breadth with a coal that jumped out of the fire when I was raking it in a hurry just before I ran for the doctor. I ought to have fixed it before, but the baby has been so very sick—Maybe I can get time to sponge and press it and turn a pleat or two so the holes won't show. Anyhow I don't mind. And I've got a good linen skirt and a blouse, and I can wear the jacket with them."

"You need a suit," said Martha, "and there's no time to do any sewing and pressing today. Your job is to get that baby ready with as little fuss as possible, and you don't want to get all tired out either. You'll need every bit of your strength. So you better let me do some thinking for you. Suppose you leave the baby with me for a while, go back and get some milk or whatever he eats, and bring it here and then you go right down town and get whatever you need. That baby will be all right with me I'm sure, and we can make a little bed here on the couch with two chairs beside it. You've got to get what you should have quickly or you won't get off tomorrow. You buy a suit! Get good material. That's economy in the end. I'll give you the name of one of the saleswomen down at the store when I used to work. She'll help you decide. It's got to be the right color, and she'll know a good bargain. They always have them this time of year. Get something simple with good lines, and stylish enough so it won't get right out of fashion. That lasts longer. You better get some shoes and gloves too, and a nice little hat to go with your suit. Anything else you need. Don't be afraid. And charge them all to my account. Then I can settle with your husband later when he gets to building for me. You needn't worry. Your husband is going to succeed in his business, and you'll have enough money to live comfortably pretty soon, I'm sure. Can you go right away?"

"Oh, you're so good—" gasped the little mother. "But I couldn't go just yet. There's some washing I should do—"

"Of course," said Martha. "I'd thought of that. But isn't there someone in your neighborhood who does washing? Just bundle your wash all up in a sheet and take them to her. Here, hasn't she a phone? Call her up right now. What's her name?"

"Johnson. But—"

"No buts. You call her up and see if she can do it all today, and you go right home and pick up the clothes, send them over to her house. Then fix the baby's milk and make your husband bring it over to me. I want to see him again anyway about something. And here. Here's my charge coin and a card from me saying you are buying for me. Now, it's nine o'clock, and you ought to be able to get all this done and get started by half past ten or eleven anyway."

"Oh—" began the little mother.

"Never mind the thanks," said Martha. "We'll tend to that when baby gets well. We can make a bed for him right here on this couch. I'll try to be a good nurse till you get back. Suppose we see if he'll come to me." Martha put out her arms and had a sudden fear lest she was too much of an old maid to be attractive to a baby.

But something leaped up in her heart as the little fellow put out a thin arm feebly, and she gathered him to her heart.

The mother laughed softly.

"He knows a fairy when he sees one," she said, the happy tears choking her voice. "Well, I'll go if you say so, though it seems awfully presuming of me. But it's like having Heaven open when everything was as black as could be. But I guess I better take baby back and fix him up for the day. It won't take me long. I can do it while his milk is preparing. I don't know what Will is going to say to all this. He's terribly proud about accepting favors, but you've been awfully good and he was real desperate."

She took the baby and hastened away, and Martha stood still watching her walk away and taking account of stock while her Adversary the devil, who interferes in all money transactions stood at her elbow and advised:

"You're a pretty fool, Martha Spicer! Do you know what you've done now? Let yourself in for a whole family! Put your charge account at the store at their disposal, and turned your home into a day nursery! At this rate you'll run through your inheritance before a year is out and have to go back to work again. What do you think folks would think of you if they knew? The folks at the store? Your own friends and relatives? They'll think you've gone crazy. You've taken a wild sick girl from the streets, a thief perhaps, or worse. You've made yourself a companion of a common little street urchin who is going to bring all sorts of creatures down upon you. You've agreed to pull down this fine substantial house your relatives left you and fill it with all sorts of new-fangled gimcracks, and all to help a lot of strangers who must be very unworthy or they wouldn't need the help. Nobody ever did the like for you, Martha Spicer, did they? Send those people to the seashore? Why you never could afford to go yourself when you were earning a good salary. Nobody ever looked out for *you* to nurse you when you were sick, or send you to the seashore. You've just got enough to be comfortable on and now you're sending a lot of good-for-nothings off for a holiday! Why, the money it costs to send those Robertses off would pay your way at a fine hotel for several weeks, and you really need the rest, you know you do! Think how you've slaved for years! Like as not they'll never pay you back what they owe you either. Then where will you be?"

"Get out!" said Martha Spicer springing to her feet and speaking so emphatically that Ernestine picked up her astonished tail and scuttled under the big rocker. She didn't know but her new respectable owner was losing her mind. She bristled her fur up around her ears and turned on the green baleful lights in her eyes to be ready for an emergency. Really this was too much, with all the goings on the last few days! And just when she thought she was going to like Miss Spicer! And a *baby,* too. What would a baby be like in the old house?

Martha went to the kitchen and got ready the beef tea for the girl upstairs, and then hurried around getting her house in order. She had suddenly remembered that the baby would be back in a few minutes and she must be free to look after it. A baby was a great responsibility. She began to plan how she could make a sort of pen for it on her bed, putting chairs and pillows around for a wall so it couldn't roll off. The Adversary for the time was vanquished. She felt suddenly like a child with a first doll, and eagerly looked forward to its return.

The baby was in his coach fast asleep when he finally arrived. The father and mother were flushed with excitement. They hadn't been shopping together since they bought their first housekeeping things just after they were married.

They had found the washerwoman ready and willing, who had promised the wash by six that evening. The baby's bottles were neatly packed in a tin pail ready to be put in the refrigerator. The process for heating and administering the food seemed simple enough. The mother's white blouse, linen skirt and worn serge jacket looked neat, although the broken black straw hat she wore showed plainly she needed the new felt Martha had advised.

Armed with advance-payment money, several addresses, and a couple of letters of introduction to tradespeople, the young couple left in high feather. Then Martha went into the parlor and stood beside the little coach looking down on the sweet baby face, marked the wax-like transparency of the delicate flesh, the long sweeping bronze lashes, the gold curl that strayed out over the white forehead. A little living soul in a tiny body! And some day if he lived, this flower-like baby would grow into a great boy like Ronald. How wonderful! And Ronald had been little like that once, too! Yes, he would grow into a fine boy like Ronald. With such good parents he would never be a bad boy like the ones who tied poor Ernestine to the doorknob.

There were still things, of course, that Martha had to learn about boys in general, and Ronald in particular, but, of course, she didn't know it. She thought that in perceiving some good in Ronald she had arrived at the ultimate conclusion concerning boys.

"Meow!" said Ernestine softly, not to wake the baby. She was not accustomed to children, but she showed a human interest in this one, and was willing to let bygones be bygones for the sake of the baby.

Martha spent much time that day standing by the baby

coach watching the baby. It came to her that once *she* was a baby lying on a pillow with her mother and father watching over her. She recalled the glances of the Robertses as they were leaving this child. Such looks of utter devotion. Strange new thoughts. It gave her a different view of life, of herself, of her own father and mother.

Upstairs there was no appreciable change in the patient. Still that quiet steady sleeping, that utter apathy to food or anything outside herself. It filled her with awe. Each time she entered the room it seemed as if Death stood there in the offing waiting to claim the girl who had almost gone with him before. Each time she approached the bed cautiously, watched to see if the breath was still there. Yet the girl kept breathing steadily on, and sometimes it seemed that she was growing a little stronger.

It was an exciting moment when the baby at last stirred in his warm nest and turned a sleep-flushed cheek away from the pillow. He opened bewildered eyes to the strange room, and the gray-haired woman who stood over him with a bottle carefully wrapped in flannel to keep it warm. He gazed with troubled eyes and puckered his lip, but at last succumbed to the first taste of the bottle, stopping now and then to murmur: "Mam-mam-mam—" and the word went to Martha's heart like a stab, so that she put forth her best efforts, gathering the little stranger into her arms comfortably and adjusting the bottle to his convenience. So they sat in comfort and conversed in an unknown tongue about the deep things of life, and Martha found she was learning a lot she hadn't dreamed of before. The cat, not to be impolite, hopped velvetly up to a chair near by and tucked herself into compactness within vision of the baby, who stared at her with round astonished eyes, and finally consented to smile.

At four o'clock Ronald breezed in, took up the baby who gurgled happily at his coming, proving that he was an old acquaintance.

And at last the father and mother arrived, laden with bundles and boxes galore, and after exhibiting some of their purchases, took the baby and went home to pack.

The girl upstairs on the bed opened her eyes as usual that night when Martha fed her the chicken broth, but when it was finished she sighed and nestled against the pillow and murmured softly, "Thank you!"

On sudden impulse Martha stooped over and kissed her tenderly on her little white hand. Such a pretty frail little girl she was to be floating all alone through the world!

But there was no further motion, no more words, and Martha went down to make all tidy for the night, and to reflect on how empty the downstairs seemed without the baby. A baby! She had always thought of babies as burdens and troubles, nuisances! And behold they were Heavenly blessings!

The Robertses stopped on their way to the bus to say good by and show her how well everything fitted. Mrs. Roberts looked so pretty in her new suit and new hat. She had gathered her little son into his pink blanket and he was already sleeping soundly. The father had folded up the little coach and carried it and the two suitcases. They poured out a lot of eager thanks, both talking at once, and then rushed for their bus and Martha stood on the front steps and watched them out of sight with a smile on her lips. She caught the last flutter of the mother's hand from the bus window at the corner, and she saw the father swing himself aboard as the bus started.

And then she realized that her first big benevolence was launched.

"Well, fool woman, what are you going to do next?" said the Adversary, standing in the doorway behind her.

"Meow! I hope you're going to have a little time to pay attention to me now," complained Ernestine, arching her back petulantly under Martha's feet. "I'm so faint I can hardly stand on my paws."

"You poor cat!" said Martha with compunction, picking up the furry creature, but she swept by the Adversary and slammed the door in his face. She had no time to listen to his advice just then.

DR. Sterling started out on his self-arranged vacation with high hopes. He had spent the night thinking out a plan of campaign. He had tried to guess where the girl would have taken refuge. It hurt him terribly to think that she had not come to him for help when she might so easily have done so. And yet he knew her proud nature, her fear of making any trouble in the institution. Besides, though she had for a time seemed to enjoy the warm friendly fellowship they had had together, he had never been able to understand why she afterward held herself so aloof. If he only knew the secret of her sudden coolness he would be better able to answer that question of "why" to his own satisfaction.

However, though for some reason she had decided to be less friendly with him, that did not make him less anxious to find her and help her. Indeed as the days went by and no word came from her his heart was in anguish. Every little movement and habit of her lovely face, every expression, every turn of speech seemed to return and to grow upon him, until it sometimes became almost a torment to him, and he went more feverishly to work than ever on his almost hopeless task of trying to get a clue.

With the help of his detective friend he combed the country round about Willow Croft and Enderby, and then proceeded out west, trying his best to find relatives or old friends where she might have gone, or who would have known of her whereabouts.

Several times in his journeys he came into crowds of people hurrying to some train or boat, and he would think he saw her in the distance among them, only to meet with terrible disappointment when he came up with the person he had thought resembled Janice. In his frantic search he visited schools, hospitals, orphanages, and various institutions where she might have sought a job as nurse, but day after day there came nothing but disappointment. He fell into the habit of studying faces when he entered a train or bus, and with a swift glance he would know at once whether or not she was there.

He had arranged to have his mail and telegrams forwarded to him wherever he went, so that he was never more than two days without definite knowledge whether he had been called on the telephone or whether any mail was awaiting him somewhere, but there came no word.

In the long lonely watches of some of the nights of his anxiety and disappointment he had come to know that he loved her deeply. That she seemed to be to him the one whom God had sent to his care. And he had let her get away and go into all sorts of perils. He blamed himself continually for having allowed her to wait upon that inebriate. And yet, of course, if there was something in him for her to fear it was as well that she should have discovered it in time before the man himself recognized her.

At last he felt that he would go crazy if he went on

this way any longer, and it would be best for him to go back to Enderby. If she ever wanted to communicate with him suddenly, that would be the natural place for her to find him. Anyway he must go back.

And on the train on the way back he fell asleep and dreamed of the day when he and Janice had been out in the open watching the lovely cloud formations, and she had suddenly exclaimed that God had been so good to her, helping her to a place where she could go on living. And when he had asked if she really believed that God took notice of His creatures and arranged their lives for them she had said that if she didn't believe that she wouldn't have the nerve to go on living. Was the little girl still believing that? Was she still comforted by it? He found himself wishing that he had the same faith in God.

That night he prayed again. He asked God to take care of the girl, to find her and keep her and comfort her, and if it wasn't His will that he should find her again, wouldn't he please send somebody else to take care of her and keep her from harm? And some day might he find her and be able to tell her how he loved her.

So he went back to the sanitarium where every turn reminded him of her, and the days were one long torture because she was not there.

The new patient, Herbert Stuart, was supposed to be cured. At least he was gone, and Sterling did not attempt to find out much about him beyond the fact that he had gone to New York. How much further no one seemed to know. If the girl whom he loved was in danger from Herbert Stuart how could he hope to save her? He could only pray that God would do so. And in that growing belief he got through the days.

"Doctor Sterling doesn't look well, does he?" said

Brynie to Ray. "I wonder why? You don't suppose that Rose Bradford turned him down, do you? Maybe he's been off trying to make up to her again and she wouldn't have him!"

"Well, I wouldn't blame her much," said Ray, "the way he ran around and buddied up to that little white-faced scrap we had here for a nurse! My word, the idea of her trying to train for a nurse when she couldn't stand the sight of a drunken man! Well, I'm glad she's gone, but Doc Sterling has no one to thank for his being turned down by a wealthy girl but himself. He ought to have known a girl like Rose Bradford wouldn't stand for that!"

By spring Dr. Sterling had definitely decided to leave the sanitarium, and had handed in his resignation, to take effect early in the fall. He would certainly have applied at once for a position in the army if it had not been that he had a strong feeling that he must be somewhere available if that dear girl needed him. At least he would wait until fall, to give her more opportunity to communicate with him. Also he felt that he owed this to the sanitarium to give them time to find the right successor for his work. So many had gone into war work that it was not easy to find just the one for important places at home.

But more and more he was troubled what to do. Had not God put it upon his heart to search out and somehow help this poor child who had wandered away again, into a frightening world? Or was this merely a selfish thing, that he wanted to stay here because he loved her, and wanted to be the one to help her again as he had helped in the first place?

So it was that Sterling fell into the daily habit of prayer, putting the whole matter off his own heart, beseeching the Lord to keep her, and to make it plain to him what he ought to do. If only he knew that she was safe how gladly would he go and do his part for his country. "Oh, God, open the way. Make this plain to me. I want to be a child of Christ, an accepted believer. So now take this trouble over and do for me, and for her."

And one day he got a letter from an old medical college friend who had bought a practice in a city nearly two hundred miles away from Enderby. It said:

Dear Howard:

I heard the other day in a roundabout way that you are resigning from Enderby. I don't know what your plans are, or whether you are already booked up, somewhere, but if you aren't I am asking you for the sake of our old friendship that you will honestly consider what I have to ask.

About six months ago, I began to develop a serious physical condition, which I am told can definitely be cured if I will submit to an operation and a drastic course of treatment. This would entail giving up my practice for at least six months, perhaps longer. But I have some very sick patients whom I hesitate to leave except with the right man.

I have thought of you. Would you be willing to undertake it for me till I can return and take over? I know your reactions. I would feel entirely happy if you were here. Some of the cases are unusual, worth your study.

I know not what the future holds for either of us, but if you will help me now I pledge my best efforts to repay, or work with you, afterward. We can talk that over later.

I am asking an immediate reply. They say I

should begin my treatment within a few weeks at the latest.

Whatever your answer may be,

Yours as ever,
Ted Blackwell.

Sterling had just been breathing one of his anxious inarticulate prayers when the mail was brought in, and somehow the letter seemed as if it might be a sort of answer, a door opening for him somewhere that he did not seek for himself.

He waited only a few minutes to think it over before dashing off a brief reply:

Dear Ted:

Sorry to hear you are under the weather, old man, but of course you knew I would be glad to do anything in my power to help.

I am pledged to stay here till the end of the month, and then I am free and at your service.

I shall await your further advice, and most earnestly hope that all will eventually be well with you.

Yours to command,

Affectionately,
Howard

After that letter was mailed Doctor Sterling took new heart of hope. For some reason he felt that the answer to his queer prayers was on the way, and he went about his daily duties in a cheerier way. He made definite plans to leave his work in good order, cleared his desk, checked up on all records with which he had had to do, and in short got entirely ready for leaving.

This helped his whole morale so much that the nurses began to notice it.

"Well, Rose must have taken him back after all," said Nurse Ray to Nurse Brynie. "Look at the smile on Sterling's face. I haven't seen him smile like that since little white Mary left. Something's happened, that's sure."

"Oh, yes?" said Brynie. "If you ask me I think he's simply glad to get away from here where he's reminded of Mary. I don't believe for a minute that Rose Bradford would take him back, not after all this interval. She's got too many after her. And anyhow he's not entirely cheered. He looked as grouchy as a sour apple tree when I took that report down from the head nurse. He's just trying to buck up and leave a good impression in case he wants to come back."

"I think you're wrong," said Ray. "I heard him talking. I think he's definitely going into the service somewhere as soon as he gets done this taking-over for the doctor who is sick."

"Well, army or no army, whatever it is, he's not for us much longer, that's sure, and I think some of the nurses have wasted a whole lot of ammunition running after him. I don't mean just us underlings. The head nurse smiles her prettiest every time he comes around, but he doesn't see her any more than a fly on the wall. I think he's off us all for life. He never takes anybody out driving any more, do you take notice? Not since Mary left."

"Oh, that's just because of the shortage of gas."

"Gas, my eye! It's just because he's not interested!"

"Well, have it the way you please, I'm not interested in him any more either, so what?"

The discussion ended with the advent of a patient in the hall within hearing, and the day of Sterling's release drew nearer and nearer.

13

MEANTIME in the faraway city where Dr. Blackwell ministered to his patients, no one suspected the state of things, and least of all Martha Spicer, who was congratulating herself that Ronald had brought them such a good doctor, a man they could absolutely rely upon, so good and kind.

She told him so, too, a little later when he made his nightly visit to see the patient. She told him about the faint little "thank you" that the girl had murmured, and his face lighted with interest.

"I think that is decidedly a good sign," he said, and gave directions about watching very carefully, being sure to talk casually, and not put abrupt questions. Let the girl volunteer information about herself. At least for the present until more normal conditions became constant.

And then as Martha bowed him out, she said in her warmest tone, "We're so very glad that we have you for a doctor. I feel as if I would like to tell you. It was such a blessing that we found *just you*. You've been so exceedingly kind. You've seemed to take such a personal interest in us as if we were a part of your own family!"

The doctor smiled a sad wistful little smile.

"Well, I'm sure I've enjoyed being in and out here among you," he almost sighed as he said it. "It is not always that the relationship between doctors and patients becomes so exceedingly pleasant. I am sure this young girl's case is most interesting, and I have enjoyed watching it and helping a little now and then. I do hope that she is soon to come out of this vague stage, and be back to normal again. I think you can watch for that almost any day now. Well, good night. I hope you and your patient will have a pleasant restful night." And then he went away, and Martha nipped a tear in the bud as she locked the door, for somehow his tone had sounded lonely. So she thanked God again for her doctor.

But the very next morning when Martha went into the guest room she found the girl crying softly into her pillow.

Down on her knees beside the bed went Martha and gathered that forlorn child into her respectable maidenly arms.

"You poor little girl," she said tenderly, "now stop crying and listen to me. What is it you are crying for? Do you feel badly again?"

"No," she said sobbingly, "but I was wondering why you didn't let me go. I was almost gone that night. I know for I heard the doctor telling you yesterday when you thought I was asleep. And it would have been so much better for everybody if I could have gone then. There's nobody in the whole universe that wants me, nobody cares, and I've no job, and no place to go!"

"Now listen!" said Martha, surprised tears rolling down her own cheeks. "That's not true what you are saying. Somebody does care! *I* care! And somebody *does* love you and want you. I'm a lonely old woman and I need you."

The girl turned and looked at her in astonishment with solemn tear-wet eyes.

"Do you mean it?" she said. "Do you mean you would let me stay here till I could find a job and pay you for what you have done? Me, an entire stranger?"

"Certainly I do!" said Martha. "And you're not to talk about pay now. You are visiting me now, and by and by if you want a job we'll look around together and find one. I've been alone all my life and have been working hard. I've just got to a place where I can do as I please, but I find I don't please any more. I need somebody to help me, and I believe you are just the one, if you will."

"But why do you do it? I'm a stranger. You don't know what I am."

"Yes," said Martha, "I think I do. I think you are one of God's little ones. And I want you to stay with me. I want you for a little sister. I never had a sister. I think we could have a happy time together; and if you want to work when you are able, why that will be all right. But just now you are visiting me."

"Now you've done it!" said the Adversary, "and if you're not sorry before this business is done—"

But Martha wasn't even listening. She was watching the light in that girls' eyes, as she flung her arms about Martha's neck and cried out, "Oh you are good, good, *good* and dear! I don't see how you could possibly be lonely as I am. You are so dear that everybody must love you wherever you go."

"No," said Martha, almost laughing, "they haven't, but that's another story and a long one. And I've brought you a tray. Suppose you see how well you can eat this morning. You've got to eat every crumb to satisfy me."

The girl ate with more appetite, slowly and with a faint smile between the mouthfuls.

"You're better," said Martha joyfully.

"Yes," said the girl, "I'm better, and I'll soon be able to get up and get out of your way. Excuse me. I do appreciate your invitation, but I know I must have been an awful burden. But sometime if I find work, I'll hope to be able to pay you back."

"Now look here," said Martha jumping up, "what kind of nonsense are you talking? You certainly are not going away. That is, not unless you don't *like* it here. You are staying with me till you are really strong and have pink in your cheeks and can enjoy life."

"Oh, but I *do* like it here!" cried the girl. "It is like Heaven! But I must get a job first, and then if you want me I'll be glad to come back and stay with you."

"Very well," said Martha pleasantly. "You shall have a job. I can get one for you the minute you are well enough to take it. I've had a fine position in a big department store, and if I ask them to take you they will I know. But I shan't do a thing about it until the doctor says you are able to work. Now, will you be a good girl?"

"Yes," murmured the girl wonderingly.

"Very well, child. And now don't you think it's about time we were introduced? I'm Martha Spicer, I've been supporting myself for over twenty years. Now I've retired, been doing nothing but what I please for more than a week, and I find it rather lonely living here alone. Now suppose you tell me your name."

"I'm Janice Whitmore. My parents are dead, and a little while ago my only sister died, and I'm on my own. That's about all. I told you the rest when I barged in on you."

"There now, child. You're not going to talk any more now. No more tears. I want you smiling. What a pretty name you have! Janice Whitmore! I like it!"

"Meow!" said Ernestine, suddenly giving a velvety bounce up on the bed and walking impertinently up to the visitor's face with her cold little pink nose and her furry cheeks to investigate for herself. She felt it was high time some attention was paid to her, and now that the strained tones of the conversation had somewhat relaxed she might bring herself into the limelight.

Martha tried to sweep her off, but Janice reached welcoming arms and snuggled the big cat close to her cheek, begging to have her remain, so Ernestine settled down with a smirk of triumph toward her mistress and closed one eye, mumbling her content in loudest purrs.

"I would like to get up," said Janice suddenly. "I want to help do something around the house. I will get well quicker that way."

"You'll not get up till the doctor comes! If you are tired of this bed you can come into my room and lie in my bed. That will give you a change. Can you walk that far? I'll fix the bed for you."

"Oh, please don't go to all that trouble!"

"Why, it's no trouble at all!" and Martha was off like a young girl, and soon had Janice propped up in her own bed, her hair brushed and a pink kimono around her shoulders, looking like a washed out apple blossom after a storm.

The doctor arrived about that time and was startled to be ushered into the pleasant front room. He stood for a moment in the doorway and marveled how the little pale waif from the street had turned into this beautiful girl.

"How soon do you think she will be able to go to the shore?" asked Martha smiling.

"Shore?" asked the doctor. "Oh, yes, shore. The very best thing you can do for her. Why, by next week I should say. Or perhaps sooner. Say the end of this one."

"Oh, but doctor, I can't possibly do it, I've got to look for a job and earn some money first," cried Janice.

"Doctor, tell her she's to obey orders for a while yet. I have to go down to the shore on business pretty soon, and she is going with me just as soon as you think it's all right for her to go," said Martha.

"That's fine!" said the doctor. "Of course you'll do what you are told. You couldn't possibly do any sort of work at present without running great risk of putting yourself back into bed again. You wouldn't want to do that, would you?"

So Janice subsided, but when Martha came back from attending the doctor to the door where they had had a few words about the patient, she found Janice weeping again.

"I can't go to the shore," she wailed. "I haven't any decent clothes, nor shoes, nor anything, and my suit is shiny and soiled."

"Now that's all nonsense!" said Martha. "You're my little sister, you know, and I'm giving a house party. Ronald is going along and we're going to have a good time. Don't you know, you represent the girl I used to be, who never had any of the good times she wanted, nor pretty clothes. So now I'm going to have the pleasure of getting some of the things I never could get for myself. They wouldn't be suitable for me now, pretty bright things, and nice girlish things. I'm far too old, but you are going to wear them for me, and in that way I shall enjoy them. If you don't like some of them you can give them away or send them back, but I want to have a good time buying pretty things for you, just this once before you get to be a grand independent lady with a job and refuse to let me do it any more. And now, little Janice, will you call me Martha and dry those tears? What colors do you like best?"

"Brown," said Janice promptly, smiling.

"And what next?"

"Blue. But you won't be extravagant, will you—Martha?"

"I will if I like," smiled Martha. "And now, little girl, it's you for a sleep, and after that we'll have a talk about what we're going to do. When you wake up you're going to have ice cream. Do you like ice cream? And while you are eating it I'll tell you about all the bay windows we are going to build in the house, and you can help me decide what kind of curtains we'll get."

"Oh," said the tempter. "How foolish you are! You ought to have told her she could stay only a few days, at least until you find out what she is like. You may regret this bitterly."

But Martha paid no heed.

The next morning Janice announced she was going to get up, and wanted to know what Martha had done with her clothes.

"No getting up till the doctor has been here," said Martha firmly. "Remember you promised to be good."

"All right," said the girl submissively. "But, Martha, I've got a suitcase down at the Central Station. It has a few clean things, underwear and a clean blouse. I had to check it I was so tired, and then I didn't have the five cents to get it out again."

"Get out the check and I'll send Ronald for it this afternoon when he comes by. Now I'll get your breakfast. Ernestine can keep you company while I'm gone."

That was a breakfast fit for a king. There was oatmeal cooked all night, rich cream, the top of the bottle, orange juice that had stood by the ice all night, and a tiny omelet. Martha brought her own breakfast upstairs too, and while they ate they talked.

Afterwards while Janice took a nap, Martha went to the telephone, called two or three of her former colleagues at the store, asking them to select such things as she wanted for a girl friend, and have them sent out by special messenger that day. With her knowledge of the store it was easy for her to make selections from the saleswomen's descriptions.

She came back to Janice when she awoke with a smile on her lips and her eyes dancing. She had had the time of her life buying that outfit. There was a brown and white tweed suit with a brown velvet collar, and several blouses to wear with it. There was a leaf brown crepe, and another crepe of aqua-marine blue, a few cotton prints for warm mornings, with brown or blue for the predominant colors, a lovely brown wool jersey for cool mornings. That was enough for a brief trip. She also had a warm tweed coat sent up and a small soft brown felt that was sure to be becoming. Some underwear and stockings from her own old department, gloves and collars and handkerchiefs. She gave her friends in the store carte blanche and knew their selections would be in good taste. There would also be needed shoes, but a local store would send those up to be tried on, and Ronald could take an old shoe to them for size. She could hardly wait for afternoon and the things to arrive.

The doctor's visit gave them promise. Janice might try sitting up in a chair that afternoon. Ronald came in early, attended to getting the suitcase, and brought up several pairs of shoes to be tried on. Everything was moving fast.

Then the things from the store began to arrive, and had to be opened and admired. Martha would allow no trying on till the next day, but Janice was delighted with everything, and so excited she had to be put on the bed and made to take a nap.

They had a jolly little supper together, the three, for Ronald invited himself. He was wild with delight over a package that Martha had ordered for him. Two new neckties and some gay handkerchiefs.

"Some class!" he said as he strung both neckties around his neck, and cocked a red handkerchief in his grubby front pocket. "I'll be all dressed up and pretty as a red wagon."

When he finally went home slamming the kitchen door happily they looked after him lovingly.

"Isn't he a dear boy?" said Janice, and a warm glow came into Martha's heart as she assented.

But Janice could not go to sleep that night till she had thrown her arms around Martha's neck, showered her face with kisses, and murmured many thanks for the lovely garments.

They were awake early the next morning, and Janice tried to make Martha let her get up and get breakfast, but Martha was firm. Ronald rushed in for a minute or two at quarter to eight. He had been up since half past five working in the grocery. The store boy was away and he had the job of sweeping and straightening up for the day. Ronald had designs of his own and he wanted money for his trip. Money that did not come from Martha Spicer. He meant to be a bit independent.

It was a happy day, and one by one the new garments were tried on, and fitted beautifully. Janice was very happy, though still deprecatory about accepting all this munificence.

But Martha went about her work, putting things in order for leaving with a song on her lips, something that she could not remember ever to have done before. Singing at her work!

> *"Children of the Heavenly King,*
> *As ye journey, sweetly sing!"*

Ernestine couldn't understand it and looked at her inquiringly. It was quite a relief to have Ronald come in for a few minutes. But then she heard them talking. They said she, Ernestine, was to be left with Ronald's mother, who had once thrown a brick at her for sitting down on a clean dishcloth that was bleaching on the grass! How was she to know the woman would object? No indeed! Ernestine had no intention of being left in a fix like that. She would hide in the cellar the morning they left, and live on mice. She knew where there were plenty, nice tender juicy ones. And now and then a dusty little city bird for a change. But they wouldn't put anything like that woman over on her, not on your life!

Martha did some packing the next day after the doctor had been in and said that Janice would be able to go for the week end. That would allow for Ronald to finish his school week if they took the afternoon train. Then Martha went over to see Ronald's mother and arrange for Ernestine's care, promising that she would look after the boy to the best of her ability while they were gone.

The cat was sitting trustfully in the window blinking and watching for her return when she got back, and Martha almost felt a pang of remorse for this poor creature who was not going along. Fancy Martha Spicer thinking about a cat's comfort!

So Ernestine had a nice saucer of cream for her lunch and a piece of a chop that was left over. She ate it gratefully and sat licking her whiskers without a suspicion. But the next morning when they were about to start Martha suddenly gathered the cat up, bundled her into a big shawl, and carried her out of the door.

Ernestine was wise enough to realize that the worst had come. She backed and scratched in a dignified way, but Martha's arm was firm and determined, and the shawl was bewildering. She felt herself presently transferred to another arm even more firm and determined, felt a gentle pat on her still covered head, and heard

Martha say, "Good-by, Ernestine, we'll soon be home. Thank you, Mrs. MacFarland. I hope Ernestine won't make you any trouble."

"Ernestine make trouble, *indeed!"* protested the cat in one long dismal howl. "It was far, *far* more likely that the woman would make trouble for Ernestine!"

After a little the shawl was removed and Ernestine, from the window, was permitted to watch her traitoress-mistress and the stranger-guest depart in a taxi. After which she was allowed to get down on the floor, when she immediately took refuge behind the sofa, glaring out greenly and watching every time the door opened.

She bided her time till Ronald rushed in leaving the door open, and then like some belated comet, she fled, making a bee line for the hole under her own steps, where she took refuge in trembling rage in a dark corner of Martha's cellar, her green lamps shining out balefully into the silence and darkness.

So, Martha started on her first real vacation.

Ronald arrived at the station only two minutes later than his ladies and took possession of the suitcases, bought the tickets and swelled around generally as if such duties were a regular part of his daily life. The trip was an exciting one, personally conducted by Ronald who had made it before, and therefore could identify and introduce every sight by the way.

The big plain cottage, to which they presently came, needed painting, but was spacious and looked toward the sea. The new boarders didn't mind the shabbiness. And there were wide piazzas running all around the house on every floor.

As they climbed the stairs the Robertses came out in the hall to greet them and ask if there was anything they could do for their comfort, and then immediately apologized as they saw the offended look on Ronald's face.

"Oh, excuse me, Ron. I didn't know you were along. Of course you've looked after everything."

It was soon time for supper, and Martha looked proudly at Janice as she came down in her pretty plaid skirt and trim white blouse. She certainly was a pretty girl.

Ronald escorted them into the dining room with the air of owning the place, and said "Hello" to the colored waiter, who grinned back. Ronald pulled out the chairs for the ladies as if he were an old hand at the business, and Martha's heart swelled with pride in him.

Janice wasn't equal to doing much walking yet, but after supper Ronald came flourishing up to the piazza with a double wheeled chair and putting both his ladies in it wheeled them off triumphantly.

They leaned their heads back and looked off to sea, and felt suddenly intimate with the great ocean.

"Oh," said Janice with a sigh of delight, "I've always wanted to be alone with the ocean for a little while and really get acquainted with it. I used to get up early in the morning when I was a little girl and we went to the shore, just so that I could see the ocean before the crowds got there and trifled with it. It always seems to me that the ocean gets reserved and kind of retires into itself, gets that far-away look in its eyes you know, when a great lot of people come around it and prance up and down on the boardwalk looking at each other, and never casting a glance out to sea. Don't you think so?"

"Why, I never thought about it," said Martha, looking in wonder at this shy little girl of hers who had suddenly turned out to be a sort of poet. Were such thoughts really learned, or were they merely childish fancies? Her life had been so entirely practical that somehow she was at a loss to know. But the fancies pleased her, and she smiled indulgently on the sweet girl.

The next morning Ronald wanted to teach Janice to swim, but Martha said she wasn't strong enough yet, so Ronald compromised on a crabbing expedition.

They rode to the inlet on the trolley, with the ocean spray dashing up around the wheels of the car at one place. They found a boat awaiting them with all the paraphernalia for crabbing, and even Martha submitted to climbing in and taking a part in the frolic. Ronald had paid the fare, and when Martha protested he said:

"Whaddaya think I am? A tight wad? Whaddaya think I earned all that money for working at the grocery if I didn't have a place to spend it?"

They climbed down the wooden steps into the wide comfortable boat, held their skirts away from the pile of wet strings, raw meat, and long handled bag nets, and sat where they were told. Then they were rowed silently, breathlessly out into the bright golden and blue water, still as a piece of glass, out amid the tall fringing grasses that rose like a hedge and shut them in, with fleecy white clouds, reflected here and there in the water, like spirit boats out on cruises of their own.

At last they drew up near a big island of grass and anchored. Ronald attended to the details with the air of a professional, for while the others were sleeping he had thoroughly acquainted himself with the business, and knew just what to do next. He already knew more than the man who had taught him.

Yes, this was the crab bed, those voices over the other side of the island that sounded like detached spirits were more people crabbing.

"There's one, be careful! Oh, I lost him," he shouted, and Martha suddenly became filled with a desire to see one of those creatures they had come out to hunt—a creature to whom she had often been likened in the old days in the store.

"Yes," said Ronald, "those dirty wet strings are lines, and the pile of raw meat is bait." But when she perceived that she would be expected to take those dirty wet things in her hands, and manipulate them, drop them into the grassy water to lure the crabs from the mud in which they hid then she shuddered. She even began to feel a little sorry for her victims.

When at last there came a tug at the end of her line and she dipped the net and lifted it and two fierce angry eyes like long piercing telescopes appeared above the water and looked at her she shrank in horror. Was that what they thought she looked like? With a cry she almost dropped her net, till Ronald, always ready for emergencies, rescued the crab and landed it in the box in the bottom of the boat.

"He's a honey! He's a lulu!" cried the boy. "I guess they'll be astonished at the house when I tell them you caught him."

Martha smiled. She liked the praise but she hadn't got over her fright, and the curious feeling that the ugly frantic creature with the mad vindictive gaze might be herself thus embodied. Nevertheless the enchantment had fallen upon her and she went on working as hard as any of them to catch a lot of crabs.

The sun was high when they turned back, and people were singing all sorts of tunes as they came out of the lagoons, and wended their way back to their hotels. Gay modern lays most of them were, but one boatload was singing "Brighten the corner where you are." Martha, looking at the big old crab she had caught, as he sat blinking and belligerent in his box, wondered if even a crab could possibly change—that is a human crab—and brighten the corner of any old box where he might find himself! She would see!

They went to a football game that afternoon. Martha Spicer at a football game! *Think* of it! But Ronald had the tickets, a gift from an old pal of his in the city who worked at the powder mills and played on their ball team. He was down at the shore playing a local team and had met Ronald and given him the tickets. Martha wouldn't have gone, but she saw the wistful look in Ronald's eyes and heard the exclamation of pleasure from Janice, so she went.

A fresh sea breeze had come up and it was really chilly.

"Ronald, go and get your overcoat," said Martha as they gathered on the front piazza about to start to the game. "There's a sea breeze and it's really chilly."

"No chance!" said Ronald amusedly.

"But you *must!*" said Martha. "I can't have you getting sick from catching cold, away from home."

Ronald sobered. *"Can't!"* he said firmly.

"Why not?"

"'Cause I haven't got any." He said it with a grin.

"Do you mean you came down here without your overcoat?" she asked severely.

"Sure!" said Ronald, still grinning. "Didn't have one to bring. Never owned an overcoat in my life and never expect to."

"Oh!" gasped Martha. "Well, haven't you got a sweater or something?"

"Sweater wasn't fit to bring. Got it half tore off me at the last football game."

They walked on a few steps down the boardwalk and then Martha looked up at the window of a big shop along the way and a sudden idea struck her. Her practiced eye scanned the display in the window, and halting at the door she said:

"Wait here just a minute. I want to go in. I won't be but a minute or two."

Ronald frowned, but tried to look polite.

Martha went in, held a brief conversation with a man behind the counter, and came out with a white sweater over her arm. She held it out to Ronald.

"Will that fit you?" she asked. "Put it on and see if it's all right. It's yours."

The boy looked at it, bewilderment, delight and incredulous amazement in his face.

"Aw, *gee!*" he said. "Oh, *Boy!* You didn't go and get that *for me?* Oh, Boy!" His eyes were like blue stars.

Martha nodded, her own eyes full of pleasure.

He whipped off his coat and on with the sweater in no time. It proved to be all right. Years of experience had made Martha a pretty good judge of size.

"Some class!" went on Ronald, admiring himself. "Boy! Won't the fellahs at home envy me! Boy! I never thought I'd have a *white* sweater! Gee, I gotta crush on myself."

He stared at himself in the store windows they passed, and turned around to Janice and demanded admiration. He stuck out a bashful hand and shook Martha's vigorously.

"I certainly do thank you," he said. "It's what I always wanted." Then he straightened up and walked with his head held high in a self-respecting way.

Of course they had a good time after that.

Martha learned a lot about football too. She found she knew what a touchdown was, and which colors on the sweaters represented which teams, and who was left-tackle and a lot of other things. And then they met Binnie the bashful left-tackle himself and Martha remarked, "We must invite him to supper some time!" and filled Ronald with supreme delight. But he only said, "Oh, Boy! That'll be swell!"

And so Martha arose with the crowd and added her elderly voice to the yell that arose in favor of Binnie, and went home numbering yet another boy to her list of exceptions in the way of boys.

14

SUNDAY began with a difference of opinion between Martha and Ronald on the subject of church attendance, but in the end Ronald went to church to please her, and sang with the rest.

But in the afternoon they went to sit out on a pier for a little while to watch the ocean, and Ronald was telling all he had learned from an old sea captain down by the light house. He informed them what kind of boats were passing on the far horizon, interspersing his knowledge with bits of sea stories.

A little child not more than three years old had wandered away from its parents who were sitting on the other side of the pier, came up to laugh and talk with Ronald for a few minutes and then ran away to play with some shells that someone had given her. She had gold curls and great blue eyes, and made a sweet picture in the distance. Ronald slumped down in his chair and watched her between the fringes of his eyes. Suddenly they heard a piercing scream, a little bright flash of blue skirts and gold hair, a frightened baby face going overboard, and then the great gulf of angry waters frothing with foam swallowed her up!

Three men looked down from the railing at the boiling waters beneath and shook their heads.

"Not much chance for anybody down there," they said gloomily, and looked off toward the creeping speck of a life boat from the upper pier. "Who does she belong to?"

But Ronald was up like a flash flinging off his sweater, kicking off his shoes.

"That boat's too far off to get here in time," said the second man pointing to the life boat.

"Which way is the current?" asked the third man, looking uncertainly down into the water. "Which way will it carry her? I wonder if there is a rope anywhere around we could throw down to her!"

"Chances are she'll strike the piles," murmured the fist man. "There might be a rope back by the casino. I wonder where the life savers are?" But he made no move to do anything.

But Ronald was vaulting over the rail, diving into the water, and being engulfed in its flood.

People rushed to the rail now as a great murmur arose from the throng of watchers who had suddenly gathered, and watched the brave boy battling with the waves. And in the forefront stood Martha and Janice, white and frantic.

"Plucky little fellow," said one of the three men behind them. "Too bad we didn't see him in time to stop him. He'll never make it! No use! The baby's gone!"

But out to the right away from the pier were two specks on the top of a pillow, a tiny one, yellow and floating, like golden seaweed, and a dark one a little nearer the pier, fighting outward toward the golden speck.

It was then that Janice picked up Ronald's white sweater and began to wave it frantically toward that little boat that was coming on nearer and nearer. And now the watchers saw the boat had sighted the trouble and was steering toward it. They stood and held their breath and waited.

It was some minutes since the golden speck had been seen on the water and now the dark one disappeared. Oh God, were they gone? Was it too late? The boat was almost there!

Hours and hours it seemed they watched, as the boat drew nearer, seemed to halt, maneuver, and then come toward the shore. Oh, the long distance to come before they would know. The weeping of the child's mother could be heard.

But at last the boat drew near enough for them to see. There was someone—*something* lying in the bottom. And then the strong men who manned it sprang out, each with a burden in his arms.

It was then the three men who had been watching bestirred themselves to show what men they were.

A great rough sailor in oilskins came splashing through the water bearing the little maid with dripping golden hair, clinging blue dress, and laid her in her mother's arms. She was alive, they said. The boy had saved her. He had caught her by the hair and held her till the lifeboat reached her. But they must both have attention at once!

And there was Ronald lying white and still in the bottom of the boat, one arm hanging limply by his side. He had broken it against the pile in that first wave after his dive.

With grave faces and tender hands those rough men lifted him and bore him to the blankets that kind hands had brought. A watcher from the life station hurried up on a motor cycle, a doctor came, a plain gray-haired woman knelt silently by the boy's side, and the crowd waited and watched. Everything that science could do for Ronald's flickering life was being done. And yet it was an hour before the boy opened his blue eyes and set them upon Martha's face. He gave one comprehensive glance around and then weakly said, "Aw, gee, Miss Spicer, that wasn't nothing. I'm gonta get up in a minute."

They got him to the house wrapped in blankets and plied him with hot water bottles and stimulants. At last he looked up and asked, "Did I get the little kid? I somehow got kinda nutty and can't remember."

And when they told him she was coming around all right he murmured softly, "Boy, she was a pretty little kid, and awful light!"

It was then that Martha broke down and wept, and cried out softly to him, "Oh, my dear, *dear* boy! How I love you!"

Kneeling there beside his bed where he lay with a contented grin on his young face, and her hand held tight in the grip of his unhurt right hand, she did not remember how she used to think all boys were a torment.

The baby's father came hobbling in on crutches to thank the young hero, and after he had gone Martha and the Robertses, and Janice made some plans. Ronald, of course, would not be able to return in the morning, but Janice and Mrs. Roberts could easily look after him with the help of a nurse if necessary. Mr. Roberts declared his intention of going to the city in the morning. He had men who were finishing a job that he must look after. He said he would tell Ronald's mother, and ask permission to keep him at the shore till he was able to travel. But Martha felt that she should go herself. Besides if Mr.

Roberts wanted to set his men at work soon she must be there at least for a day or so to put away some things and superintend some men to move her things into a place of safety where they would not be in the way while the workmen were busy.

"If your house is in shape for the work to begin, I'll start tomorrow," said Roberts. "We'll get that other job finished by noon and I can start my men pulling down partitions right away. There'll have to be some beams set and some shoring up to prevent any cracking of walls."

Martha gasped and felt suddenly frightened at her temerity in going so far, while yet a thrill of delight passed over her that this lovely change was really about to begin.

"I could get things ready for you by noon if I can find a couple of men to help me move things," she said. "If it were not for Ronald of course I'd go up and stay."

"We can look after Ronald," said Janice capably. "Remember I'm a nurse. But oh, I wish I were able to do the work in the city. Couldn't you tell me what to do and let me go in your place?"

"No indeed. And remember you are an invalid yet yourself."

So it was all arranged for Martha to go up with Mr. Roberts in the morning.

Martha was awake and astir very early next morning. The sea had put on its sweetest calm with no hint of the angry tempest that had raged in its waves yesterday.

When she was all ready for her journey she slipped softly to Ronald's room and listened outside his door.

To her surprise she heard footsteps thumping around the room, and when she tapped at the door the boy's voice bade her come in. And there was Ronald fully dressed all but his coat, and struggling with his necktie. Somehow he had accomplished the feat of drawing his shirt sleeve over the broken arm, bandages and all, and was standing in front of the mirror, one end of his necktie in his teeth, doing wonders with the well hand in knotting the other end. He was pale but resolute.

"Ronald. *Child!* You ought not to be out of bed," cried his visitor aghast.

"This doggone tie won't get right," he complained.

"Sit down and let me fix it for you," she said gently, as one would lure a little child away from danger.

The boy approached her warily. He was white but determined, scarcely a fit subject for feminine petting.

"Now, Ronald," said Martha determinedly, "you know the doctor said you would get along nicely if you would rest a few days, but you've been under a severe strain—"

"Aw, rats! Strain nothing!" interpolated Ronald contemptuously. "Just a little knockout. That wasn't nothing. I've been hurt worse a dozen times playing football. Say, could you just tie that shoe for me? I can't make it tight. I gotta hustle. It's most train time."

"But, Ronald, you're *not* going home today! I've got it all arranged. Mr. Roberts and I are going to the city, and I'll explain to your mother so she won't worry, and you are to stay down here all this week. Janice will help you with whatever you need. She's a nurse you know, and I'll fix it all right with your mother. I'm sure she won't worry."

"Aw, gee!" said the boy with a grin, *"she* won't worry. This is only the third time I've broke my arm. She's used to it. And I ain't going to stay down here, not on your tin type! What would be the good of staying down here? I can't go swimming with this rag on my arm, can I? No, *ma'am,* I'm going back. I got a lot to do."

She laid her hand on his sound arm saying, "Ronald, be reasonable," but he only laughed.

"What do you take me for?" he asked. "A baby with a rattle? It ain't any use to nag. I gotta beat it. I got something to do today."

At the breakfast table the other ladies tried their persuasions, but all to no effect, and Martha realized that any further remonstrance was useless.

"I shall go with him, of course, and you will stay here with Mrs. Roberts and help her with her baby. Then she won't be so tied down," she said to Janice.

When they had almost reached the city Ronald sidled into Martha's seat with her.

"Say, Miss Spicer, don't you go getting any men to move your things. I got some fellas that know how to do things like that. You just decide where you want them and we'll move everything in no time."

She gave him a radiant smile.

"Thank you, Ronald, that's fine. But you know *you* can't lift a finger yourself. I won't stand for that! But you could direct them, of course. I'd hate to tell them to be careful, but you can, you know."

"Okay!" said Ronald, relieved that he did not have to have an argument.

At the station he arose and said:

"Well, I gotta beat it if I wantta get my men. So long. See you sub-se," and he vanished in the crowd.

"Oh, he oughtn't to," said Martha distressed.

"He'll be all right," said the architect in an easy tone. "He's tough. You can't kill him. He's no sissy."

Arrived at her home, Martha changed into an old dress and gathered her cat into her arms, laying her cheek against the dirty fur lovingly. Ernestine had evidently missed her. It touched her to hear the pleasant satisfied rumble of her purring now.

Soon she was at work, with the cat following her from room to room. She made short work of gathering books, papers, magazines, the pictures on the walls, everything movable, and stacking them in piles to be carried upstairs. She sent to the store for a tack puller and hauled up the old carpets. They were not to go down again, so they didn't have to come up carefully. How she hated their ugly faded colors and how glad she was to see them out of the way. Some could be sold, some given away, some thrown away. And with their going would vanish a lot of the gloom the house had held.

Ronald appeared a few minutes later with three tall boys, a little older than himself, nick-named Lengthy, Lappie, and Pace. They were awkward and shy, but strong and willing. They carried out the old carpets to the yard, brushed them off and rolled them up for further disposition. One of them possessed himself of a broom and mop and got the worst of the dust on the floors out of the way. They carried the piles of small things upstairs to a designated closet, and then attacked the heavy furniture.

"Say, I was thinking," said Ronald. "Why don't you store all that stuff in the laundry? It's clean and almost empty, and you could lock it. It would be out of the way, and not have to be moved so far."

So that was what they did.

And when the last piece was moved and the boys returned to the dismantled room, they found four large dishes of ice cream, and four big wedges of chocolate cake from the nearby bakery set out on the kitchen table.

"Oh, Boy!" said Ronald. "Stick around, fellahs. Good eats! Some class!"

And while they were eating Martha watched them furtively, and couldn't find a trace in one of their faces of the old boy-character she used to hate. Could it be that *all* boys were different?

They accepted the generous pay Martha offered when

they were done, and grinned, and one said: "Let us know when you get ready and we'll move 'em back for you."

They had not been gone long when the workmen appeared with Architect Roberts at their head, and almost at once the house resounded with hammer blows as they put in braces and beams to reinforce the walls when the partitions came down.

And then in a little while they began to hack away at a partition. Martha hung around until that began, but there seemed something reproachful in the rending of nail from timber, the rattle of plaster as it fell, bringing down the hated old wall paper with it, and Martha put on her hat and coat and went out to get some lunch at the confectioner's, while Ernestine fled to the cellar and wasn't quite sure she was safe there, finally taking to a seat on the back fence. Had everybody gone crazy, or was this the end of her world?

When Martha came back from her leisurely lunch the hall and parlor yawned in one, and the back parlor was no more. She stood amazed that so much destruction could be wrought in so short a time, and her soul triumphed in the thought that it was too late now to undo it. She was embarked at last irrevocably for the changes, and Aunt Abigail and Uncle Jonathan needn't come around and complain any more.

The men were working late that night, as they had had to be so late in beginning and wanted to make up a whole day. So Martha ran in to see Mrs. MacFarland and explain to her about Ronald's heroism, for, of course, he never could be counted on to praise himself.

Mrs. MacFarland took her into her chilly dark front room and opened the blinds half way so one could see the prim company chairs, and Martha entered wondering if Ronald ever spent much time in this dreary room.

"I thought I ought to come and tell you what happened to Ronald, and how wonderful he was in saving a little girl's life," she said as she sat down. "I'm so sorry he had to break his arm while he was under my care. But I suppose he has told you all about it."

"No, he hasn't told me nothing. He never does. Not unless he wants something. He's awful close-mouthed, Ronald is. He knows his pop would whip him if he ever found out half his goings on, so he never complains. I see he had his arm done up so I s'posed he'd been up to something as usual, climbing a light house or something. But I wouldn't blame *you*. I'd know *you* couldn't help it. If Ronald wanted to go somewheres he'd go, no matter who said not, so I never worry any more. I got enough to do without that. Broke his arm, did he? Well he likely deserved it. I hope there ain't going to be a big doctor's bill. His pop won't stand for that no matter how it happened. It's awful expensive knocking around the way he goes. It's hard on his clo'es, too. Well, I'm glad he got the little girl out. It seems a pity for little children to drown when they ain't had a chance at life, but mebbe they're just as well off! Yes, I'm glad he saved the little girl's life, but it would have been just like him to get drowned doing it. He came in awhile back and lay down on the couch. I s'pose his arm hurts him, but he knows better'n to let his pop know."

Martha went back to her house a sadder and a wiser woman. No wonder there were some bad boys in the world if that was a sample of some of the houses they came from and how they were treated. Poor Ronald! No wonder he was interested in helping her make a cheery home!

The next two days were very exciting. There were so many questions to decide. Which way the stairs should turn, and just where the windows should be located.

The workmen seemed interested in all they did, and gladly worked overtime that the plasterer might get started soon. It was hard to keep away from the scene of action, for she delighted to watch every nail that was driven and every board that was sawed. She wished she could take hold and help. It seemed fascinating to her.

Martha had talked with Janice by telephone every night and found that all was going well at the shore. It was doing all three of them good. Mrs. Roberts looked like a new woman, the baby was getting fat, and Janice said she felt better than she had for a year.

So Martha stayed on till Saturday, and then asked Ronald to go back with her for over Sunday, for he was still rather pale and she knew he would get little sympathy at home if he stayed. He was working at the grocery now, doing light work, earning a little money for himself, but he was rejoiced to go back to the shore for over Sunday.

The doctor had come in for a few minutes and gone over Ronald, fixing him up with clean bandages and making him comfortable. Before he left he told them he was going to have to go away to a hospital himself pretty soon, perhaps within a very few days. He made rather light of it, said he was bringing a friend of his to take his place until they would let him come back on the job. He didn't make much of his own ailments, just said there was something wrong that needed righting, and it would mean taking a rest after the operation was over. But he said a great deal about the doctor who was taking over in his place. He told how they were in medical college together, told some amusing incidents of their young days, and what a fine chap the other doctor was, until Ronald, watching grudgingly, almost felt he *had* to like him, although he *wasn't* going to let him into the place in his heart that had hitherto been occupied by Dr. Blackwell. Ronald was very loyal to all first loves, and he thought there was no doctor in the world like the one he had first discovered, who had brought Baby Roberts and Janice back to life when they were practically dead.

Martha as she watched the doctor talk, thought that now she understood the sadness that had seemed to be growing in the face of the kindly physician. He didn't say how serious his trouble was, he spoke of it as a trifling ailment but she wondered if there was danger that he might not be returning.

"Can't you come down to the shore over Sunday?" she asked. "We'd love to have you as our guest, and you would certainly have at least three patients while you were there."

"I'm afraid not," said the doctor with a smile. "I've just about all I can possibly do here before I go. Besides I have two patients who are still very low, and I would not dare leave them till the other doctor gets here. But I certainly appreciate the invitation, and shall think of it in the lonely days when I am in a hospital room by myself, recuperating, I hope," and he smiled again, such an endearing smile. Martha couldn't bear to think he was leaving them.

"But I've just been thanking God for you, Doctor," she said protesting. "I thought it was so wonderful that we had found you. Or rather I thought it was so wonderful that God had sent such a fine doctor to just us."

"Well, thank you," said the doctor, much touched. "I am flattered that you thought of me that way. So perhaps I can presume to ask that you will wish me well in the experience I have to go through. God might help there, I have been led to suppose."

"Oh!" said Martha, her cheeks turning pink, because she was always embarrassed when religious topics were mentioned. It seemed almost irreverent to talk about God in ordinary matters. "Why, yes. We'll all pray for you. That you may get well and come back to us."

"That's great!" he said. "Good night, and God bless you."

15

THE Roberts baby was getting fat and rosy. Its mother declared there was no longer any need for them to be at the shore, and besides she felt she ought to be at home again and be watching that her husband was eating his meals all right. There was one other time when she was away that he went entirely without lunches. Didn't bother to put them up. And anyway he was very busy and hadn't time to eat he said. So when she got home he was thin as a rail. She didn't want that to happen again.

Martha laughed at her, and told her *she* was looking after his lunches. Every day she either sent him off to a restaurant or gave him some coffee and a sandwich in the house. And so she managed to make her subside for that week. But the next time she came down they went at it again and this time Janice had joined the rebellion and declared she simply would not stay there another day at Martha's expense. That she was perfectly well now and must go back and get that job she had to have at once.

Martha held them off a little longer by saying that she and Ronald had come down for a few days' rest and fun, and they must all stay at least to the end of the week.

Martha wanted to have the house a little farther along before Janice returned. But at least the second coat of plaster was on and it was dry enough to be perfectly safe to sleep in, they said. Besides, they didn't sleep on the first floor where the plastering had been done, anyway, and the upstairs walls were dry as a bone.

So at the end of the week the little company packed up and migrated back to the city, a rosy healthy group, and Mr. Roberts met them at the station and received his well baby and happy-looking wife with great thanksgiving.

They all stopped at Martha's house for a minute or two to see how things were progressing, and even Martha was surprised to see how much had been accomplished in this last week. Mr. Roberts had put on three extra men who just happened to have a few days off from their regular jobs, and things were going fast.

The men had somehow all come to be interested in getting this house in shape for the return of the owner, and they had themselves come a little early that morning and swept up and tidied around till the place looked almost livable.

"We would have had it nearly done if we hadn't been held up on the mill work. You know it is hard to get things done these war times," said Roberts. "I had to change the design twice before I could find windows that would fit our spaces."

But it seemed marvelous to Martha. She hadn't expected to have anywhere near as much done.

Then Mrs. Roberts went home to begin living again, and Martha and Janice went down to the store, for Janice was not satisfied to stay at home and wait. She wanted to be on the job at once.

So Martha left Janice in the waiting room while she ascended to the office of the manager and had her talk.

The manager was beset by a double rank of people in his office waiting to see him, but when Martha sent her name in she was to supersede them all and come at once to the inner sanctum.

"My word, Martha Spicer!" said the manager.

"You're the very person I was wishing I could see! Do you know what a fix you put us in leaving this store? What do you think happened this morning? Your nice little substitute that you took so much pains training to take your place announced that she is going to be married the end of this month! Sprung it on me just like that! And I don't know which way to turn to get somebody in her place. Do you know, we've discovered it isn't everybody can take that place. Your little Miss Janeway did well enough, though we weren't crazy about her. You see you spoiled us, Spicer. We want you back! Say, don't you want to come back at least for a while till we could look for another paragon like yourself? Not that I think there is one, for we want *you* back! How about it? Aren't you about tired being a lady of leisure? We'll double your pay and give you half time whenever you want it, and you can choose any assistant you want. We'll really make it worth your while if you care to take it up."

And so, instead of talking about a job for Janice, Martha found herself actually considering whether she would go back herself.

"You could make money enough in a short time to cover all those improvements you've made," whispered her good angel. "And besides, you'd have a chance to undo some of the impressions of yourself you've been regretting. Then too, since you can have any assistant you want, why not take Janice? You could work together beautifully, and also watch that she didn't overdo. You couldn't have anything better."

She tried to think why she had not wanted to go back. Her old hatred of the store? Why, where had it vanished? She was thrilled to be there again! Her recent delight at being free? But she had found it was lonely to be free. And how pleased she was to think they had actually missed her and *wanted* her back! Besides, it wouldn't be the same old monotonous grind. She could stop now whenever she wanted to. She had her home, her lovely home, and friends who loved her. After all, why not be independent like a man? Have business hours and then come home and enjoy life making people happy with the money earned?

All the way down to the waiting room the Adversary was calling her a fool.

"Now just see what you've done to yourself! Just because you are troubled about having spent so much money on other people who are nothing in the world to you, you are planning to go back into slavery again. You've taken a lot of fool responsibility on yourself! That boy and that silly girl, and those other long-legged fellows that harem-scarem boy brings around and will land on you, you'll see! If you didn't spend your money on other people you wouldn't have to do another lick of work. You ought to spend your money on *yourself*. It's your just due!"

Then out of the annals of her childhood-Sunday-School days Martha murmured, "It is more blessed to give than to receive," and again, joyously, triumphantly, "Give and it shall be given unto you; good measure, pressed down, and shaken together, and running over, shall men give into your bosom. For with the same measure that ye mete, withal it shall be measured to you again."

"And," she murmured to herself as the elevator stopped at her floor and let her out, "it looks as if that is just what has happened, having this offer of double salary and short hours, having all these sweet friendships. I never gave anything before in my life, not even a smile, and I never got anything. But just as soon as I began to give, things came my way."

And then she marveled at the way the Adversary had fled at the first sound of the "sword of the Spirit, which is the Word of God."

They went to the tea room for lunch, and had such a beautiful time together.

"Did you get me a job?" asked Janice anxiously.

"Yes, little girl, beautiful work and a good salary. And the best of it is we can be together. That is, *I* think that's the best of it. Janice, they want *me* to come back to the store, and bring you for my assistant! And they're going to give me double what I used to get and shorter hours. Janice, I think I'll say yes! You see, the girl who took my place is going to be married!"

"Oh, but that sounds too good to be true," said Janice with a radiant face. "Listen, Martha! Now I'm *sure* God cares and looks out for His own. Martha, are you sure you're not kidding? Are you sure we are not dreaming?"

"No, little girl, not dreaming. I'm to take you back to the office at three o'clock and introduce you, and we'll tell him then that we'll come, if you think you want to do this."

"*Want* to!" said Janice. "How could I ever not want to, dear friend? Such a grand, beautiful thing to happen to me!"

So Janice met the manager, who seemed pleased with her, and Martha told him they would come.

The end of it all was that the bugles were blowing for the half-past five closing time when they got up to leave the office, and they went home to get supper in the little crowded kitchen. Not a large supper, but good. A little tender broiled steak, fried potatoes, lettuce and a dish of cut up peaches with cream. It didn't take long to prepare. And Ronald dropped in when they were half through and shared the peaches and cookies. So Ronald had to hear the story.

"That's swell!" he said. "Why, you can make money! You could buy a Ford, couldn't you? And ride down to business the way men do, you and Janice, and not have to sit around those old trolleys and busses."

"Why, of course," said Martha. "That's an idea! I'll do it. And we'll have a piano, too. I never played a note in my life, but I'm sure you can play, Janice, can't you?"

"Why, yes, I can play. That is, I'm not wonderful or anything like that, but I can play."

"I thought so," said Martha excitedly, "and we'll have some real music in our new house. Ronald, you aren't old enough to drive a car yet, but when you are we'll have some grand rides together."

"No, I ain't old enough to get a license yet," said the boy glumly, "but I can *teach you now*. I *know* how, of course!"

The doctor came in and heard the news, and rejoiced with them almost sadly.

"Well, I'm glad you've got your jobs if that's what you wanted, but I don't want you to let that girl work too hard at first. You know she was rather down and out not so long ago."

"I know," said Martha, suddenly grave, "but she'll be working with me and I can send her home when I think she is tired. I'll be very careful of her. And we want you to be careful of yourself too, doctor, and get well quickly and come back to us."

"Well, I'll try," he smiled sadly. "That's some incentive."

"And, oh, doctor, we're thinking of having a house-warming pretty soon, when the place is in order again, and we hope you can come. You must not go away before that."

The doctor looked gravely at her.

"I'll be delighted if I *can* come, but it will have to be soon, for I may be called away within a few weeks now. But thank you just the same!"

That night Janice lay awake a long time. It was sad to think Dr. Blackwell had to leave, sad to think there was pain and suffering and peril ahead of him. But there was something sadder back in her heart that she did not dare take out and look at nor think about any more. It seemed to make life almost unbearable when she did. Yes, even since other people had been so very kind and loving to her, the thought of Dr. Sterling and all he had meant to her when she was so alone in that sanitarium seemed to touch a sore nerve that ached for hours afterwards.

But tonight she deliberately went over the memory of her life after she woke up in that hospital bed and let her memory bring its pictures one by one, hoping that now the sweet pain would have worn away and she could look life in the face again and not carry a torment into the new environment which she was soon to enter.

But it was still there, the memory of the way Sterling had looked at her sometimes, the memory of his gentle voice, the touch of his hand on her arm. And he all the time engaged to that beautiful rich girl! And yet she could not resent his kindness to her. She could not somehow believe that that other girl was really in his heart at all. Of course, though, she felt herself very young and inexperienced. She wasn't a judge of men. Oh, why did life have to be this way? Why should one doctor mean so much more to her than another? Why was there a hungry ache when she thought of Dr. Sterling, and nothing when she thought of the kindly, somewhat sad face of Dr. Blackwell? Well, those were questions she could not answer. But the final result of her self-examination was that the only thing that was likely to cure her tendency to keep Dr. Sterling's memory fresh in her heart would be to write to him sometime and explain why she had run away from the sanitarium without leaving him any word. Surely a long enough time had now elapsed since her flight from Enderby to make him understand that she was not trying to crawl back there again. Not seeking for any benefit from him.

She had a job now, and would probably be making money enough so that she could even offer to repay some of the kindness that had been shown her at the institution. Also, she would be of age now in a few weeks. And she wasn't really afraid of Herbert Stuart any more. God had shown her that He was protecting her. Moreover, she had a legitimate home with a woman who really seemed to love her and want her. There was no real reason why she might not write and tell him how sorry she was to have felt she must go silently without explanation. Well,—perhaps—after she got settled in her new job, she would think it over again, and then write. She was certain it would take some of the ache out of her heart to do so.

She turned over, settled her head on her pillow, and found that her meditation had definitely eased the heavy burden she had been carrying. Then her heart broke forth into thanksgiving to the God who had provided her a place where she might work and earn. She should not let any sorrow burden her when so much had been wrought in her life. And yet, she felt that if she could just once see Dr. Sterling, and explain it all to him, and read forgiveness in his eyes, if she could once know that he did not blame her for running off in that way, say he understood why she did it, why then her heart would be at rest. She did not love Dr. Sterling, of course. She couldn't, for he belonged to another girl, and she abhorred girls who fell in love with another woman's man. But she did honor and respect him and she did want him to understand.

That was the way the thoughts formed themselves in her mind as she dropped away to sleep. And then far into the night there came a vision. She seemed to see him bending over her bed as he had bent so many times when she was ill, and looking down at her and smiling, saying, "It's all right, little girl. I understand!"

And when she awoke in the morning, and the sun was shining brightly, she found a great joy in her heart. A joy that perhaps she had no right to have. Yet it was there, and it brought a glory into her face and her eyes that others could see. They did not know what made it. They thought it was her new job, and rejoiced with her, and she let them go on thinking that. She could not tell them how she had been hearing her doctor speak to her in her sleep, and that she was happy because she believed that he really understood.

16

MARTHA Spicer went back to the store two days later and introduced Janice to the business world.

The night before she spent some time on her knees, asking for help to live a different life, and to show those about her a better way than they had known. Now that she had been learning many things, and had come to see how wrong she had been, it seemed as if her Heavenly Father had graciously given her another chance to go back to the place where her Christian witness had been worse than nothing, and to relive those years of selfish unpleasantness in a different way. She wanted to live now to the glory of Him who died for her, and not to please herself. She realized that this was an opportunity that came to few, and she was thankfully accepting it, and meant to do her best, but as she stood thus on the very threshold of the new-old life her heart trembled and she felt a strange shyness begin. She knew old habits would bind her, and draw her back to old ways. She understood that she could not do this thing in her own strength. It must be the strength of the Lord, not any force of her own. He must show her continually what to do, what to say, even how to feel.

There were the boys especially. She knew she had been so disagreeable to them, and had thought herself justified. And now that the Lord had sent Ronald to teach her how much worth there was in the soul of every boy, she knew she had much to atone for. Some of the boys at the store had known her well, and hated her. They would have much against her at the start. She would try to undo the dislike which she had fostered in them. She would have to win them. Perhaps she could bring some of them now and then to this new home she was planning. Get Ronald to put his strong shoulder to the job and help her to know them. But most of it she must do alone with God, and therefore she prayed.

Then there were the young girls who were under her, with whom she was so closely associated. They too hated her and had done all they could to make things hard for her. Yet they were girls like Janice, some of them working hard, and living in little hall bedrooms, keeping themselves straight in a world full of sin. She ought not to have blamed them for wanting to chew gum and paint their nails and giggle with the young salesmen, and try always to have just as good a time as possible. Of course they ought to have limited their amusements to time that was not paid for by their employer, but then they were just young girls, young things with hard disappointing lives to lead, and she might have made their way easier many times and didn't. She had been an old crab, as she knew they had called her. She was going back to try by the grace of God to be different now. She was going to try through the sweet girl Janice, to let some sunshine into the lives of those other girls, who needed sympathy and comfort and advice, and got only sharp words and fault-finding from a world that ought to have cared for them. Well, at least she was going back with her eyes open. Therefore she trembled and prayed.

She had thought it over and almost decided to take some flowers with her that first morning and give a few to each girl in her department. But then it seemed better to her after all to go back quietly into her old place and let her life day by day show that she had a different spirit toward them. It would be harder perhaps, but it would be more genuine in their eyes, and maybe in her own.

So she went back that Monday morning as if she had not been away for nearly three months. Just took off her coat and hat and hung them up on the old hook, and sat down at the old desk to look over the mail orders and see what needed immediate attention for the day. Miss Janeway was to come in presently and hand things over formally, but the first few minutes were hers, quietly there, to gather the reins of the old rule in her hands and take over the power. And so, before the manager or Miss Janeway came, or Janice had finished fluffing up her hair by the little mirror in the inner dressing room, she bent her head on her hand and prayed again for strength and wisdom and guidance.

The manager entered a few moments later, greeted her and Janice, and almost immediately Miss Janeway came, did her part, and got away as soon as possible, with the light of coming freedom in her face. The same kind of a look of relief that Martha knew there must have been in her own face three months ago when she handed over her place to Miss Janeway and thought never to come back to it again. And now, how thankful she was that the opportunity was hers! She had to think back and remember the sunny living room with its bay windows and its landing stairs, the trim little garage that was even at that moment in process of erection in the tiny back yard for the neat little Ford she was buying, before she could quite believe she wasn't the old Martha Spicer who used to come so grumpily to her work. Only she was happy now, very happy.

And there was Janice with her sweet face all bright with smiles of anticipation over the real work she was to begin that morning, and the salary she was to earn.

And there was Ronald at school, getting ready to be a man, and meantime a continual joy to the woman he had taught to love him as if he had been her own.

Later she went out with Janice to the old department, and immediately her heart was saddened, for she saw the dark looks coming over the faces of the girls as she approached, and she saw the cash boys slide away and duck under the counters. She knew they were whispering one to another, "Old Spice Box has come back!"

The old Martha Spicer would have gone directly to her work without even a nod more than necessary to anyone, giving orders as if she had never been away. The new Martha Spicer went from one saleswoman to another, speaking a word of greeting to each one, and introducing Janice as "My assistant, Miss Whitmore."

The girls all stared at Janice, but her sweet smile disarmed many of them at the start. At Miss Spicer they looked coldly, wondering that she smiled. It was not like her to smile. What had come over her? All the morning it was so, though she did her best, and into the afternoon.

Just before closing time, Martha was stooping inside a counter to arrange some goods that had been stacked there for her to mark, and as she worked she was down out of sight for a time, so that all the girls at the counters round about thought that she had gone home. There was a lull just then in the business of the day and a girl from the mail order shoe department came over for some stockings to match a piece of goods, and while she waited for her needs to be supplied she idly talked.

"I see old Spice Box is back. Crabby as ever, I suppose. I declare, I think you girls ought to have gone to the manager and made a protest at her coming back. I can't see what the management sees in her. Why, even the customers hate her! Did she start in bad?"

"Oh, so-so," answered the yellow-haired girl with a shrug. She was a girl who was always getting into trouble with customers. "She hasn't done much yet, but I believe she's jealous of that pretty pink-cheeked thing they've got for an assistant for her. She looks at her as if she could eat her."

"I shouldn't wonder if they are going to put that new assistant into the place pretty soon and old Spice Box is just here to show her the ropes," put in another girl who had just come up. "You needn't worry. She won't stay long. Not if she's just got a fortune like they say she has. What would anybody want to stay in the store for if they didn't have to?"

"Did she get a fortune?" said the first girl. "Aw, I don't believe it. Who would leave a fortune to an old cranky woman like that? I shouldn't wonder if that was all bluff. Or maybe it didn't pan out. I've heard of such things. Anyhow, she isn't going to try any more of her sarcasm on me. I won't stand for it! I'll report her, even if I lose my job for it!"

Then up spoke another girl, frail, pale and sad looking. "Girls, I think you're real mean to talk that way about Miss Spicer. She came and shook hands and smiled at every one of us. She said she was glad to get back and she hoped we'd have a nice time together. And she was just lovely to me at noon. She noticed that I had a headache and she took me into her own office and made me lie down on the couch. And that Miss Whitmore bathed my head with lavender water, and gave me some aromatic ammonia and got me a cup of tea. She was just dear. She talked to me about Miss Spicer. She says she lives with her and they have beautiful times together. She says they have a piano and a cat and she is buying an automobile. And I'm to go home with them pretty soon and stay over Sunday. What do you think of that?"

"Aw, bologny! What's she sucking in with you for?" asked the yellow-haired girl. "I wouldn't trust anything she did as far as my nose. She wouldn't invite anybody to see her unless she wanted something out of her, I'll bet. You better watch out. If I was you I wouldn't go."

"Oh, shut up, Jennie, you're jealous," said another girl. "You'd go in a minute if you ever got invited, if for nothing else but out of curiosity. I know *you*. But you *won't* be, so don't worry."

The floor walker came hurrying anxiously past them just then, looking askance at the girls, because they were not supposed to be there at that time, and they scattered precipitately without another word. But Martha, when she thought she would not be noticed, marked the last lot, closed the boxes, arose from her cramped position, and walked quietly to her office. As she passed them, busy with some papers she was carrying, the girls looked in horror at one another.

"Do you suppose she heard us?" they whispered. "If she did she'll get it back on us somehow, you see if she doesn't."

The bugle for closing sounded and a moment later Miss Spicer stepped out of her office and came walking down the aisle laughing and talking with one of the cash boys as if they had had a joke together. What could it all mean?

"For the love of Mike, girls, what can have come over her? She's been smiling all day!" whispered one girl, "and now she seems to have a case on Bobbie!"

"I'll bet she's going to be married to some rich old

guy," said the yellow-haired girl. "Wouldn't that be something?"

"Nothing like that," said another. "She wouldn't come back and work in the store if she was marrying a rich guy, would she?"

It did not take many days to make the people in the store realize that there was a wholly different Miss Spicer at the head of the underwear department, but it did take many weary weeks of perseverance and patience with impudent lazy self-sufficient people before the young women under her began to understand that while she still meant business and must be obeyed in any command she issued, yet she could and would be tender and sympathetic and loving to them all at all times. Not until a number of them had been to her pretty home and breathed its loving atmosphere did they quite understand. And even then they came back puzzled and thoughtful, and wondered what had done it.

But gradually, one by one and two by two, they capitulated to her, till it got to be quite the thing for the girls, and the cash boys, to seek Miss Spicer in any time of need, and to know that she would be a rock of strength, and always a sympathetic friend.

Her little world grew gradually larger and larger, as one by one she added new people to her list of friends, who later shared the hospitality of the rejuvenated brick house. Almost every day somebody who needed a ride and some advice rode home with Martha. And so in time many people from the store came to know and love Ronald, and some of Ronald's friends, and many of the neighbors in the street. And Ernestine, of course, was beloved by all of them.

Janice got along beautifully at the store, both with her work and with her co-laborers. Her smiling face and charming ways were part of the great attraction to go and see Martha Spicer. And always at the pleasant little dinners and teas, Janice acted the part of the young hostess, like a daughter of the house.

"How they all love you at the store!" said Janice to her one evening as they went up to their rooms for the night. "They are so fortunate to have had you and known you all these years."

"*Love* me?" said Martha with a smothered sigh. "My dear, they used to hate me. Yes, I know, for I have heard them say so!"

"How *could* they!" said Janice aghast. "You are so good, good, good, and dear!" She flung her arms about Martha's neck covering her face with soft little kisses.

"I don't see how you could possibly have been lonely, as I was. People everywhere must love you wherever you go."

"Oh, my dear, you don't know. You don't understand. Do you know what they all used to call me at the store? Spice Box. I have heard them many a time. Old Spice Box!"

Janice was quiet for a minute or two, her arms still around Martha's neck.

"Oh, but a spice box is a lovely thing," she said with a smile. "Don't you know it is? It goes to make everything taste just right. Without it things would be flat. Why, I can remember how lovely my mother's spice box used to smell when I was a little girl! Besides, Martha dear, those people didn't know you the way I do. You've just been an angel to me!"

Martha suddenly hid her shamed tears in the girl's neck and tried to get control of her feelings.

"You are a dear child," she said chokingly, "and I thank God every day for sending you to me!"

THOSE were days of delight to Martha and Janice. Every morning they got up with some new idea about how to fix something for the house, and every evening they developed some new corner or window or bookcase for the admiring inspection of the workmen who were getting tremendously interested in this house they had been making over.

The work was going forward rapidly, and if one might judge from the number of people who dropped in from the street to see what in the world Miss Spicer could be doing to her perfectly good respectable old house, Mr. Roberts must be gaining name and fame. One and another householder would come the second time and ask the architect his price for taking down a partition, or putting in a window, which showed that the new neighbor in the district had started something that wouldn't stop at her own house. It began to appear that almost every family on the block, and a few on the next one, were contemplating alterations. Those who had no alleys and couldn't hope to have bay windows would have to be content with taking down partitions.

Although, there were a few who looked on such innovations as unnecessary, almost unrighteous, and clung to traditions and old customs with a stolid zeal. They declared Miss Spicer might better have rented out a room or two in these war times if she had so much room to spare, rather than to make a great big room with no hall and only a little vestibule to keep out the cold in winter. Entering into the parlor right like that wasn't decent, they declared. But Martha went on her serene happy way and never knew.

Martha and Janice went about the store almost every noon now, and browsed around among curtains and furniture, coming home at night with something pleasant. And then among the art works Martha came upon the little head of exquisite marble, a representation of Joan of Arc, the one she had admired so long. She recognized that its beauty had had some effect upon her. She could see that a bit of art like that would somehow bear a message of sorts to anyone who looked at it, and when she brought Janice to see it and found that she too felt its power, she bought it. Shades of the ancestors, how they would have raved! But she had long ago ceased to listen to them. This was an acquisition that would do something beautiful to her home, and to all who came to it, and she felt she must have it. It represented all the things that had been starved out of her young life. It was a little expensive of course, but so was everything that had real intrinsic value, and she felt she could not afford to pass this by. In fact she was beginning to see that it did something to both herself and Janice to be in that store and feel that they were a part of it.

The morning came at last when Mr. Roberts announced that the living room and dining room, even down to the catches on the windows and the fasteners on the delightful corner china closets were complete, and they might take possession of it.

They had watched the painters and paper hangers in their slow, tedious process of finishing, and now they were all eagerness to move in. For indeed the kitchen and laundry were over-congested with things new and old, and it was growing more and more difficult to get any meals at all.

It happened that Ronald and his gang, as he called them, came strolling in as if by appointment, probably having received a tip from Mr. Roberts, and presented themselves for work. They took their orders from Ronald and started a procession of furniture out of the kitchen and laundry and into the grand new apartment that the old house had become. Ronald got his directions in a low tone from Martha if he wasn't just sure where something went. It was remarkable how often he knew without asking.

Janice and Martha had been at work every night rubbing up and polishing the fine old mahogany, and now the boys brought them carefully in and set them in place almost as if they were sacred articles. The sideboard, its brass handles shining brightly, the table and chairs, the high chest of drawers, the couch, the rockers, the round center table, and the old secretary with its high glass doors and its desk that would draw out. These all appeared with new dignity and beauty in the pleasant setting of the new rooms. There was some new furniture, upholstered in fine bronze leather like billows of air, a couch and chairs, the color of the woodwork.

The walls were pale cream like faint sunshine, and there were curtains of silky woven sunshine. The three helpers came down stairs with their arms full of books and paused in amazement. They couldn't tell what unearthly atmosphere had suddenly fallen into that place to make it different from anything they had ever seen before. There were pictures being hung upon the walls, one of the ocean upon which they gazed and gazed. There were bronze-green velour curtains hung from the arch where the partition between dining room and parlor had been, and there were cushions to fit the seats around the fireplace to match the curtains. There were built-in bookcases, and Martha was bringing beautifully bound books and placing them. Every touch was telling now. Then Ronald pointed to the rugs and showed the boys where to place them. Two big ferns and some scarlet geraniums were in the bay windows. At last Ronald, with great awe in his face, and cautious handling, brought forth Martha's one great extravagance, the little head of Joan of Arc.

Carefully they undid the wrappings until the exquisite bit of art stood forth in all its beauty, and the group of helpers and the men who had helped to build, all stood around and looked with reverence as if in the presence of something holy. Perhaps it was the feeling the artist had put upon the stone that they should bow in soul before it as did those who recognized the purity of the consecrated girl. It was just as Martha had hoped. That little statue with its lovely profile had power to arrest attention and uplift the thoughts of even the lowliest, for as they looked, those men felt this was a living, breathing mortal before them—calling them to higher purposes and nobler aims. The soft tints of the amber and deep brown in the coloring of the marble, the strange trick the artist had of chiseling life into the pupils of the eyes, deepened the impression.

But nothing could keep Ronald, the irrepressible, still very long. He was the first one to come to himself.

"S-o-m-e *Looker!*" he drawled. "Who-*wis*-she? Say, Janice, she looks like you!"

That broke the silence and the company began to move about and try to express their delight, but ever as they moved they kept turning back to look at the girl in marble, and to recapture that fleeting impression that she was a real living being wishing to speak to them all about something most important.

"Who is she?" It was Pace who asked the question again, timidly. He could not get away from feeling she was somebody real.

"Joan of Arc? Oh, don't you know her?" said Janice. "She's a wonderful character in history. You must have studied about her in school."

"Oh, sure!" said Ronald confidently. "She was a dame that could ride horseback to beat the band, wasn't she? And had all kinds of nerve, and got a lot of men to follow her, but couldn't get enough, so she had to beat it. Or did she croak? I forget. Janice, why don't you tell us the story about her?"

"Why, I will," said Janice pleasantly, "if you will all come over when you have the time. How about tomorrow afternoon, Martha? It's a good story for Sunday."

"By all means," said Martha smiling. Her extravagance was doing its work all right. There ought to be enough in one of Janice's stories to help those boys a lot.

So the boys shuffled away, chiming forth "So-long" at the door as they went out.

After they were gone there was a patter of velvet feet and Ernestine came and stood in the archway, the first time she had ventured alone into that room since that horde of awful strangers fell upon their house and devastated it with their poundings and sawings and rendings and thumpings. And so this was what they had done to it! If Janice and Martha hadn't been there she wouldn't have recognized a thing in the place. She felt her world had come to an end. Such a vast space where there used to be narrow walls! Such myriads of little woolly mats where an ugly carpet used to be! Such grand chairs upon which to curl up and take a nap! She had never read of Aladdin's Palace or she would have thought herself in it surely. She uttered a low "Meow" and advanced cautiously over the slippery polished floor till she was safe beside Martha. From this haven she took a survey, snuffed the new odors of plaster and leather and varnish, gave a glance at the bay windows, and the big staircase with its landings, and then her eye fell upon the fireplace and straight to it she went with almost a sigh of joy, and stood there looking. "Meow!" she said, as if to say, "This is what I have longed for all my days, and dreamed of all my nights. I am content."

Then on a little old rose prayer rug she curled, rumbling a joyful purr, and sat staring into the empty grate.

"She wants a fire," said Ronald, and dashing out to the kitchen came back with some shavings and matches and a small stick of wood. In a moment there was blaze enough for Ernestine to realize what life was going to be like that winter.

It was then that Janice threw her arms around Martha's neck and cried out, "Oh, Martha, it's so wonderful! Your dear house and everything! I'm so happy I have a part in it."

"Yes," said Martha happily, "I'm glad too. I'm glad you and Ronald are both here with me. I'm thinking if it hadn't been for Ronald I never would have had this made-over house. He was the one that put it into my head. And I'm so glad. I think it's lovely, don't you, Ronald?"

"Swell!" said Ronald joyously, tickling Ernestine's ear.

And about that time Dr. Howard Sterling stood in the wide entrance hall of the sanitarium at Enderby, saying good-by to the nurses, and internes, and the new house doctor.

Now that the time to leave had come he was feeling sad about it. This was the place where he had come to begin his work, and the place in which one of the sweetest experiences of his life had occurred. He hadn't known he would feel sorry to leave it. The nurses smiled and watched him and wondered if he was going to see Rose Bradford before he left that part of the state. They whispered that he looked tired, and was awfully handsome, and it was such a pity he was leaving. And then Sam drove up with the house car and he was whirled away.

"Yes, ma'am," said Sam when he got back from the station, and was being questioned by the nurses, "he took that samest train that he took to go to Martin's bof times, but I couldn't say whether he were going to Bradford Gables or not."

But Sterling did not go to Bradford Gables. Instead he took the taxi and drove to the cemetery at Willow Croft.

At the gateway he left the taxi and walked in the moonlight, in through the gate, and over to where Louise Whitmore Stuart and her baby girl were buried. He stood there alone by the side of that dead unknown sister, thinking of the girl he had loved who had gone from him, whom he perhaps would never see any more. Before he left he knelt by that sister's grave and said aloud: "Oh God, take care of her!"

Then he walked back to the Junction and took the late train which brought him, a little after midnight, into the distant city that was his goal and there he found his old friend Ted Blackwell waiting for him.

They drove to Blackwell's quarters and had a long talk, and when they parted for the night Blackwell said: "I'll never forget this that you are doing for me,

Howard! It's as if you were giving me a hope of life again, for I'm satisfied that without this operation I cannot live. And now there are three or four patients I want to take you to see in the morning, or during the day, and the next day I'm off, if all goes well. I hope you won't have too rotten a time of it carrying on for me. I have some very good friends among my patients I want to introduce and I know you'll like them. And now good night! I'll see you in the morning."

18

THE new piano arrived that Saturday night and was put in place where its voice could be heard to best advantage, and Janice and Martha had hard work to drive themselves to bed that night, it was so interesting to listen to it, as Janice rippled off different portions of melody out of her past. Ernestine was really startled by it at first, and looked at Martha as if to say:

"Now what do you think Aunt Abigail and Uncle Jonathan would think of having a thing like that in the house?" But after a little she settled down and tried her voice with it, deciding that it would be all well enough for her to sing to if they played *her* time. She couldn't be expected to learn new-fangled time, like ragtime or swing, or modern music. She didn't hold with that.

And so the piano was there in the room when the boys entered that first Sunday afternoon. It startled them because they didn't know anything about its coming. Except Ronald, of course, who always knew beforehand everything connected with the house.

The boys came in in awkward silence following Ronald. Coming there in their old clothes to place the furniture was one thing, but coming there all dolled up in what they called their Sunday best and seeing that room in all its finished glory when other people were present was entirely another story. They felt for the first minute or two as if they wouldn't have come at all if they had realized. And then they got so interested in looking around and getting the amazing effect of all that had been done that they forgot to be awkward, and just sat and enjoyed.

The Robertses and three of the workmen had asked if they might come too and hear the story, and they were sitting back by the kitchen door, unobtrusively, enjoying the changes that they had helped to bring about in this commonplace house.

Janice was there, and as they all settled down to look around she stepped across to the piano bench and sat down, letting her fingers ripple over the keys in what seemed to them a marvelous shower of beautifully colored sounds. They sat and stared and stared and drank it all in, till the music suddenly broke into a well known hymn that they all had heard more or less everywhere, even though they were not regular attendants at church. And when the music had sounded through a verse and chorus Janice turned toward her little audience smiling and called a challenge, "Come on, let's sing! You all know this, don't you?" And she began to sing:

> *On a hill far away stood an old rugged cross,*
> *The emblem of suffering and shame,*
> *And I love that old cross where the dearest and best*
> *For a world of lost sinners was slain.*
> *So I'll cherish the old rugged cross,*
> *Till my trophies at last I lay down,*
> *I will cling to the old rugged cross,*
> *And exchange it some day for a crown.*

Suddenly she whirled about toward them and said engagingly:

"Come on now, sing that chorus with me. I'm sure you all know it. Everybody knows that. And then I'll sing the next verse and you all come in on the chorus. Now! Sing!" and she stuck a great chord on the piano that fairly drew the song from their lips. One by one, the boys began to growl out a note now and then, till when they reached the last line everyone was singing cautiously, trying not to be heard, but singing.

"Again!" she said, and they all sang it again, gaining in volume. Then sweetly her voice rang out alone:

Oh, that old rugged cross, so despised by the world
Has a wondrous attraction for me,
For the dear Lamb of God left His glory above,
To bear it to dark Calvary.

This time the chorus was very good, and by the time the last verse was finished the whole roomful were singing heartily.

"That was good!" said Janice. "Do you know another as well?"

"Onward Chrisshun soldiers!" shouted Ronald helpfully, and Janice smiled and went into the melody, the whole company following her clear voice and making fairly good music. And the beauty of it was that none of them felt they were doing much singing themselves.

Ronald still had a high clear soprano voice when he chose to use it, though usually he tried to growl a low uncertain bass, thinking it was more manly. But now he led off and the chorus rang out,

Onward Chrisshun soldiers! Marching as to war,
With the cross of Jesus going on before.

They sang the four verses with Janice's help, and then she felt she had her audience right where she wanted them, and she swung around and went over to the round table where the lovely little head of Joan of Arc was standing, just where the light from the new bay window could shine across and show the exquisite profile.

Janice turned the marble head around, till the eyes seemed searching the eyes of the boys seated in front of her, and their mumbled talk was hushed, as they looked at the statue and wondered what this story was going to be.

Janice was standing now not far from the lower steps of the stairs, the landing of which would shelter her somewhat, in case anyone should happen to come to the front door. She was facing the row of boys, and farther back were the Robertses and the workmen who were regarding her with eager eyes.

The Robertses had become very well acquainted with Janice during the stay at the shore, and admired her greatly. She had been a great help to Mrs. Roberts all the time, and dearly loved the baby. So she did not feel that they were strangers. The workmen were friendly fellows who had passed a pleasant word with her now and then going about their work every day.

But it was to the four boys that she began to tell her story. The others were just people who had slipped in because they wanted to. She smiled around upon them all before she began.

With one hand softly touching the marble shoulder of the statue she began:

"Joan of Arc was born in Domrémy, France, on January sixth, fourteen hundred and twelve!"

She paused a moment to let that fact sink in.

"That is just eighty years before America was discovered by Christopher Columbus," she went on.

The boys looked duly impressed, gazed at the statue with awe, and a soft drawing in of the breath. That seemed to put Joan almost out of their comprehension.

The doorbell rang just then, as doorbells have a way of doing just at a critical moment, but the boys did not notice it. Their attention was entirely centered on that beautiful girl's face. And Martha, with forethought, was seated very near the vestibule door. She softly slipped out, drawing the door shut behind her.

It was the doctor, with the new doctor in his wake! She greeted them pleasantly and explained what was going on. A hungry look came into Blackwell's eyes.

"May we come in?" he asked. "We'll be very good and not make any noise!" He gave her an affectionate grin. "Couldn't we just slip in by this door, behind the stairlanding and nobody will see us? We'll do it so quietly they won't be disturbed."

"Why, yes, I suppose you may," said Martha. "I don't think anyone would really mind, only you know how shy boys get sometimes. But there are two chairs right here beyond the door, behind the landing. You'll be entirely out of sight while the story is going on, and afterwards I'm sure you'll be forgiven."

She laughed softly and slipped inside the door like a wraith ahead of the two men, and went back to her own chair. The two doctors proved that they could be as silent as two cats. Not even Ernestine could have done it better, and there they were sitting within the room yet not in sight. Janice had no idea who had come to the door, or if anyone had come in, and not even the boys looked up to see if anyone was sharing their story. So Janice went on with her tale without losing even a little faction of the dramatic opening.

"Not much is known about little Joan's childhood because it was so long ago and her people were not very important people, and therefore did not keep records of their children's sayings and doings as young fathers and mothers do today. But we know that she was a sweet good child. She lived next to a church and loved to go to church. Her mother taught her to pray, and prayer must have been a real thing to her, because she seems often to have had regular conversations with God. They called her pious in those days, but that is just an old-fashioned name for loving to learn about God, and trying to please Him. A name for being a real, what we would call today, Christian. Nowadays the word pious is used to make fun of religion and discredit people who make a great show of their religious beliefs and yet do not live up to them, but in Joan's days it did not mean that. It meant true religion, truly trying to please God and walk in His ways. And when they said it about Joan they meant that she was sincere and real in her thoughts with God."

Dr. Blackwell looked up at his friend Sterling to see what impression his young patient Janice was making on his friend, but he was not prepared for the look of startled wonder and joy that radiated from Sterling's face.

That voice, oh, that dear voice that he had listened for in his night watches! The little nurse Mary who had vanished like a spirit. Had he found her at last? He couldn't see her face because he was sitting behind the stairlanding, but he bent forward and tried to look around the corner and see her, and he fairly held his breath not to lose a single syllable.

The sweet voice went on:

"One day when Joan was about thirteen years old she was walking in her father's garden and she heard a voice. Somehow she knew it was God speaking to her, telling her what He wanted her to do, and how He wanted her to live. And while she was still out there in the garden, when their talk together was over, she made a vow or promise to God that she would live for Him always. That she would never marry, but would make her life entirely devoted to His service. And after that she began to hear that Voice again, sometimes two or three times a week!"

"Was it a real voice," put in Ronald, "or did she just *think* she heard it? Was it just imagination?"

"No," said Janice, "she *said* it was a *real* voice. And we have no other means of knowing about that except from what she said, so I guess we have to believe her. She certainly suffered enough to be believed."

"But God doesn't *really* speak to people so they can *hear* Him, does He?" asked Ronald skeptically.

"Why, He used to," said Janice. "Don't you remember how He talked with Adam and Eve in the Garden before they had sinned, told them there was just one rule they must keep in the beautiful Garden-home He gave them in Eden? And told them if they wouldn't trust Him enough to keep that rule they would bring Death into the world for themselves and their children. That was what happened that made everybody have to die now, you know. And then God called them, don't you remember? After they had sinned and were afraid to answer. And when they finally answered He told them what was going to happen to the whole race of their children that were to come after them. Sin and death. Oh, and He talked to them, and to Abraham, and Moses, afterward, and a lot of other men, of how He would send His own Son to die in their place, and rise again to make them all right before God. Sometimes He only came to them in dreams in those days. But whether it was a voice they could hear, or a dream they could remember, or only a still small voice in their hearts, God really spoke to them. And so I am sure God spoke to Joan of Arc. He had something special for her to do for Him, and He wanted to have her know Him so well that she would obey just what He told her to do. But anyway, whether they were voices other people could hear too, or only voices she heard in her heart, I am sure she *thought* they were real voices, for she said they were, and the people who knew her in the days when she lived, all testified that she told the truth and was a good and honorable girl. She would not have told a lie."

Sterling, as he listened, unable to see the face he knew so well and longed to look upon, closed his eyes and let the sweet voice and the great truths she was telling flow over his hungry spirit like a soothing flood. He wondered as he listened, where she got the knowledge to talk like that, where she got the power to make such things plain to those untaught boys? He could just see the lovely little statue that stood on the table before her, and wished she too was within his range so that he might study her as she spoke. Oh, was this real? Or was he only imagining it? Was that his little Nurse Mary out there?

He had not yet learned to call her Janice, even in his thoughts, although he had by this time of course learned that her real name must be Janice Whitmore.

But the voice went on, making the story out of an age that was past, live again for that little audience.

"The voices kept coming," she said with conviction. "For five years she heard them two or three times a week at least. There was war in that time, too. Her own country, France, was in trouble, and she was aware of the horrors of war, and the dreadful things that were going on all about her. That was between 1419 and 1428. You can read all that in history. And then the voices commanded her to go to raise the siege of Orleans, a great city of France. That was in October of 1428. It was a distinct command that she, a girl, should raise an army and go and fight to set the people free from their oppressors. England was gathering an army to conquer the young crown prince's territory south of the Loire River. And the voices told her to go and do something about it. Everybody she told about it thought she was crazy. Joan went and told her father about the voices' command for her to go to war and her father said: 'I would rather drown her with my own hands than to have her do that.' But Joan was determined to go anyway. She felt she must obey God's voice, even beyond her father and mother. So she went to other friends of hers to beg them to help her do this great thing, but they one and all did their best to persuade her she must not do it. But on she went, determined to carry out God's purpose for her life. At last she went herself to the commandant of the Prince's army and begged him to write a letter to the Prince and say that she was sent by the Lord to lead him to his crowning. He paid little heed to her words and sent her back to her parents. But still Joan continued to talk more and more of her great mission. Later when the news of more fighting around Orleans came she went to visit some cousins in Vaucouleurs, and sought once more to convince Baudricourt to let her try her fortune at war. He had just learned of disasters, and was perhaps ready to try anything once, so he gave Joan permission to go. He gave her a sword and said: 'Go, and let come what may.' She wrote to the Prince asking for permission to come and give him information that no one else possessed. There was a great disturbance and the council met to decide whether the young king should hear her or not, but at last she was led into his presence, and with meekness and simplicity she said: 'Most noble Dauphin, I am come to help you and your kingdom.' The Prince talked with her for more than two hours. As she addressed him she said:

'I am God's messenger, sent to tell you that you are the king's son, and the true heir to France.' She was trying to urge him to come forward and fight for what was his by right. But even then there was much to hinder. The king insisted she be examined by an assembly of learned theologians. She told them that she would raise the siege of Orleans and have the king crowned, and she dictated a letter commanding the English to depart. They sent to her home, but could find nothing but good of her, and finally she was sent to Tours. She put on white armor and had sent to her from the church a sword on which were five crosses, and so at last she started. On the night of April 28th, 1429, she entered Orleans, bringing hope to the beleaguered citizens. The Maid and her companions stormed the 'bastille,' the Tower of the Augustines. They also captured Tourelles which commanded the head of the bridge. Joan herself planted the first scaling-ladder, and was wounded in the shoulder by an arrow. But Orleans was saved. Joan entered the city in triumph. They marched on Reims and two days later the king was crowned. Beside him stood the Maid, a banner in her hand. 'Gentle King,' she said, kneeling before him, 'now is fulfilled the will of God that I should raise the siege of Orleans and lead you to the city of Reims to receive the holy coronation, to show that you are indeed the king and the rightful Lord of the realm of France.'

"As time went on there were other battles. And now, successful, she found that she was allowed to lead the royal forces to an assault on the Porte Saint Honoré at Paris. It failed, however, and Joan was wounded in the thigh, but had to be dragged from the field by force. There were more battles, and more troubles, and Joan was distinguished by patience and a power to persist against all odds."

On went the story, briefly told in simple language and

the little audience was held at the point of keen attention as Joan's trial came on. Janice made it plain that the reason for the trial was based on those twelve points, the main ones being that she claimed to be acting under the command of God, that she had really heard voices, and that she was responsible only to God and not to the church. They censured her masculine dress, and insisted she should wear woman's garb and not soldiers' garments. Janice brought out how plainly envy and hate and bitter jealousy were at the bottom of this. Joan's claim that she had prophetic power was another sore point. And then Janice made very plain how Joan was suffering for her own country, desiring to lead it to victory.

"We today," said Janice, looking at the four boys in front of her, "are fighting just as earnestly for our country's freedom as they were in Joan's time. But if Joan could come back today and fight for us, and insist that the way she urged was the way of righteousness, the right way, God's way, and that God had told her what to say to them, would there be some today who would cry her down as they did then? We are urging our women to do all they can in this war. Is there anyone like-minded with Joan? Perhaps there are many, and hundreds of years from now the people who live then may be studying about them. But there could be none who would excel this lovely girl, who devoted her life, under God's direction, to fighting even to the death for victory, for freedom. That is what our boys are fighting for today. But if you go, boys, go in the strength of the Lord, for that is the way to win, and the only way. Joan had printed on her white banner the name of Jesus. It was in the strength of Jesus that she conquered, and when it came time for her to die, she died a glorious death crying out in her last breath 'JESUS!' For Joan did die for her faith. Her enemies pursued her to her death. They insisted that she should be burned at the stake. And though there was a long and bitter trial, and though she just escaped the torture chamber, she was finally sentenced to be burned at the stake. It seems a terrible thing to hear that this lovely girl—for all the records show that she was very good and beautiful, and most devoted to her Lord, serving Him with an honest heart, accepting Him as her sole Guide to whom alone she owed allegiance—should have had to meet her death in fire! They gave her a cross from a neighboring church and she kissed it while she was being chained to the stake. As the smoke and flames swept up over her lovely form she cried out 'JESUS!'

"They took her ashes to the bridge of Rouen and threw them into the Seine River. A lovely servant of the Lord, brought into the world perhaps just to serve in a special way to carry out some of God's great purposes, and if she did some things in different ways from those we know now, who can criticize her? For she surely served the Lord Christ and was loyal to His commands as she understood them through the Voices. And boys, I think it would be wonderful if every one of you should learn to know God, as lovely Joan did, and to follow the Voices with which He will surely speak to your hearts if you will let Him, through praying to Him and through reading the Bible. Then you can take your knowledge of His Bible which He Himself has said is the sword of the Spirit with which He wants you to fight, and go out to fight the enemies of the Lord Jesus Christ. Not to do good works—no, that isn't of value, but to conquer His enemies because He has sent you to do it, and because you love Him who died to save you. There is another woman in the Bible named Esther who was something like Joan of Arc. Sometime I'd like to tell you her story if you would like to come another day and hear it."

"Oh, *sure!*" interpolated Ronald. "That'll be swell!"
Janice smiled.

"But don't forget this beautiful Joan," said Janice.
"Carry home the lovely memory of her in your heart,
and think about how she listened to God. And someday
perhaps you will hear voices in your own hearts. Voices
of God, setting you apart to get to know Him, later
sending you on some errand for Him! Now, come up
closer and take a nearer look at Joan so you will not
forget her story."

As one man, those boys arose and approached, stood
looking into those beautiful chiseled eyes that almost
seemed to speak, so real they were, and then Ronald
looked up from the marble face to Janice's, and broke
the hush that had come over the little company.

"Say, Janice, she *does* look like you. Only I think
you're better looking!"

"Oh, *Ronald!*" reproved the girl in a kind of shocked
voice. "Don't say that!"

Quick to get her idea, the boy subsided.

"I see what you mean," he said in a low tone and
added, "I'm sorry!"

The two doctors had forgotten to keep out of sight
now. Dr. Blackwell had quite come out into the open,
with Sterling not far behind him. And so it was that
Janice turning away to hide her embarrassment, came
suddenly face to face with her dear doctor, and almost
thought for a moment that this story had gone to her
head and that she was seeing visions and dreaming
dreams.

But Sterling, with a great light in his eyes, went
forward and took both her hands in his.

"Mary! My little lost love! I have found you at last!
Thank God!" he murmured.

Perhaps nobody heard him, unless it might have been

the other doctor who had been studying that group of boys and marveling at the effect this story had had upon them.

But he came up now to introduce his one-time patient to the substitute doctor, and lo, he found them holding hands.

"Oh," he said smiling. "You've introduced yourself I see, Sterling! Well, that's pleasant. You don't waste much time, do you?"

"Oh, but she's an old friend of mine," said Sterling in a moved voice. "She's one I've been searching for for more than a year. You see, I *lost her!*"

"Yes?" said Blackwell with a peculiar twinkle in his eyes. "I see. Well, that being the case I guess my services are not required and I'll go and help Miss Martha pass the lemonade."

He slid away to Martha's side and passed lemonade and cake most efficiently, until Ronald corralled him and asked in a disgruntled voice, "Say, who is that guy over there holding our Janice's hand? Who does he think he is, anyway? Seems to me he's a little bit fresh right at the start this way."

Blackwell grinned.

"That's the new doctor, kid! Get close to him as soon as you can. He's an all right guy, and it seems he's an old friend of your Janice so I guess we can't put in any objections at this late day. But I'll tell you this much, he's going into army work as soon as he gets done substituting for me, so he won't likely be around forever. Enjoy him while you can. But take it from me, he's an all right guy!"

"I see!" said Ronald, narrowing his eyes and looking across the room at the new doctor. Then he got his own glass of lemonade and went across the room where he could get a good view of the new man, studying him hard, with the eyes of a man who has precious things to protect, and is growing up fast.

And then it was Martha who sighted the two happy faces looking at one another, and marched over to her doctor, and asked: "Who is that guy?" or words to that effect, uttered in more Marthaian phrases.

19

THEY were all gone at last except Ronald and the cat. Even the two doctors were gone, because Dr. Blackwell remembered suddenly that he had made an appointment to meet one of his patients just at six o'clock and bring the substitute doctor to see him, and there was barely time for them to reach the place before six.

"It's important, Sterling," said Blackwell when he saw the desperate look in the other man's eyes, "and the girl will be right here when you come back again. She lives here."

"Oh, yes, of course," said Sterling, wondering why there was always a desperate situation where this girl was concerned. "Well, if I must I must, but—I *must* speak to her for at least a minute before we go."

"Very well, I'll tell her," said Dr. Blackwell, and he went over to Janice's side.

"Could you come over and speak with Dr. Sterling, Janice, for just a moment? We have an appointment to meet a patient at six and we've barely time to get there." He spoke gravely, firmly, trying to let her know she must somehow get away from these people and come with him at once. Also, he was watching her keenly. Was she as interested in his substitute as Sterling was in her?

But the quick flush of interest in her eyes and the bright flush in her cheeks told him without any words. Yes, she was.

"Of course," she said at once. "Boys, will you excuse me a moment? I must speak to someone."

They stood watching her as she hurried across the room, watching "the strange guy" as they all instantly called Sterling. They had seen the bright look in her face. Was he good enough for her? That was the question in every boy's mind. And what about "Doc," the other Doc whom they knew and liked. The Doc who was going away to be sick, and maybe—just *maybe*—never coming back!

Sterling watched the girl as she hurried toward him, watched the banner in her eyes, the joy on her lips, and his heart leaped with hope. Still—there had been so many setbacks. Dared he hope? Yet—she was here! He had seen her, had heard her! What a wonderful girl she was!

His smile met hers half way across the room, bringing out more banners in her cheeks, and when she came and looked up into his face there was a new dignity about her that he had not seen in her first surprise at meeting him, a dignity that had grown in the interval of her absence. She had suffered of course to bring that look in her face. Oh God, must she suffer any more? Was there still something insurmountable that would keep them separated?

But he began to speak, rapidly, eagerly.

"I have to go," he said, and there was wistfulness in his voice. "It seems to be important to Dr. Blackwell. But may I have your assurance that you will be here when I can come back? That you will not vanish into the wide world again? I have spent much time in searching for you. I know that when you go you have some mysterious power of disappearance, but I beg of you that you will not do so again. For the love of mercy let us have an understanding this time."

"Oh, yes!" said Janice eagerly. "Yes, I have so wanted to explain it all to you, and yet there didn't seem any way before. I have thought of writing pretty soon just to let you know what really was the reason I had to hurry away without explanation."

"Oh, yes," said Sterling, *"that* I know already. It was Herbert Stuart and he had some power over you. Of course I don't know what, but I know he is a scoundrel of the lowest type. But what I didn't understand was why you did not come to me, why you didn't tell me he was your brother-in-law, and ask me to help you. I had promised to do so. I thought you trusted me."

"Oh, I did trust you. I do!" she said, deeply moved. "But—how did you know he was my brother-in-law?"

Sterling smiled sadly.

"I have not been over a year hunting you everywhere I could think of, without finding out a good many things about you and your family. But the thing that hurt was that you did not confide in me. You had ample time when you came back to consciousness, while the nurse was out of the room."

Her eyes grew suddenly deeply troubled.

"Oh—I thought—It didn't seem that I had the right to bring my troubles down upon you—and the institution—I—"

"Excuse me, Sterling!" said Dr. Blackwell, "I think we shall have to go at once! I know Janice will understand and excuse us. You can come back!"

"Oh yes," said Janice, putting out a cold little trembling hand. "You will come back?"

He gripped the small hand in a quick firm clasp that told her how deeply he was feeling.

"I shall come back," he said, "and—*You* will be *here?*"

"Oh, yes, I will be here. You will let me know how soon that will be?"

"I'm afraid not tonight," said Dr. Blackwell firmly. "We have yet a number of important calls to make on very sick people. I'll try to figure it out for you, Howard. Janice is working and her hours are nine to half past four or five. Are you free tomorrow night, Janice? I'm afraid I'll want Howard every minute till I leave, but I'll try to find a place somewhere, and meantime, won't she keep?"

"Oh, I trust so," said Sterling with a great anxiety in his voice.

"Sure she will!" assured Blackwell. "Man, I'm glad you are so much interested in my very best prize patient! But I don't know but I'm a little jealous also. Come on, fellah! We can't wait another second!"

And so the two doctors went away, and Janice turned back to those boys and tried to think where she had left off in talking to them. She found herself trembling from head to foot with a great gladness.

That night after everybody had gone home, and the house was very quiet, Martha got to thinking about this new doctor, and the fact that he had seemed to be holding hands with Janice, and she wondered what it all meant, and what it might mean to herself. She didn't get much sleep.

And Janice in her room, hugging to herself the thought of her dear doctor, and that he was here and she was to see him soon, suddenly remembered Rose Bradford, and her heart went down, down to the depths. How silly she had been! He was here of course, and she was going to see him soon, and talk with him. She could explain all about Herbert, and her other job perhaps and how she'd had to run from him again. But how after all was the situation enough changed to give her such great joy? There was still that Rose woman, and she still must keep her admiration to herself. She must not let her heart get the uppermost for since she definitely knew that he was engaged it would not do for her to even get very friendly, for her own heart was not to be trusted, she saw that now. One couldn't be awfully good friends with a man who belonged to somebody else, because the line between friendliness and love was very closely blended, and one never knew when it was going to get closer, so it was better to keep away.

Over and over she canvassed that subject, and came again and again to the same conclusion. She must be very careful in that talk she was to have with Dr. Sterling pretty soon.

"Oh, God, help me. Keep me from going in a wrong way even in my thoughts!" she found herself praying.

And then would come the agony of returning to the same aloof relationship she had been enduring for a long time, and she finally went to sleep without getting anything settled, except that she must be careful, and not say too much. But there was one thing that was a relief. She was glad he knew about Herbert and had no very high opinion of him. He would be able to understand whatever she thought it right to explain and she need not worry over whether she should tell him any more or not.

But at last she fell asleep.

And over in the next house Ronald had tossed about a bit and yawned and got up and got drinks of water, and when his mother asked him what was the matter he growled out that he guessed his old arm was "feeling the weather tonight" although the weather that night was unquestionably fine, so that not even a broken arm could hope to give excuse for any rheumatic pains. But Ronald was definitely worried about that new doctor and Janice. Who was he, anyhow, and what did he want to put Janice into such a conspicuous position for, right before a lot of fellows? Holding her hand all that time. Suppose he did used to know her somewhere, did he have to barge in on a perfectly good time she was having and bring that up? Boy! whyn't he wait till Monday at least? That was the swellest time they'd had yet, that story and that statuary, and the lemonade and cake. And then he had to hold up traffic *holding hands!* Well, there wasn't anything he could do about it and Doc had said he was a right guy, so, of course, he had to shut up about it and let come what would. No, he couldn't do anything about it. But tomorrow night he'd go over to Miss Martha's and they would talk all about their Sunday gathering, and how well they sang, and what a swell story it was, and how good the lemonade tasted, and maybe he would feel better. But anyhow, if he didn't pass his algebra exam, Miss Martha would have to find out about it and feel bad, so he better go to sleep right now. Likely everything would come out all right after all, and he mustn't forget to pray for Doc and his operation. Gee! It would be bad to have anything happen to Doc. And it was sort of good that his new man was willing to come and take Doc's place when he might have gone to war and got to be a Doctor-captain or something. Maybe he'd try to like him after all. So finally Ronald went to sleep.

Sterling was not free to go and see Janice until after eight o'clock the next evening, and he called up to see if that would be all right for her.

"Oh, yes," she said, with a joyous welcome in her voice, "I'll be glad to see you."

When he arrived he found the coast clear, and Janice

opened the door for him. He took both her hands in his and led her over to the couch where he drew her down beside him.

"Now," he said, "I've got to talk fast because I must take Ted over to his train. He leaves around ten and I told him I'd be back in time to see him off. But I couldn't go any longer without a talk with you. And besides he has a lot of old patients coming in for last directions and I didn't want to spoil their fun by being so constantly on the job. And now, will you tell me why you didn't come to me for help?"

"Why, I told you," said Janice, suddenly looking very uncomfortable. "I didn't want to complain of one of your patients. And I didn't want you to know that a man like that was my brother-in-law. My sister Louise spent a good many years trying to hide what he did, and I know she would want me to do all I could to keep up the illusion."

"But that, you know, is all a lot of hooey. There shouldn't have been a reason like that between you and me."

He was looking straight into her eyes so that she dared not raise her own to look at him, and he still held her hands very firmly. She looked down at them in a troubled way and thought of his beautiful fiancée. She oughtn't to let him hold her hands, yet perhaps he didn't think anything of it. Some people didn't. And she didn't want to begin to act unpleasant and aloof when he had just come. She had needed him so long! In a minute perhaps he would realize what he was doing and let her hands go. She would rather it would come about in that way. She didn't like to fight and wrench them away. It didn't seem ladylike. It didn't seem friendly.

He was holding her hands warm and close in both his own now.

"Tell me, my dear, what has come between us?"

She looked up quickly, more stirred at his touch than she wanted him to see. Suddenly she spoke. Her lips were quivering; and she tried to draw her hands away.

"Nothing has come between," she said softly, "only we ought not to be doing this," and she pulled her hands firmly but gently away from his.

"Wait!" he said, his lips set. "Just what do you mean? Is there some reason—Janice, are you *married*? Is this something I don't know?" and he put his hands firmly about her wrists. "Wait! I must understand this! We can't go on through life with misunderstandings. *Are* you married?"

She broke into a nervous little ripple of laughter, and then was suddenly grave.

"Oh, *no!*" she cried. *"Of course not!* But *you*—you are *engaged*, and it isn't fair to the other girl—! It isn't *right!*"

"What? I, engaged? I certainly am *not* engaged, and never was! Where did you get that? It is you I love, and *only you!* Of course, if you don't love me, and feel you never could, you have a right to draw away from my touch. Is it that, my dear? Am I hateful to you?"

"Oh, *no,*" she said softly, her earnest eyes looking into his now. "But—they said—"

"Yes? What did they say? *Who* said it? I insist on knowing who told you this?"

"The nurses. They didn't exactly tell me. I overheard them talking, but I think they meant me to hear. And, of course, probably they thought I ought to know. I had been awfully thoughtless."

"You? Thoughtless! Nothing of the kind! You had been like a lovely clear icicle most of the time those last weeks. You wouldn't come near me if you could help it, and you smiled so sadly and distantly, like a lovely star! Oh, my dear! It broke my heart some of those days when I

was searching for you and you only seemed farther and farther away each day. I wondered why I kept on, when it seemed so clear that you didn't *want* to be found. And yet I *had* to go on and find out where you were if it was humanly possible. But why did you think you could credit what those nurses said? Didn't you know they were a jealous, catty lot? Not all of them, of course, but a group who always want attention themselves. I would have thought you would understand what they were and not have trusted them."

"Oh, but I had no reason to doubt them. You had always been honorable and fine. And when she came she was so lovely!"

"She? What on earth are you talking about? When *who* came?"

"Why, Rose Bradford, the one they said you were engaged to. And then you went away several times and they said you had gone to see her. Why wouldn't I think it was true? I was only trying to be right and true. And they had been talking about me, too. They said I was trying to *catch* you! Oh, I was so humiliated! I had been brought up to be decent and self-respecting, and a Christian. I did not want to do anything that would be supposed to be otherwise. I wanted them all to know I was not chasing anybody. You had been very good to me when I was in dire distress, and you saved my life! I could not help being grateful to you, and admiring you greatly, but I did not want to be misunderstood. And I did not want to compromise you in any way for the girl you had chosen. I wanted to go quietly about my duties and keep your respect through life if I could, but I did not want to be thought to be silly and wanton!"

"You were never that, Janice! And only a fool could ever think you were. The trouble was those girls who talked that way were so lost to all sense of righteousness themselves that they couldn't conceive of anybody wanting to live on a higher plane. But as for Rose Bradford, I never loved her, nor even wanted to be engaged to her, though she tried hard enough to make me think I did. But after I knew her she was definitely out of my thoughts. She couldn't ever be compared to you. And now, Janice, let's forget Rose Bradford and those fool nurses, and let's talk about you and me. Janice, I love you, and I've learned through these long months of searching for you that I shall never be happy or satisfied without you. Do you feel that you could ever come to love me?"

He searched her face anxiously, the sweet eyes downcast, the lovely lips curved into the lines of great happiness.

Then she raised her head and let the joy in her eyes shine into his.

"Oh, I *do* love you!" she breathed softly. "I've loved you from the first! That was what was the matter. I thought I ought not to."

"You precious love!" said Sterling, suddenly reaching yearning arms to draw her close. "Oh, my darling!" And then his lips were upon hers, and a great joy descended upon them both till it seemed as if God stood there with His hands upon their heads blessing them.

All the months of pain and uncertainty, and distress and separation vanished, and they almost saw why the hard things had to be, that this perfect blessing should be theirs. More perfect because they had suffered, more joyous because they knew what it was to think they would never have it.

They were sitting so with the realization of their new happiness upon them, when suddenly the little new clock on the mantel that Martha had bought only a few days ago, chimed out the half hour, and beat upon the consciousness of the young doctor with sharp insistence.

"Great Scott!" he said, and looked at his watch. "Can it be possible the time has gone like this? I can hardly get to the office and down to the station in time for the train! It hurts to tear myself away but I shall have to rush!"

He lifted her to her feet and stooped to put his lips in one more quick kiss before he rushed to the door.

"I can't be back tonight, for it will be too late, but I'll be seeing you. I'll be calling you. Good night, darling!"

It was during that last quick kiss that Ronald, approaching over the back fence, stopped to reconnoiter at the end window that looked over into the back yard. He placed a cautious eye where it would take a full view of the big room before he ventured into the blessed precincts. But what he saw filled him with dismay.

He waited until the front door shut, waited another decent moment or two, and then slowly, dejectedly, he entered the kitchen door which Martha generally kept unlocked for his benefit.

Martha was at the kitchen table cutting out cookies and placing them in the baking tins. There was a delicious smell of pleasant baking in the atmosphere. Ronald usually tried to get in on the baking nights. He was always on hand to sample them.

He stood around till the first batch came out of the oven, helped to take them out of the pan and spread them on the big china platter that stood ready. Then after he had finished two hot cookies and pronounced them "swell," he stood back and sighed heavily.

"*Good night!*" he said gloomily, "I don't see what people wantta fall in love for! I don't see what they see in *love!*"

Martha laughed.

"Well," she said with an amused half-bitterness in her face, "I guess there's nothing we can do to stop it."

"No," he said sorrowfully, "but why did *she* fall for *him*? He's all right I guess—if he had only stayed away. But good *night!* Why did he haveta go and spoil everything?"

"Well," said Martha, endeavoring to be cheery, "a good many people have fallen in love through the years. The world is still going on, and *some*times we have good times."

"Yes? Well, that Joan of Arc didn't ever fall in love, did she? Why can't everybody be like her? Gee! I thought Janice had more sense. I thought she was just like Joan of Arc!"

"Not everybody has to be burned at the stake!" remarked Martha crisply. "But then, perhaps there are more kinds of stakes than just wooden ones," and Martha sighed.

There was silence for a minute and then Ronald said:

"Well, *Boy!* We've got *God* left *any*way, and He *can't* change! I'm glad of that!"

"Cheer up!" said Martha. "It maybe won't be as bad as we fear."

"No," purred Ernestine, coming out from under the table to see if they were going to give her a cookie, "it won't. I went in a while and jumped up beside them on the couch, and he seemed quite pleasant. I guess we're going to get along."

And out on the highway Dr. Blackwell's car was speeding along, taking him and his old friend to the train, and one of them had a heavy heart as he went away into pain and loneliness and uncertainty, but the other's heart was light like Heavenly sunshine.

About the Author

Grace Livingston Hill is well known as one of the most prolific writers of romantic fiction. Her personal life was fraught with joys and sorrows not unlike those experienced by many of her fictional heroines.

Born in Wellsville, New York, Grace nearly died during the first hours of life. But her loving parents and friends turned to God in prayer. She survived miraculously, thus her thankful father named her Grace.

Grace was always close to her father, a Presbyterian minister, and her mother, a published writer. It was from them that she learned the art of storytelling. When Grace was twelve, a close aunt surprised her with a hardbound, illustrated copy of one of Grace's stories. This was the beginning of Grace's journey into being a published author.

In 1892 Grace married Fred Hill, a young minister, and they soon had two lovely young daughters. Then came 1901, a difficult year for Grace—the year when, within months of each other, both her father and husband died. Suddenly Grace had to find a new place to live (her home was owned by the church where her husband had been pastor). It was a struggle for Grace to raise her young daughters alone, but through everything she kept writing. In 1902 she produced *The Angel of His Presence, The Story of a Whim,* and *An Unwilling Guest.* In 1903 her two books *According to the Pattern* and *Because of Stephen* were published.

It wasn't long before Grace was a well-known author, but she wanted to go beyond just entertaining her readers. She soon included the message of God's salvation through Jesus Christ in each of her books. For Grace, the most important thing she did was not write books but share the message of salvation, a message she felt God wanted her to share through the abilities he had given her.

In all, Grace Livingston Hill wrote more than one hundred books, all of which have sold thousands of copies and have touched the lives of readers around the world with their message of "enduring love" and the true way to lasting happiness: a relationship with God through his Son, Jesus Christ.

In an interview shortly before her death, Grace's devotion to her Lord still shone clear. She commented that whatever she had accomplished had been God's doing. She was only his servant, one who had tried to follow his teaching in all her thoughts and writing.

Don't miss these Grace Livingston Hill romance novels!

If you are unable to find any of these titles at your local bookstore, you may call Tyndale's toll-free number **1-800-323-9400, X-214** for ordering information. Or you may write for pricing to **Tyndale Family Products, P.O. Box 448, Wheaton, IL 60189-0448.**